## FIGHTING FIRE WITH FIRE

"A man who'd turn on his own kind's no better than a rattler," Sutter declared, lurching to his feet. "And we know how to handle snakes in these parts."

Random began a flippant reply. Then he saw the big man's hand move. Firelight danced along the blued barrel of Sutter's Colt as it swung inexorably up. Fast as Random was, he had no chance to draw.

As the pistol roared, Random threw himself into the fire.

Sutter squealed like a wild horse as he pulled the trigger three times, the yellow flashes of his handgun rupturing the dark. To his horror, though, he saw an unearthly figure suddenly loom at the edge of the fire—a blazing man, tall and terrible—with a pistol in his hand. . . .

# THE
# WAR PARTY

**Victor Milán**

A DELL BOOK

*This book is dedicated*
*with respect and gratitude*
*to the memory of my aunt, Dr. Mary F. Woodward,*
*whose legacy made it possible.*

Published by
Dell Publishing Co., Inc.
1 Dag Hammarskjold Plaza
New York, New York 10017

Dell ® TM 681510, Dell Publishing Co., Inc.

ISBN: 0-440-19716-3

Printed in the United States of America
First printing—February 1984

# ACKNOWLEDGMENTS

*I would like to express my deepest thanks to the following: Joseph Wm. Reichert, Esq., for sharing of his stock of lore; Martha W. Milán, for encouragement and proofreading; Ricia Mainhardt, Barb Miller, Joan-Marie Moffitt, Patricia Jackson, Jim Bakke, Betsey Gardner, Donna Sutton, John Brooks, Melinda Snodgrass, Mary-Rita Blute, and Edward "Wyoming Slim" Bryant, for support, moral and otherwise; to Cherry Weiner for running interference; to Jim Frenkel for ideas and patience; to Peter Guzzardi for forbearance (lots of forbearance); and finally to Karen Flowers, for helping me keep it together. May you walk in beauty always.*

## NOTES ON APACHE PRONUNCIATION

The Apache vowels sound approximately like those of Spanish, except for "i," which sounds like the English "i" in "wit." The doubling of a vowel does not change its pronunciation, but merely means the sound is prolonged— the exception being "ii," which has the sound of the "i" in "machine." Each vowel may also be nasalized, as represented by a "nasal hook," as in "ą," "ę," "į," "ǫ." The nasalized vowels sound like French nasal vowels: "ą" like the "a" in *dans*; "ę" like the "e" in *rien*; "ǫ" like the "o" in *bon*. "Į" has no equivalent, but isn't hard to figure out.

Consonants are roughly as in English. There are two unfamiliar ones, however: the glottal stop and the voiceless "l." The glottal stop is represented by an apostrophe, as in *naa'tsili,* "cattle." It is made by shutting and then opening the passage through the larynx. In English it occurs as the break between the syllables of "oh-oh." The voiceless "l" is written as "ł," and has no English equivalent. It is similar to the Welsh "ll," and is made by positioning the tongue to say "l" and forcing air out around it without voicing.

Apache is a tonal language. Since it consists of only two tones, only high tones are shown, represented by accent marks: á, é, í, ó, ń.

This scheme of pronunciation uses the orthography developed for the Navajo language, and which has been adopted by the White Mountain Apache Tribe.

"I don't go so far as to think that the only good Indians are the dead Indians, but I believe nine out of every ten are, and I shouldn't inquire too closely into the case of the tenth."

—THEODORE ROOSEVELT, 1889

# PROLOGUE

Little Italy, New York City
March 28, 1896

Darkness filled the room like fog, scarcely touched by the yellow flicker of the gaslight. It was a damp spring night. Nights like this seemed filled with hateful things, from the fumes of old cigars seeping from the carpet, to the moaning of an old drunk in the cells downstairs rising hollow and desolate around him. Outside the shuttered window boots tapped counterpoint to the rain drumming on the sidewalk as the residents of Little Italy scurried home, slipping on wet pavement and casting nervous looks at the blue-coated, high-helmeted officer getting soaked on the steps of the dingy marble police headquarters building.

His pen scratched rapidly across a sheet of yellow paper. He was a big man, chunky and solid, who wrote with that famous hard-driving force of his. Two words ran together and he flung the pen down in irritation.

He was near the brink of exhaustion. Still he drove himself. Only in work could he find refuge: refuge from the jeers of his opponents; from the bitter battle with Parker, his rival on the Police Board; from the inexorable approach of June and the Republican convention in St. Louis, which, barring a miracle, would dash his presidential hopes by nominating another man.

Like a man probing a sore tooth he glanced around his office. It depressed him. His blocky mahogany desk, bearing the scars of his predecessors' cigars, stood in the middle of the clammy cubicle, a brass telephone handset perched on one corner. A couple of wicker-backed swivel chairs stood by the walls, while a clock above the mantel ticked with the maddening persistence of the water-torture. The only illumination came from a lamp that sprang like a growth from the wall, giving off a mean and cheerless glow. These were no settings for a man of Destiny.

A coughing spell seized him. He coughed into his fist, thick shoulders jerking. He heard the scrape of heels on a desk in the next room, and the thin singing of the telegraph. Another drunk had joined the moaner in the cells below, droning out an obscene song. He grimaced. Perhaps he should call for an officer to go and club the beasts to silence. He hated drunks, he hated noise, he hated obscenity. Maybe he would go and do it himself.

Instead he sighed and reached for his pen.

A tattoo of heels approached his door, and it opened. His secretary poked her head in.

"We just received a telegram for you, sir." She looked perplexed. "It's from the Department of the Army."

He sat up abruptly. "Bring it here, Miss Kelly," he said in his high voice. He took the flimsy sheet briskly from her, spread it on the desk before him with firm sweeps of his hands, and tipped his glasses forward to read.

Smoothing black hair from her forehead, his secretary watched him with her mouth a thin line of concern. He seemed drained, his cheeks gray, his center-parted brown hair lank and disarrayed, the undersides of his eyes rimmed with dark smudges like smears of charcoal. His normally immaculate coat was wrinkled, his highboy collar limp with overwearing, and his tie was askew. She worried about him, though her own eyes were dark-circled too.

His head began to nod as he skimmed the message, picking up tempo like a bandmaster swinging into a Sousa march. Slowly the ends of his moustache crept up, showing his famous teeth, square and bright and even. What could it be? Miss Kelly wondered. He had many contacts with the Navy, she knew. What could the Army have to say to him?

Whatever it was, it had a pronounced effect. Finishing, he reread the telegram and then bobbed his head once sharply. He slammed his fist down on the desktop, making Miss Kelly and the telephone jump.

"By Jove," he said. "By Jove!" He was showing the whole awesome array of his dentition now, grinning like an overjoyed rabbit. "This could be it. Yes, this could well be it!"

He sprang up and strode to the single window, flung open the shutters with a pistol-crack sound, tugged the shade and let it snap up, and then hauled up the window to draw the heavy sweet-wet air into his lungs. He gazed out into dark Mulberry Street as though upon conquered domain.

"But what is it, sir?" Miss Kelly asked.

He swung to face her. He stood straighter than before. His clothes had somehow lost their crumpled look. His cheeks glowed with a ruddiness she had not seen for days. "A miracle, Miss Kelly," he said, and laughed his boyish laugh.

# THE TASK

The Española Valley
New Mexico Territory
April 2, 1896

# CHAPTER ONE

Whistling his defiance, the stallion reared and pawed the air. Juanito hung onto the rope, letting him go up on his powerful hind legs while his forehooves flashed inches from the small Indian's face. The object was to tire the animal out.

The stallion once more vented the whistling scream of the wild-born horse and sunfished. Without warning he lashed out with a sharp front hoof. Juanito moved surely and fast. The blow went harmlessly by.

He heard LaMontagne bellowing encouragements from the corral fence. The big, bearlike ranch owner knew better than to offer his help; he understood Juanito's Apache pride and respected it. He paid Juanito to handle his horses for him and knew enough to stand back and let him *do* it. Besides, LaMontagne would most likely get in the way if he interfered. He'd spent most of his adult life as the foremost architect in Rouen before moving to the wilds of the United States and buying a few hundred acres of choice bottomland in the lush Española Valley.

Gradually the horse wore himself down, jumping skyward off all four hooves, kicking, twisting, snapping at the lead. Juanito hung on, not letting him get twisted in the rope, not letting him go. Finally the struggles began to subside.

He was not a show horse. He was a big-headed swaybellied mustang with a Roman nose and one ear chewed off short. A pinto, white and faded-out dun like a pair of brown corduroy pants left out in the sun too long. He was one mean, ugly son of a bitch. He could also live on a few mouthfuls of water a day and run a longer-legged animal into the hardpan deserts and rocky mountains of the Southwest.

The West was opening up. The Frontier had been declared officially closed in 1890. The demand for good cowhorses was growing rapidly. Pierre LaMontagne was trying to help meet that demand.

He took the wild mustang stock, tough, rangy, and smart—descended from the original Barbs and Arabs of the first Spanish settlers by way of just about every kind of horse that had found its way

west of the Ohio—and crossed it with modern horses of various
standard breeds. The wild horses tended to be wormy and disease-
ridden from life on the range. By breeding them with bigger, sounder
animals he hoped to produce an ideal all-round working horse. He'd
been at it for ten years now, and people were beginning to take notice.
Ranchers around Española spoke highly of LaMontagne horseflesh.

The mustang's fury spent itself in a headshake and final resigned
expellation of breath through flaring nostrils. He stood with legs
splayed wide, head down, muzzle dripping foam, rough coat shiny
and spiked with sweat. The rancher clambered over his peeled-wood
fence, another hairy rope coiled for action. The horse could only bob
his head in protest.

When the second rope was in place a third man, a stocky Tuba City
Navajo named Ramírez, came over the rail with an orange-glowing
iron in his hand. He took aim and pressed the iron firmly to the horse's
haunch. It bucked and screamed. Ramírez scampered away, holding
his round-crown black hat clamped to his head, leaving the triple-
mountain brand burned into the seal-brown hide.

"That's one mean *hombre*, *hein*?" LaMontagne said to Juanito. He
slacked his loop and whipped it off over the stallion's head. "Think
I'll breed him to that *grisette* of a chestnut saddlebred. Their offspring
will breathe fire." Juanito slipped his lasso free. The animal nodded
his head, bucked once in place like a rocking horse, then spun off into
a tail-high kicking run around the corral while both men dashed for
the fence.

On the safe side of the rail, watching the mustang kicking up dust,
Juanito pushed back his hat and wiped sweat from his forehead with
his blue kerchief. The sun was low over the Jemez, the day poised
between light and twilight. A breeze blew from the shade of the
cottonwoods clustered around the big house, smelling of flowers and
spring moisture. The rains were good this year. Grazing would be
excellent in the valley.

The green Española Valley was a far cry from the Mimbres
Mountains of southwestern New Mexico where Juanito had been
born, and farther still from the parched emptiness of the San Carlos
Indian Reservation where he'd grown to manhood. But life was good
here. Better than he'd ever known before.

"When he cools off, take him out to the north pasture and let him
go, Ramírez," LaMontagne said. He looked at his foreman. "We're
finished for today, Juanito. Go on back to your lovely wife."

He turned and started off toward his whitewashed adobe farm-

house, whistling an Offenbach air. After a few steps he swung back.
"Perhaps we go hunting this Saturday, hey, Juanito? There's a black
bear making trouble up by Velarde. He's a clever one; it'll take a real
marksman to bring him down." He laughed, shaking his barrel belly.
"I'll let you use my elephant gun. We'll show those people some
shooting!"

He laughed some more. Juanito grinned. What LaMontagne
jokingly called his "elephant gun" was a custom-made Sharps Model
1874 .50-140 express, a very accurate, extraordinarily powerful, and
inordinately expensive piece that was the French-born rancher's pride
and joy. Though designed to shoot buffalo, the .50-140 Sharps in fact
*was* used as an elephant gun, with a great deal of success. Its
awesome recoil always punished little Juanito's shoulder, but he loved
to shoot it anyway. "I'll be glad to, *jefe*."

LaMontagne frowned. He disliked for Juanito to call him chief.
Then he saw the Apache's half-hidden grin and laughed, knowing he
was being teased. He waved a burly arm and lumbered off for the
house.

Still smiling, Juanito started for his own house, the house he shared
with his beautiful White Mountain wife Mariana. He enjoyed teasing
LaMontagne, and one of the reasons he enjoyed it most was that he
could do it. He was fortunate to have the big man's friendship and the
big man's job. Too many of his people were starving on the San Carlos
or coughing their lungs out in Fort Sill. *And my father?* he thought,
but put the question quickly from his mind.

With the aftershocks of the Crash of '95 still rumbling through the
economy, exacerbated by the government's clumsy manipulations,
there were a good many whites who would have given almost
anything for a job such as that of foreman on the Three Mountains.
Even now, ten years after the final surrender of the Chiricahua and the
end of the last true Indian war in North America, it was all but
unheard of for a white to give an Apache a responsible, well-paying
job, still less so to call him friend—and least of all to trust him with a
valuable rifle.

LaMontagne's trustfulness did not go unremarked. When Juanito
took the wagon into Española for supplies, he was almost accustomed
to the hate-stares and the comments, spoken aside and none too
quietly. And he knew the talk his employer had heard—about "good
God-fearin' white men starvin' for work," about how he'd be sorry
one day for giving an Indian, an Apache in particular, his trust.
Juanito would turn on him one day, he was assured. Or maybe his

neighbors would take matters into their own hands. These were
lynching times, angry times, with violent labor unrest on the one hand
and calls for a war, any war, on the other. But LaMontagne just
boomed that mountainous laugh of his and ignored everyone.

Juanito wasn't smiling anymore when he walked through the front
door of his little three-room adobe house a hundred yards south of the
main building. Mariana appeared in the kitchen doorway, wiping her
hands on her apron. "You're brooding again," she said sternly. "You
must stop it, or you'll wind up looking like your old Uncle Nana."
Then she laughed, which spoiled her attempt at seriousness. It came
to him again how the White Mountains lacked much of the reserve of
the Mimbreños—the Chíhéne, or Red Paint People, among whom he
had been raised. It was often in his mind to chasten her for it, but
somehow he could never bring himself to do so.

She glided to him, kissed his cheek, and danced away. He shook his
head. She definitely had a frivolous streak.

She returned to the kitchen. He went out again and sat on a chair
under the pole-and-rush awning that covered the porch to watch the
dusk give gentle way to night. Leopard frogs began to trill in the small
creek that watered LaMontagne's apple orchard. The smell of the
stream and of transplanted honeysuckle enriched the air. It was a calm
and lovely evening.

Juanito found his thoughts, once again, turning toward his father. It
gave him a twinge, a coldness. *Ten years*. He remembered crouching
in the scrub, watching the federal troops herd the last of the hostile
Chiricahua like animals aboard the cattle cars that would bear them to
Fort Marion, Florida, and exile.

It was a bitter irony that he had to hide to see his people deported
from their own homeland. Despite his own heritage he had always
refused to take the warpath. But General Crook had gone, and with
him honor, at least as far as red men were concerned. General Nelson
A. Miles now had charge of Indian affairs in Arizona.

It had been promised that only those who had taken arms against
the whites would be shipped away. But it would have been politically
inexpedient for Miles to allow the Chiricahua to remain in Arizona.
Like his former comrade-in-arms George Armstrong Custer, Miles
had his eyes fixed firmly on the White House. So all Chiricahua—
Chíhéne, Chókánéń, and Ndé'indaaí—would go to the humid,
stinking swamps of Florida—even those who had served the Americans as scouts against their own.

Juanito remembered the look on his father's face. The exterior was as calm as the granite cliffs under which he had been raised. But his son knew his heart. The old man was desolated. But not defeated.

Aguilar, the Old Eagle, would never be defeated.

Now his older son felt the familiar guilt well inside him. *Should I have gone with him?* He had refused to join his father in war. Should he then have chosen to share his exile?

"Tse'e." It was an evening-quiet word from the doorway. Mariana stood in the indigo glow before full dark, her hands ghostly-pale with flour from rolling tortillas. It was his name she used, the name her people had given him when he married her and so became one of them. *White-tailed Deer*, the name meant in the language of the White Mountain Apaches. It was derived from the Power he had that made him such a renowned hunter as a young man—a power not of markmanship, but of finding deer. He had always preferred the name to Young Eagle, his birthing-name.

"You remember."

He looked away.

"Those days are gone, Tse'e my husband. You're fortunate now, you walk in plenty and peace. Why recall other times?" She shook her head. "Sometimes I think you need to feel sad."

He said nothing. There was nothing to say. She reached out, took his hand, and held it tightly a moment. Then she let it go and went back to the kitchen, and shortly a rich blanket of smells covered him, heat and meat and bread and spices. He loved those smells, those odors that said home as surely as the weathered doorpost.

His thoughts turned to Mariana. She was a beautiful woman to his eyes. Unlike many women of the People she was beautiful in the eyes of the whiteman too. Like him, she was of the lean-faced variety of Apache, not moon-faced or broad of jaw like some. She was slender, her shape still lovely, though she was past her early twenties, only two years younger than her twenty-eight-year-old husband. Part of this was due, he knew, to the fact that her willowy small body had not borne the burden of many children. Of none, in fact—a lack he saw as his failure and her sorrow. She saw it as neither, but he could not accept that, just as he could not accept that she saw him as strong and brave and good. The eyes of Old Eagle's son were keen, but they missed some things.

Of one thing there was no doubt: that he loved his White Mountain girl desperately and wholeheartedly. Even had the whites not abolished multiple marriage, he would have asked for no other woman. He asked nothing but to be allowed to live his life in peace with her.

Without her he would not wish to live at all.

She called him in to dinner, and he ate with good appetite and talked of LaMontagne's plan to go after the marauding bear in Velarde. He would get to shoot the "elephant gun" again—though LaMontagne would in fact allow him to do so any time he wished, he preferred to save it for special occasions, so it would have a greater savor for him. As he talked, he lapsed into Apache, which he still spoke as a jumble of White Mountain and Chiricahua when he was with her. Usually they spoke English together, both of them being justly proud of their command of that difficult alien language. But when he was excited, or happy, he always lapsed into his boyhood tongue. Hearing him, Mariana smiled to herself. She said nothing, but the candlelight danced in her dark eyes.

After dinner he smoked a cigarette in the *sala*, the sitting room that shared the house with kitchen and bedroom. Mariana busied herself washing dishes and doing the day's-end chores, and he found himself thinking back yet again.

He thought of his best friend. Strange as it was for a wealthy white rancher to befriend a refugee Indian, stranger still was it that the older son of one of the greatest—and most irreconcilable—of the Chiricahua war-leaders should take as his closest friend one of the most effective enemies the wild Apaches ever faced.

But it was not so odd, perhaps. Random was a mercenary, a kind of man most white soldiers spoke of in contempt. Yet after they got to know him, the Apache, at least, felt no contempt for him. Only a handful of white-eyes spoke the Apache tongue, and most of that few haltingly, like children. In a year's time Random spoke it as if he'd first seen daylight in a mountain arroyo rather than in some huge whiteman house back East. He knew Apache wisdom and Apache ways, and where most military men of his day turned to the campaigns of Napoleon and Lee for inspiration, he studied the tactics of the greatest generals of the Southwest: men like Mangas Coloradas and Nana and Juh, and greatest of all, the Old Eagle's own cousin, Victorio. In time he earned the ultimate backhand accolade the Territory could bestow—they called him Indian-lover, the lowest form of life to virtually every white in Arizona.

But he drew comment from the Apache too. Some said he was a shaman, some said he was Nndé, an Apache in an earlier life cursed by being reborn as a white-eyes. But all said he was a good man, a true man—and a hard man to have as foe.

His skills, as a "civilian" scout and liaison with the Apaches, had played a major role in the final defeat of the irreconcilables, as great perhaps as those played by Iron Man Al Sieber or Long Nose Gatewood or Fat Boy Davis, or any of the other handful of whites who had the intelligence and integrity to treat Apaches as human beings, though unlike the rest he was never officially acknowledged in any way—something to do with having served in the army of another country, so that it was illegal for the Army to hire him. Crook appreciated him. Miles, of course, had not. And Random became, with the Chiricahua, and the men of good faith who had fought them, one of the losers of the final Apache war.

He took it well. And he had what the whites called the last laugh too. When trouble broke out between the Americans and their allies the White Mountains a year later, the Army called in Random to prevent full-scale war. He had done so, bringing back Thunder Knife, war-chief of the Fir Tree band and formerly an important ally of the whites in their war against the White Mountains' traditional enemies, the Chiricahua, who had fled on hearing that the whites had falsely accused him of murder and plotted to hang him. Against the resistance of whites, the Mexican Chiricahua, and Kosterlitzky's *federales*, Random had succeeded. The young Juanito had gone with him. By marrying a White Mountain girl, Aguilar's son had become one of that tribe, and so his friend Random had asked him to come along to help convince the chief that the rumor was a lie concocted by the Tucson "Indian Ring" of government contractors eager for another war to bring federal dollars pouring into the Territory. The former Young Eagle already owed the man Nndé, called Green Eyes, a favor, since Random had warned him of Miles's treachery and hidden him when the Agency police came searching. But the youth had a deeper stake still.

Because the White Mountain girl he had married was Mariana—first and only daughter of Thunder Knife.

They had gone and come back, and in later years Juanito often laughed with Random over the agony the return journey had caused him, since he was ritually supposed to avoid the father of his bride. But he never did mention, even to his friend, that at one point during the desperate drive for home, fighting off the Ndé'indaaí, the justly named Enemy People, at every step, he had had his rifle sights lined up squarely on the chest of his own brother.

Nducho, the Mountain Lion, was Tse'e's obverse. Physically he resembled his older brother, small and dark and hawk-faced. But in his mind and spirit . . . Nducho was *heshkéé*, a wild, vicious fighter to whom killing was an end in itself. If the Young Eagle had never trod the path of war, his younger brother had walked it more than enough for both of them.

But Juanito felt no compulsion to dwell on thoughts of his brother. He had not seen him in eight years, nor had any word of him. Probably his bones lay bleaching somewhere in the Sierra Madre of Mexico, with none to give them proper burial. Even though he hadn't been able to bring himself to shoot him, on that long-lost day, now at last, he was content to forget him.

After the return from Mexico there had been more trouble. The whiteman did not recognize the Apache law that made him a White Mountain; he had been born Mimbreño, and Mimbreño he still was. Once more Random saved him, spiriting him and Mariana off the reservation and eastward into New Mexico Territory, where Random had a friend.

So Tse'e had come to the Three Mountains ranch. Pierre LaMontagne and his flamehaired wife Jeanine, as petite and quiet as her husband was exuberant and huge, had adopted the fugitive pair. And so Tse'e became Juanito, foreman of the LaMontagne ranch, and life was good.

But still the memories came back.

Mariana returned from the kitchen, eyes shining. He rose and took her hand and, almost shyly, led her into the cool darkness of the bedroom.

A gunshot jarred him from sleep. He sat upright. Mariana stirred beside him and sat up too. She made no sleepy, truculent inquiries, only waited, alert and wholly awake.

A second shot broke the night. A dog barked. More shots came, quickly, tumbling over each other like eager children. Juanito leaped from the bed. A Winchester 94 hung on the wall of the *sala*. He grabbed it down and threw open the door.

And found himself staring full into the face of a man.

It was a face out of nightmare: a gaunt, craggy Chiricahua face, with a yellow scalpband tied around the forehead, made eerie and horrific by the single wide band of white painted across the nose and beneath both eyes. It was impossible, but somehow *bronco* Apaches had swept up like wildfire from Sonora, to shatter the peace of the Española Valley. But that was not the worst thing.

The face was that of his brother.

Juanito fell back, stunned. "I greet you, *shikis*," Nducho said in the singsong tongue of the People. "Don't you wish to invite me in?"

Without waiting he stepped into the room. Others crowded in behind. Juanito had never seen the three before, but he knew what kind they were. They were killers.

Apache killers.

Nducho encompassed the room with a sweep of his gaze. His face had matured into austere handsomeness, but in the moonlight his eyes shone with something much like madness. "Take the White Mountain bitch," he ordered his men. "But don't hurt her." The eyes returned to Juanito. The knife-slash mouth smiled. "Yet."

He plucked the carbine from his brother's fingers. "What do you want?" Juanito asked, in Spanish. It was a small defiance.

The Mountain Lion didn't deign to notice. "For you to act like a man," he answered in Apache, "a Chiricahua man. Not a White Mountain lapdog of the *'indaa ligai*."

In panic Juanito glanced around. The largest of the intruders stalked toward his wife. Looking frail and helpless in her flannel nightdress, she retreated to the door of the room she shared with her husband. Juanito felt his brother's challenge: *You held a rifle in your hands, brother,* he could hear the warrior thinking, could hear the contemptuous inflection of *shikis,* "brother." *Why weren't you man enough to use it?*

Now, with two painted warriors clinging to his arms, glancing back nervously over his shoulder at the huge man closing on Mariana, he would gladly shoot his brother, though he had not been able to nine years before. He should have shot at once. But the shock had numbed him. And now it was too late.

The hulking warrior seized Mariana, gathered her in. Juanito gave a cry of rage and tried to tear himself from the others' grip. He heard a grunt, looked back over his shoulder. The big *heshkéé* who had been grappling with Mariana wasn't grinning anymore. As Juanito watched, orange light came flooding in from behind him, illuminating a face gone taut and strangely gray. Two big hands were pressed to the warrior's belly. Between them jutted the handle of a butcher knife.

Mariana was gone.

The two released Juanito and raced to the back of the house. "No," Nducho shouted. "Let her go. We can find her if we need to."

A fresh breeze, spring-chill and crisp, blew through the house. Mariana had opened a window and fled. The two warriors cursed in Spanish. "But she's killed Big Nose."

"If Big Nose is fool enough to get himself killed by a White Mountain, and a woman at that, we don't need him," Nducho said. Big Nose stared at him, opened his mouth to speak, then fell very slowly to the side.

"Enough of this. Our father waits outside, Tse'e."

"Our *father*?" The word struck him like a blow.

"Why else do you think we're here? Haastjj 'Ítsá has broken free of the white-eyes' prison. He returns to his people to take up a holy quest. You're going with him." He turned his head and called into the night. Looking past his shoulder Juanito could see orange flames leaping high against the black sky.

"Sometimes I think you're no better than a woman, *brother*. But we need your rifle Power. You'll help us." He leaned close. "Or we'll run your White Mountain woman down, and she will have a hard time of it before she dies."

His blood turned cold within him. Nducho's wolves were capable of carrying out his threat—both parts of it. "The LaMontagnes?" he made himself ask. "What have you done—?"

"Made good whitemen of them." Nducho smiled, a feral, merciless smile. "And that stinking Yudahá dog, too."

Juanito yelled and threw himself at his brother, grasping the rifle and almost wrenching it away before the others dragged him off. Nducho stepped back, grinning as if nothing had happened. "Don't you see? I'm doing you a favor. You weren't meant to be a dog, and lift your leg whenever the bearded *'indaa ligai* tells you to piss."

Juanito kept fighting his captors, to no avail. The mad, ugly grin left Nducho's lips. "Don't be sad, brother," he said earnestly. "I've brought you a present. A very fine one."

A skinny warrior entered behind Nducho. He held something in his hands, which Nducho screened with his body as he turned to accept it. Then the Mountain Lion turned and held the gift out to his brother. The full horror and despair, the irrevocable *reality* of this night, smashed Juanito in the pit of his stomach.

Nducho's gift was LaMontagne's prized Sharps.

# CHAPTER TWO

"I'll be blunt with you, Mr. Random," said the man behind the desk. "We want you to head off an Indian war."

In a straightbacked chair by one whitewashed wall of the post adjutant's office, a portly florid-faced man cleared his throat. "Now, Colonel Sinclair, I hardly believe the situation warrants such language. Say rather that we wish Mr. Random's, ah, assistance in averting a potentially unpleasant situation." A broad mouth smiled. "No need to be alarmist."

The officer commanding Fort Apache, Military Division of Arizona, eyed the man in the rumpled but expensively cut civilian suit without approval. Then as one they both looked to the younger man in the dusty boots and trousers and gunbelt, white linen shirt and open black vest, who sat with an unmilitary sprawl in another of the uncomfortable government chairs chewing on a green squawbush stem.

Random took the stem from his mouth, spit a fragment into the gleaming spittoon that squatted beside the walnut desk. The corners of the colonel's gray moustache quirked upward in distaste. Lieutenant Colonel Edward Sinclair was like his office. Both were small, compact, without ornamentation. Regular Army all the way—nothing out of place.

"From what little I've heard of the situation, Mr. Jordan, the word 'war' doesn't seem at all inappropriate," Random said softly. "Unless you've special reason for optimism?" Jordan frowned and looked away. From the corner of his eye Random saw a grin tugging at the lips of the fourth man in the room, a man of about his own age and almost his height, who sat on the edge of the map table by the window with one leg crossed over the other and one immaculately polished Wellington casually aswing. He had more than a hint of gray at the temples of his brown hair, and gold leaves on the shouldertabs of his dress-blue coat. A *chapeau-à-bras*, plumed with yellow-dyed horsehair like the one resting on the colonel's desk, lay propped against a roll of maps by his hip. Random nodded slightly and put the stem back in his mouth.

On the wall behind Sinclair's desk hung two large maps butted together. The legs of the colonel's chair scraped on the hardwood floor as he rose and turned to the maps. "Two weeks ago, the authorities at Fort Sill informed us that an aging Apache named Aguilar had disappeared from the Kiowa-Comanche Reservation, where the Chiricahua have been kept since 1894. They were quite embarrassed. It seems that, given the advanced age of most of the leaders of the captive Indians, they have allowed their vigilance to grow somewhat slack."

"I expect they've already forgot the lesson Nana taught them about superannuated Apaches in 'eighty-one," Random said. "And Ulzanna and Chato are none too old. But go on."

Sinclair whipped a hickory pointer with a motion unthinkingly reminiscent of a saber coming to salute and laid its tip against the right-hand map. "Ten days ago, parties unknown attacked and burned the Three Mountains ranch north of Española, New Mexico. The civil authorities found four bodies, identified as those of Pierre and Jeanine LaMontagne, the ranch owners, and a Navajo hired hand and his wife. The bodies had been mutilated in what was described as a 'typically Apache manner.'"

"Mutilation of corpses isn't typically Apache," said Random.

Orders being orders, Sinclair hid his irritation at the interruption with a little bob-up on the balls of his feet. "Neighbors of the LaMontagnes report two other people living on the ranch. No sign of either was found." He paused significantly. "It is also reported that the missing couple are Indians, most likely Apache."

A perceptive man might have noticed the quick trade of glances between Random and the major. Neither Jordan nor the colonel saw. Sinclair continued, "In the Army's opinion, and in Mr. Jordan's as well, the disappearance of the Old Eagle from Fort Sill and the Española atrocity are not unconnected."

"Nducho." Random spoke the word as though spitting. The corners of his mouth dug into his cheeks.

Sinclair nodded. "It seems likely. Since the killing of Massai and the disappearance and presumed death of the Apache Kid, the Mountain Lion is the most prominent Apache renegade remaining in the northern Mexico–southern Arizona theater. Since the Mountain Lion is Aguilar's son, it doesn't seem unreasonable to surmise he had a hand in his father's escape."

Jordan pulled a silk handkerchief from the pocket of his waistcoat and dabbed at a shiny expanse of forehead. "Incomprehensible," he said. "After all the efforts we of the Bureau have expended on behalf of our charges over the last decade, that such men remain incorrigible in their barbarous brutality."

Random showed white teeth. "Perhaps a diet of short-weight rations and enforced Christian proselytization has worn thin for them, Mr. Jordan. And tell me, can a white man be convicted for murdering an Apache in the Territory these days? I've been away."

"I don't believe we need rehash the Bureau of Indian Affairs's policy just now, gentlemen," Sinclair said dryly, laying his words across Jordan's angry reply like a stick. "Keeping the peace in the Division is all I'm concerned with at the moment."

"Why did you cable me to come here directly from Santa Fe?" Random asked. "If Haastjj 'Ítsá makes for his old home in the Mimbres, I'm in the wrong place to try and intercept him."

Blank for an instant before understanding that Random had used the Apache for Old Eagle, Sinclair swept the pointer from the Rio Grande valley to where New Mexico and Arizona, and their maps alike, came together. "The war party was observed near the border, heading for Arizona and probably right here to the White Mountains." He smiled with neither warmth nor give. "You probably passed them on the train from Santa Fe to Holbrook."

"An old woman, a genuine Boston Brahmin straight off Beacon Hill, was on the AT&SF, bound for Sacramento," the major said. "It seems her daughter ran off with some writer who fancied himself a latter-day Bret Harte. He picked up an affliction in a mining camp in California—Mrs. Prewitt was none too forthcoming concerning its nature, though I gather she has surmises—and died, leaving the young hothouse flower bone-dry and wilting fast."

"Get to the point, man!" Jordan exclaimed.

The major waved him a bland look and continued, slower than before. "They were just west of Thoreau"—he said with a quick grin at Random, who rolled his eyes at the "proper" pronunciation of the name, which was "Through" to the denizens of the town, no matter what Henry David might have said—"right where the track switches northwest across the Río San Jose, when she summoned a porter and said that she had observed a party of, and I quote, 'horrid red savages, all on horseback and armed like Cossacks.'"

"She should write for the Hearst papers," Random remarked. "She's got the style for it."

The colonel snorted impatience. He wasn't used to waiting on the convenience of junior officers, to say nothing of civilians—and when the civilian he had to deal with was a goddamned mercenary who demanded money for doing his plain patriotic duty, the situation was well nigh intolerable. Bad enough dealing with that pompous lardbutt Jordan; Sinclair was at least accustomed to him, or at any rate resigned. As superintendent of District Seven of the Bureau of Indian Affairs, J. Ramsey Jordan's choleric purview included both the San Carlos and the Fort Apache Indian reservations, which meant he was an all too familiar figure to the commander of the outpost from which the latter reservation took its name.

The man named Random had no official standing whatever, which made the fact that Colonel Sinclair had been ordered, *very* officially, to treat with him quite unsettling to the colonel's orderly mind.

"The porter tried to humor her," the major said. "You know these easterners. Anyone without a stand-up collar and a bow tie is a barbarian."

"I beg your pardon, Major Carrington," Jordan interjected huffily. "I myself am from the city of Philadelphia."

"But this Mrs. Prewitt actually saw what she said she saw?" Random asked, ignoring him.

Carrington nodded. "She insisted on reporting to what she termed the 'proper authorities' on reaching Gallup. Not long after that, word came in that a prospector had been found in the Malpais over by Grants, fresh-shot and scalped."

Once more Random took the short green stick from his mouth. It was an old Apache remedy, and usually worked, but he suspected that it would not be strong enough medicine for the headache he'd been fighting off all day. He tossed it into the cuspidor with a tiny clang. "I presume Nducho's running with the usual assortment of *broncos* out of Sonora and Chihuahua?"

"As far as we know," Sinclair replied.

"Then why are they headed here? They've never loved either the San Carlos or the White Mountain people, and they've loved them less since the local Apaches sided with the Army in the wars. And I can't see them getting homesick for that hellhole you're pleased to call the San Carlos Reservation."

Jordan's face went purple, clashing violently with the rust of his three-piece suit. "Here now, Mr. Random! The Bureau has made every effort to ensure decent conditions to all its wards. As long as these Apache willfully resist all attempts to civilize them, one cannot expect them to share civilized levels of comfort!''

The two officers looked elsewhere. San Carlos deserved the title hellhole, and everybody in the room knew it. Random sucked in his cheeks and regarded Jordan, in no friendly manner.

"We don't know why he's coming here," Carrington said, bridging the comfortless gap in the conversation with the admission. "But we're damned near sure he is."

"We want him stopped," Colonel Sinclair said. "And we want it done before N—Nd—the Mountain Lion and his renegades do too much sowing of the wind. Because if they do, it's by God sure that every Apache in the Territory will share in the whirlwind that's reaped."

Random nodded. "A lot of your leading citizens would welcome the chance to clean out the Apaches your General Miles didn't treacherously ship off to the swamps of Florida."

Sinclair's lips whitened under the gray pencil-line of his moustache. "*Mister* Random," Jordan said, voice thick with the syrup of conciliation, "I think you judge the citizens of the Territory too harshly. Despite the hostiles' surrender a decade ago, they still find themselves prey to the depredations of the red wolves in spite of the unflagging efforts of our Army to contain them." He glanced sidelong at Sinclair, who did not seem pleased despite the unctuous tones. "Many believe the renegades are abetted by those San Carlos and White Mountain Indians who have been allowed to remain on their ancestral lands in return for their professed friendship and loyalty to the United States. And need I remind you that the Apache Kid, who so recently struck terror throughout the Territory, was a White Mountain." He shook his head. "The Arizonans may be intolerant, sir. But one can see the cause of their resentment."

Random fixed him with a piercing green gaze. "Just whose side are you on, Mr. Jordan? I thought you were here to represent the interests of your Bureau's wards."

"Mr. Jordan is here to represent the interests of his Bureau." Colonel Sinclair did not bother to blunt the edge of irony in his words.

Brushing long blond hair from his eyes, Random settled back in his uncomfortable chair. His skull pounded. He wished he had some of the new German wonder-drug called aspirin.

"Why hire me?" he asked.

"You're the only experienced scout available. Albert Sieber is confined to crutches, courtesy of the Apache Kid—who is likewise unavailable, for obvious reasons." The colonel laid down his pointer and resumed his chair. Arranging his hands before him on the desk, he went on: "Merejildo Grijalva and Sam Bowman have disappeared from view. One presumes they're dead. Mickey Free was deported with the Chiricahua. And Tom Horn is presently on the Powder River working for the Pinkertons, or so I understand."

"And even if he weren't, we couldn't trust him with this," added Carrington.

"Perhaps I should rephrase my question," Random said. "Why are you going to an outsider, a civilian? You've two troops of the Seventh Cavalry on-station, and four companies of the Eleventh Infantry, plus what? Eight or nine Apache scouts." He looked hard at Sinclair. "So why me?"

"I don't see how it concerns you." Sinclair bristled, unused to such questioning. A look of contempt came over his face. "You'll be amply paid."

"I'm being asked to risk my life, Colonel. So everything about this situation concerns me. And whether you mind my saying so or not, it seems there's one hell of a lot I've not been told."

"The Apache wars ended ten years ago," said Jordan, smirking openly at Sinclair, "and this is an election year. How is it going to look at appropriations time if our brave Army can't prevent a fresh irruption of savages from butchering a few dozen whites?"

"Don't push me, Jordan!" shouted Sinclair. The small officer's face was almost as red as that of the superintendent, who blinked and pulled his head back into his stiff collar like a large fleshy bird. Such an outburst was unlike Sinclair.

"If the Army takes official action, it'll come out sooner or later," Carrington said. "That will give those influential citizens you were talking about the opportunity to agitate for the removal of the Apaches who remain in Arizona. And if the Army didn't start rounding them up pronto and packing them off to Fort Sill, there are several thousand cowboys and burnt-neck miners on hand who'd be all too willing to finish the work begun at Camp Grant a few years back."

"So that lets out the United States Marshall's office as well," Random said. "What about Indian police? There's a sizable contingent at San Carlos, and you had some up here at the Whiteriver Agency too, last I heard. Why not use them?"

Sinclair looked back searchingly. Was this money-soldier trying to talk himself out of a job? "Mr. Jordan informs me he doesn't consider that the Apache police would be reliable in the present instance."

"It's the sickness of the Ghost Dance," Jordan said grandly. "It's permeated every reservation and agency in the West. Many of us believed we'd put a stop to that nonsense at Wounded Knee." He sighed. "That belief proved premature."

He favored his listeners with a look of porcine sagacity. "We all know that the White Mountains and the San Carlos dislike the Chiricahua. But they came close to soothing over their differences once before. Are you familiar with what took place at Cibicu, Mr. Random?"

"All too familiar," Random said in a flat hard voice. Jordan's small watery eyes met his and quickly turned away.

After a moment Random shook himself and shifted in his chair. The chair had not been designed to be sprawled in, but he sprawled just the same, even though it felt as if a few of his vertebrae were about to slip out of place. He knew how much it rankled Sinclair to see a civilian slouching in his office. At the same time, he knew Sinclair was probably not unaware that in earlier years Random had endured the most brutal military discipline on earth, and emerged not just alive, but a hero. It could not help but keep the man off balance. Which was fine with Random.

"So you want to save the Army's reputation, and probably its appropriation, and not incidentally your own career, Colonel. But unlike you I'm a free man; I can pick my assignments." He lifted a boot and rested it on the edge of Sinclair's desk. "I need one more reason to work for you."

The colonel glared at Random, his hatred raw as a wound. "I don't much care for the Apaches who are supposed to be your good friends, Mr. Random," he said at last, wrestling each word out past tight lips. "But I have no wish to be the officer called upon to officiate over their extermination."

The bootheel scraped off his pristine desktop. "That's the right answer, Colonel," said Random quietly, and sat up.

Tension fled like a sigh. "At what level has this been approved?" Random asked. "I don't want to go in somewhere for supplies and find the Army's disavowed me and put a price on my head."

"Your employment in this affair has been cleared at a high level, Mr. Random," Sinclair said.

"*How* high?"

Sinclair hesitated. "The General of the Army himself approved it."

Random laid back his head and laughed. Nelson A. Miles had been named to replace General Crook commanding the then Department of

Arizona in 1886. His first act had been to fire the scouts, both white
and Indian, who had brought his predecessor so much success.

For his victory half a year later Miles had been named top man in
the U.S. Army. The scurrilous, however, whispered that the last
Apache war had ended, not because of the elephantine efforts of Miles
and five thousand regulars, but because a couple of Chiricahua
defectors found old Geronimo in an arroyo and advised him to
surrender, which he did.

But Miles was the man of the hour. His was the story that the nation
would hear, and believe. But he knew he had critics, men who knew
how wanting his performance had been, and he hated them. Among
the most vociferous was also one of the most experienced, a man who
despite his youth had spent years fighting in the deserts of North
Africa with the French Foreign Legion: the former civilian scout
Random.

"My commissioner knows of this . . . *scheme* as well, and
concurs in it," said Jordan. The mercenary did not miss that the
superintendent failed to say his superior approved it.

"So the Army and the Bureau are doing this on their own, without
letting the secretaries of Army or the Interior in on the secret. And of
course no one's going to tell lame-duck Grover unless things go all to
hell. Fine." He stood; stretched. "If you gentlemen meet my price,
there's a good chance they need never know."

"Very well." Sinclair was scowling at the flippant reference to his
commander in chief. "What's your price?"

"Five thousand dollars."

"Five *thousand*?" Jordan began to sputter, turned it to a cry of
outraged disbelief. "Colonel, from the very outset I have opposed this
ridiculous plan. Now perhaps Mr. Random's exorbitant demand will
convince you to do what must be done: send out your cavalry."

"No." The colonel turned to Random. "That's a lot of money."

"You said it yourself, Colonel. I'm the only man who has a prayer
of doing the job." He smiled grimly. "Think of it this way: What
happens to me if I fail? Nducho's every bit as vicious as the
stereotyped popular image of an Apache. If he gets hold of me, not
even his father's hatred of torture is liable to earn me a quick death."

Silence gathered like dust in the corner of the room. Finally Sinclair
sighed and pushed his chair back again to rise. "Very well, Mr.
Random. I am authorized to make any settlement within reason. And I
regret to say that under the circumstances your price seems very
reasonable."

He came halfway around his desk and stood contemplating the mercenary. "I don't approve of you," he said. "A soldier should be ready to serve his country at need, and not have to be bought or bribed. But I'm aware of your record, Mr. Random. You're a brave, resourceful soldier, and"—he paused—"you're the only man who can do this. So I offer you my heartfelt best wishes." He held out his hand.

Random took it with a hard, scarred hand that seemed oddly older than his young-looking face and lithe frame. "Thank you, Colonel," he said gravely. "But there's one point that needs clearing up: I don't have such an exalted opinion of myself that I believe I can avert a new Apache war and send Aguilar, Nducho, and their friends scurrying all on my own."

The lids of the colonel's gray eyes came down like shutters. "We do have a squad of troops we can offer you, Mr. Random."

He turned from Random's look of surprise. "If you would be so kind as to ask Lieutenant Mayhew to step in, Major Carrington."

Carrington leaned back and rapped on the window with his knuckles. An instant later the door banged open with a blast-furnace rush of air. A reed-slim young officer with the yellow stripe of the cavalry running down the legs of his trousers snapped to attention as if he'd been springloaded and concealed beneath the stoop. "Yes, sir!" he yelped, accompanying the "sir" with what sounded suspiciously like a click of his heels. Sinclair frowned. Despite the pseudo-Prussian rig the Army had adopted for its dress uniforms in 1872, American soldiers were not, repeat not, supposed to click their heels when saluting.

"Yes, Lieutenant," the colonel said, returning the youth's salute crisply, but without sound effects. "Kindly send in Sergeant Brown and his men."

"Sir!" Mayhew took advantage of the salute to swipe surreptitiously at his yellow plume, which was hanging in his eyes. With the plastic grace of a marionette he turned and clomped into the white glare.

He was back in a moment. Of course he had not been taken into the colonel's confidence, but with that rudimentary instinct possessed by havetails, he knew that Something Big was in the wind, other than the aroma of the mules in the quartermaster's corral. His cheeks were pink with pride to be taking a part, however peripheral, in some event that he assumed as a matter of course would be duly gory and heroic.

Six men filed in behind him to line up smartly before the adjutant's desk. "Ten-*shun*!" rapped one, and saluted with a precise snap that left Mayhew gasping like a carp out of water. "First Sergeant Theophilus Brown, commanding replacement squad, Company G, Twenty-fifth United States Infantry reporting as ordered, sir!"

Random's eyebrows rose as he regarded them. He was beginning to understand how Sinclair could say the Army had to stay clear of this matter in one breath and offer him an infantry squad in the next. The replacement unit was very handsomely turned out. The spikes atop their white cork helmets glittered like the spearpoints of a Spartan phalanx. The eagle shields facing the helmets shone like golden mirrors. The stand-up necks of their coats were immaculately white, as were the stripes running down their trouser legs, and the gloves encasing the hands that gripped the butts of their outmoded .45-70 Springfield rifles.

But their faces were black.

# CHAPTER THREE

Two wiry painted *broncos* hustled Juanito from his home into a scene straight from the whiteman's hell.

The low adobe ranchhouse burned with a caged-beast roar, windows glaring like orange eyes, smoke spilling from them and beginning to seep through the seams of ceiling and flat roof and wisp upward, gray against the blackness of the sky. Horses screamed, drummed their hooves frantically on pine planking, as shouting warriors raced along opening stall doors to free the creatures from a stable some overzealous raider had prematurely set afire. There were perhaps twenty of the marauders, Juanito judged. Dazed and horrified as he was, he still saw with Apache eyes.

Anger burst within him like a bomb. He fought the hands that manacled his wrists. "Murderer!" he screamed at his brother, in the language of his birth. "You kill by night—you'll walk in darkness forever!"

Nducho's eyes became furious slits above the stripe of white-clay paint. "No, my son," came a calm, familiar voice from beyond his shoulder. "The Mountain Lion and his men will not walk in darkness in the Happy Place, though they slay by cover of night. Yusn has given them dispensation to do those things which must be done."

Juanito barely heard the words. Stunned, detached from the horror that had invaded his peaceful life, he raised his head and looked upon the lined narrow face of his father.

"I'm glad you've chosen to ride with me at last, 'Ítsá Bizhaazhé," the old man said.

The warriors released Juanito's arms. He staggered. How long since he had heard that name, Young Eagle, his birthing-name? Even before the last time he had seen his father he had taken as his adult name the White Mountain *Tse'e*, White-tailed Deer. That had been a decade before.

A mounted man swept up, yanked his horse to a haunches-low halt before Juanito. He led a second horse that rolled its eyes and fought the reins in fear, a gray roan mare with black stockings—Juanito's own horse, with his simple Mexican saddle on her back. He looked from the horse to his father, and then to his brother. "Mount," Nducho hissed. "Or stay here to face the questions the white-eyes will ask about the killings here. You'll have a hard time answering, with a rope around your neck!"

Nducho raced to his own mount, a big skitterish sorrel with a deep-burned Mexican brand on his shoulder, threw himself belly-down across the saddle, threw a leg over, and drew himself upright.

Juanito took the reins of his mare. But then he did a strange thing. For eight years he had mounted as a whiteman did, from the left. Now, without thinking, he went around to the right side of the panicky mare and vaulted onto her back: an Apache mount. She tossed her head with a jangling of bit and bridle, but did not try to throw him.

Aguilar flung a carbine over his head, voiced a high-pitched eagle's cry. Blinking away the tears that suddenly misted his eyes, Juanito followed, galloping for the tangle of black mesas that edged the valley to the west. As the other raiders found their mounts and joined the headlong cavalcade, Juanito chanced a single look back over his shoulder.

A Russian olive tree burned in the walled garden of the main house. Some *bronco* had splashed coal oil on it and set it alight, venting rage against the white-eyes on a thing that the white-eyes had nurtured. Looking down on the bodies crumpled in the doorway of the house, the great tree seemed to be weeping flames.

He looked then to his own house. Its door gave forth a deceptively cheery glow. He felt a leaden weight in his stomach. What happiness he had known in life was turning to ashes with his house. And the man named Juanito Aguilar died with it.

From now on he was Tse'e once more. For better or worse.

And he thought, *Oh, Mariana my love, what will become of us?*

As the war party swept like demons into the night, a slight lonely figure slipped out of the shadows and ran to the burning house of Juanito Aguilar. The thick *vigas* that upheld the ceiling were wrapped in smoke, the bright-checkered oilcloth curtains blazed at the windows. Coughing, the figure covered its mouth with a strip of flannel torn from the hem of its garment and dipped in the well. Methodically, it gathered up the carbine Nducho had tossed contemptuously aside, moved back into the bedroom for ammunition and clothing. The raiders had first fired the kitchen, and it was an inferno;

nonetheless the diminutive figure was able to rescue a pot of beans and a half-empty sack of flour before the flames drove it back.

Once more clear of the house, drinking down the relatively clear air of the outdoors with heaving gulps, the figure slipped off the torn nightdress and hurriedly donned a cotton blouse, heavy skirt, and hightopped *kéban*, Apache moccasins, ignoring the burning flakes that settled on bare skin and clung like stinging insects. Then the figure gathered up its weapon and food and hurried toward the apple orchard, where a sturdy black mare was tethered.

The figure spoke soothingly to the beast. The mare's glossy coat was smoke-dulled and singed in places from the burning stable. When she erupted from the flaming enclosure, she had almost trampled the slight form who darted from shadow to intercept her and draw her back into the night. But the familiar smell and calming touch of the figure had freed her of her panic, and the mare had allowed herself to be bridled and tied among the blossoming apple trees.

She bobbed her head and whickered softly as the figure climbed onto her back. Leaning forward, Mariana Aguilar patted her reassuringly on the neck. Then she slung her bundle and her carbine across the horse's withers, and booted the mare in pursuit of the men who had stolen her husband from her.

The war party hurtled across a moonless landscape that knew neither time nor distance. In time they mounted a low mesa, furred thick with pungent piñon and juniper, where Nducho and Aguilar judged they would be safe from the whiteman's vengeance for a time. Too sick and stunned even for mourning, Tse'e fell into a bottomless sleep, black as the volcanic rock on which he unrolled his blanket.

A blow in the ribs woke him. He rolled onto his back, blinking at a sky that was half indigo, half fire. His brother stood against the sun that rose over the Sangre de Cristos, nudging him with the toe of his *kéban*.

Nducho held something forth. "Here, *shikis*. Your drinking tube and stick for scratching."

Disoriented, Tse'e had to force his eyes to focus on what his brother offered. One was a small stick, several inches long, an inch broad, of some hard wood. The other was a short length of dried carrizo reed. "What's this all about?" he asked blearily.

"You are *dikǫǫhé*, an apprentice of war. You must use these implements to drink and scratch with, or your skin will turn soft as a woman's, and you'll grow thick ugly hair all over your face, like that fat white-eyes we killed."

Tse'e struck the stick and the reed from his brother's hand. "Murderer!" he shouted, scrambling to his feet.

The war party was scattered over a short stretch of mesa, clumped around smokeless fires. Hard faces turned toward Tse'e. He waited for one of the *broncos* to shoot him, for Nducho to snatch his knife out and come on slashing with that heedless fury Tse'e knew so well from boyhood. But the Mountain Lion was in good humor. He laughed in his brother's face.

The others joined in. "The White-tailed Deer's grown lazy among the white-eyes," one said. He was a square-faced man with a blue-checked Pima turban and a dead eye rolled up in his head, showing a fishwhite underside. "We'll teach you how to work, again, *dikǫǫhé*."

The man at his side showed stained teeth. "It's fitting you do women's work," he said. "You've never been to war. Maybe that's why you never got any children from that skinny Dziłghą'á doe." The speaker had thin limbs but a kettle belly and a second chin, which trembled as he laughed at his own wit. A sparse beard and moustache fringed his mouth. Tse'e guessed he was a Mexican half-breed.

Tse'e crossed his arms and said nothing. "Go get your scratcher and your reed, Tse'e," Nducho said. His face darkened abruptly, like the sun going behind clouds. "My patience isn't endless."

"Enough." The raiders turned their heads to look at a man sitting across the fire from Nducho. He was a stocky man with an ugly face, all knobs and angles. Except for the scalpband binding straight black hair at his temples, he was dressed all in red. Even his moccasins had been dyed that shade. It struck Tse'e like a blow to see him there.

"War's too serious for such childish games, Nducho," said the man in red.

Anger flared in Nducho's eyes. But the fire quickly went out. This man was one Nducho would be eager to keep by his side for this doomed adventure, whatever it was. He was also one he might hesitate to cross.

"But it's the old way," Nducho said. "Tse'e hasn't completed the four raids it takes to become a warrior. So he's still an apprentice, Red." A tic fluttered beneath his left eye. "He has to learn humility."

The other regarded him levelly from his skull face. "And since when do the 'old ways' require an Apache to cultivate humility?"

Tension hung like a dagger in the air between the two. Tse'e wondered how long it would be before the thin string that held his brother's vicious temper in check frayed to the breaking point. He hoped it would be soon.

"What's happening here?" a voice called. Tse'e looked beyond Red—whom he knew by another name—to see his father picking his way over the rusty black lava toward the camp.

"Tse'e won't accept the duties of a *dikǫǫhé.*" Nducho almost whined the words.

The old man stopped, looking from one son to the other. Incongruously, Tse'e felt his heart fill with love for the old man. Aguilar was old, but still magnificent, his eyes clear and black and bright as the barrel of a rifle. Erect and graceful, the planes of his face and the bladelike jut of his nose were still austere and noble and strong, yet giving hint of tenderness held rigidly within against those times it was fitting to display it. *I don't know why he's part of this evil,* Tse'e thought. *But Yusn, he's still my father!*

"He's older than you, Nducho," Aguilar pointed out. "He's too old to be an apprentice."

"But if we don't have any apprentices who'll tend the horses, fetch water, and get up early to build the fire and make us breakfast?" asked the round-bellied bearded man.

Nducho whirled on him. "You defecate through the mouth, Boca Negra! Is that why they gave you that name?" He stuck out his chest and strutted a few stifflegged steps. "If Aguilar says my brother's no *dikǫǫhé,* then he isn't one. He went through the training like any young Chíhéne. He was tough too—almost as tough as I. Even if he did turn traitor later."

"Enough, my son," Aguilar said. Nducho dropped his eyes.

They mounted and set off into the south and west, to bypass the heights of the Jemez that loomed green to the west of them. As they followed their long shadows across that dull black and green land, Tse'e found himself slipping into a haze of apathy. His friends were dead, his wife disappeared, and he, himself, was under suspended sentence of death should he try to slip away. He was trapped in the very sort of madness he had always avoided. And there was his father, always his father. No matter how vicious or insane Nducho's schemes were, Tse'e wondered if he could separate himself from them, as long as Haastíj 'Itsá went along. He did not know whether he could abandon his father again, no matter what the cause.

The sun was high in the sky when they left the ancient lava flows for the dun ridges, arroyos, and mesas of the desert. Tse'e's gloomy reverie was broken by his brother's voice, challenging from near at hand. "You're thoughtful, my brother," Nducho said. "You're not thinking of leaving us?"

Appraisingly, Tse'e looked at his brother's handsome, almost ascetic face. *Yes*, he thought, *I could run. I'm Apache too; I could find Mariana wherever she is, before these wolves ran her down. We could flee back to Española, tell the story to the sheriff or the Army—*

It seemed Nducho read his thoughts, for he laughed loudly. "Run if you will. See what the white-eyes say."

"The LaMontagnes were my friends. No one could believe I'd hurt them."

"You disappoint me, *shikis*. The white-eyes will believe anything of an Apache. As long as it's bad. No, they'd hang you, so that you went through the afterlife with your neck twisted like a chicken's—if you were lucky. If you weren't, they'd put you in a cage until you went mad." He shook his head. "And they name *us* cruel."

Tse'e looked away, trying to lose his thoughts in that angular land. He knew his brother spoke the truth.

"And consider what the *'indaa ligai* will find back at the ranch." Nducho reached down the far side of his horse. "We treated your friends the Indian way, after we killed them—*see?*"

Long strands whipped across Tse'e's face. He flinched and his pony crabstepped away from Nducho's. Then he saw what his brother held in his hand and cried out in agony.

Long auburn hair, still glossy, sprouted from Nducho's fist beside a tangle of shorter, curly hair, coal-black. Nducho had slapped Tse'e across the face with scalps, scalps matted with blackened half-dried blood—the scalps of Jeanine LaMontagne and her husband Pierre.

In his sick anger Tse'e almost dropped his hand to the blanket-wrapped Sharps tied under his right stirrup. *"Put those things down, you young fool!"* roared a voice behind them. "You're asking to get the ghost-sickness. Do you want to bring it down on all of us?"

Nducho gave a coyote-yip of laughter and spun his pony in a swirl of dust. "Are you afraid, Chi'?" he shouted, and waved the scalps in the face of the red-clad warrior.

The stocky, middle-aged Chi' raised his carbine to fend the gory trophies off. "Scalping's a filthy habit, Nducho. You don't earn any honor by doing it."

"Our brothers the Comanche and the Kiowa do it, Wears-Red-in-the-Storm."

"The Comanches also play with their penises when they're young, Nducho. Did you learn that from them too?"

Face twisted with fury, Nducho lunged his horse at Chi'. The older man's horse laid back its ears and showed long teeth. It was a ridgebacked Mexican buckskin as ugly and ageless as its owner, and fully as formidable. The chestnut shied away.

"There!" Nducho screamed, flinging his prizes into the arms of a dead piñon. "I'll throw them away if they bother you so much!" He dug the heels of his *kéban* into his horse's sides and galloped into a broad sandy wash that cut across their path.

The man in red brought his horse alongside Tse'e's. Tse'e nodded a wary greeting. Gravely the other nodded back. "You look well, Tse'e."

"Thank you, my friend. You do as well." As their ponies picked their way down a fallen-in place on the cutbank of the arroyo, he pondered how much he could say to his man, how much he dared ask. He finally settled on a neutral subject. "Why do they call you *Chi'*, Red?"

"It's short for Wears-Red-in-the-Storm," the other said. "They call me that because I do."

"But I always knew you as Lightning-Strikes-Near," Tse'e persisted. "Why don't they call you that?"

A bleak look crossed the badlands of the other's face. For a moment Tse'e thought he had overstepped. This man had owned lightning Power in years past, and had lost it—one of the direst fates that could befall an Apache. He had kept the name as long as Tse'e had known him, possibly in hopes it would help draw the Power back to him. Perhaps it had grown too painful for him to bear.

"It's to ward off bad luck," Chi' explained. "Lightning's a bad omen. Some of the weaker members of the party fear carrying such a name with them, when already we have one named Niishdzhaa among us."

"Owl?" Tse'e asked in astonishment. The Owl was the worst influence in all the Apache world, redolent of ghosts and evil. One who dared bear such a name must be extraordinarily powerful. For good or ill. "Who is he?"

"He is the prophet who brought the new word of Yusn to us," Chi' replied. "We go to meet him on the Fort Apache Reservation."

Tse'e allowed his horse to fall behind so that he might ponder this new information. *A prophet, eh.* That explained something that had been bothering him. The members of the party, his brother and father in particular, had been making much use of the name of God, Yusn. That was unlike an Apache, who normally held his religion within his

breast, regarding it as a private matter between himself and Yusn. If a
new prophet had risen among the Apache, it would explain more than
the promiscuous use of God's name. It would also explain how
Nducho had been able to assemble such a large force from the
remnants of free Chiricahua—and how he had convinced his father to
escape from Fort Sill to join him. It also told Tse'e how as seasoned a
warrior as Chi' could be drawn into something as blatantly hopeless as
a fresh attack on the white-eyes—and how a man as decent as Chi'
could bring himself to ride with a *heshkéé* of Nducho's stripe.

A shudder passed through Tse'e. Maybe he was too steeped in the
whiteman's history, but he had a distrust of prophets, whatever color
their skin. *And one named Owl . . .*

He glanced back then, and regretted it to the end of his days. A
flock of crows had appeared, as if from the ground itself, and
clustered around a dead tree that lay along the war party's back trail.
With their sharp black beaks they tore at the strands hanging from the
sunbleached limbs like black and auburn moss.

Tears drawing lines through the dust on his cheeks, Tse'e rode away
from a sun that could not touch the winter in his soul.

# CHAPTER FOUR

"Sergeant Brown and his men were sent to us by, ah, administrational oversight," said Colonel Sinclair.

Random stuck out his hand. After a moment's hesitation the sergeant shook it. He was a spare, moustached man of medium height, and his eyes were wary. Not many white civilians were eager to shake hands with black soldiers.

"I'm pleased to meet you, Sergeant," Random said.

Brown's eyes flickered. Random winced inwardly. *My accent. Merde.*

Most Americans would not have said he had an accent, or would have thought what he had to be vaguely European in its precision and occasional stiltedness. That quality was not an affectation. From the time he was eight until his early twenties, Random had spoken first German and then French almost exclusively—on the brutal Elbe-front docks of Hamburg and later in the French Foreign Legion. He no longer lapsed into one or the other tongue in times of stress. But Random's native language was English as spoken by citizens of Richmond, Virginia, and of comfortably gentle birth. And most southern-born blacks Random had ever encountered could pick out a *white* southern accent the way a magnet picks a nail out of a pile of straw, no matter how deeply it happens to be buried.

*I've gotten off to a bad start simply by opening my mouth.*

Random nodded at the gold slashes climbing the arm of the sergeant's coat like vines. "You've been in a long time."

"Yes, sir. Since 'sixty-four."

"And your men?"

"Four new recruits, one prior service, sir."

Random shut his eyes. His headache was expanding, with brass bands and carronades. *Four* new recruits. The sergeant could be a real prize, but four recruits against a Chíhéne chief who had in his day earned the respect of Cochise, Mangas Coloradas, and his own cousin Victorio—a *heshkéé* son who'd ridden with Juh and Geronimo and spent the last ten years in a wolfshead existence in war-torn northern

Mexico—plus who knew how many seasoned *broncos*! It was like issuing four invitations to a massacre.

"As I understand it," Colonel Sinclair said, "the sergeant was wounded by a rioter when the Twenty-fifth was called out to suppress the Northern Pacific strikes in Montana, back in 'ninety-four. One of the Red rabble shot him in the chest. He spent a long time recuperating in hospital, then was sent East on furlough. He had orders to report back at Fort Leavenworth, Kansas, in order to pick up a replacement squad to take back with him to Fort Missoula. This was in the fall of last year.

"When he got to Leavenworth, the squad was waiting, but no orders. They waited several months. When the orders did arrive, they were for Fort Apache. They've been here for two months," the colonel continued. "I've sent queries to Fort Whipple, Los Angeles, and finally Washington, inquiring as to what I should do with these men. So far they haven't seen fit to answer. And due to the irregularity of the situation, these men have not been entered on the post rolls as part of the official complement of Fort Apache."

This was no less irregular than misplacing the troops in the first place, as Random well knew. He was not entirely surprised to see in Sinclair's eyes an unvoiced plea for acceptance of what had to be. "They've been drawing rations from the QM over my signature, though of course their pay has fallen somewhat in arrears. In any event, since they are not officially *at* Apache, putting them at your disposal for the duration of the crisis will in no wise endanger the secrecy so vital to its successful resolution."

He allowed himself the first smile Random had seen from him. "It looks like the incompetence of those damned wooden-horse troopers of the Adjutant General's office has paid off for once."

A trumpet tootled outside. The official complement of Fort Apache was assembling for a belated Sunday parade. Random became aware that Brown's face had become a mask, perfectly immobile. He knew that his own face had reflected the doubts he felt about these troops—and that the sergeant had misread it. Random was concerned with their color all right: green. He knew Brown didn't see it that way.

*The hell with it.* "Do you know anything of mules, Sergeant?"

"Grew up with them, sir."

"Very well. With your permission, Colonel?" Sinclair nodded.

"Sergeant, I'd like you to draw six mules from the quartermaster, with saddles and tack for each. I want it made clear to him they're to be sound of wind and limb, and saddle-broke. You have until dawn of the day after tomorrow to turn your men into dragoons. Can you do that?"

"Yes, sir." He said it straightforwardly enough for Random to believe it.

"Dismissed," Sinclair said. The infantrymen turned and started to file out. "Oh. One more thing, Sergeant Brown. To keep things orderly, Mr. Random is to be regarded as holding rank of captain, United States Army, for as long he remains in the employment of the Army. Is that clear?"

"Sir."

"Excuse me, Sergeant." Brown looked around sharply at Random's soft request. White and black aside, he was not used to a de facto captain asking excuse of a noncom. "But there's one thing *I'd* like to make clear. And that's that I will order no one to do anything. If you and your men will follow me voluntarily and accept my leadership, I'll be honored to have you. But if you don't want to go, as far as I'm concerned you don't have to."

Brown looked at him as if to say, *Who're you kidding?* The white "officer" couldn't possibly mean such an extravagant offer. Of course he did, though he knew it was futile to make it. He felt he had to, all the same. Elaborating would do no good, especially with that hard look in Colonel Sinclair's eyes at this unheard-of procedure.

"We go where we're told to, Captain," Brown said. He saluted and left with his men.

Random sighed. He'd make the offer again, when they might have a reasonable chance to say yes or no.

"Well, Colonel," he said, "I don't see any reason to take up any more of your time—"

Jordan cleared his throat. "One thing, Mr. Random." The mercenary turned to him and cocked a brow. "There is to be one more addition to your expedition."

"Oh? And who or what might that be, Mr. Jordan?"

"My son, Brentwood Jordan the Third." And before Random's jaw hit his breastbone, the portly superintendent rose and walked to fling open the inner door of the colonel's office. "Brent, you may come in now. Your companions may come along too."

Random turned a wild look to Carrington. "Tom, what in God's name *is* this?" The major shrugged. He got as much mileage out of shrugs as if he'd attended St.-Cyr instead of the Point.

A resplendent vision entered the dim varnish-smelling office. Brentwood Jordan III was the all-American boy. Six feet tall, broad of shoulder, slim of hip, blue of eye. His seal-brown hair was as long as Random's, worn swept back clear of his upturned collar in a faddish "football" cut. His athletic frame was encased in a natty linen shirtwaist suit, beige and vestless. He was in short a "dude," the very picture of the casual well-to-do young gentleman, prepared, perhaps, for a quick spin down a country lane on his "wheel."

"I'm Brent Jordan," he said in a muscular baritone, extending a hand. "I'm *dee*-lighted to meet you."

Random almost groaned. There was one figure on the American scene whose silly overemphatic schoolboy manner of speaking was all the rage of eastern campuses, and Random knew him well. As a matter of fact, the last Random had heard of that prominent gentleman, he had given his private army, also known as the New York Police, carte blanche to shoot the mercenary on sight.

"Where's your bicycle?" he asked.

"Pardon?" Young Jordan looked blank.

"Never mind. Jordan, are you out of your mind? I can't have your boy tagging along with me. The Tonto Rim's a hell of a ways from Harvard Yard."

Young Jordan's well-scrubbed cheeks turned pinker. "My son is a recent graduate of Yale College," his father explained.

"I beg your pardon. But I don't care if he just graduated from the College of Cardinals. I've got enough green hands already. He's not going."

"I can handle myself quite well, *Mister* Random," Brent Jordan said, pronouncing the word "Mister" as he might to a fishmonger who was presuming to wear a silk hat and monocle. "I'll have you know I distinguished myself on the fields of honor as a member of the Bulldog first eleven."

"The *what*?"

"Mr. Jordon is referring to the Yale football team, Mr. Random," Sinclair said, not without amusement.

*This young idiot thinks "fields of honor" are where one plays football?* "I'm sure you're the very embodiment of muscular Christianity, Mr. Jordan. But this is no game you're asking to become involved in. It's war. It's dirty and grim. And there won't be any opportunity to cover yourself with glory. Just dust, sweat, and likely your own blood."

Jordan elevated his aristocratic nose. "Your words do not frighten me, sir."

"Then you're stupid."

"Now, you cain't go talkin' at Mr. Jordan like that," a voice said from the door. "He's a gentleman."

"That's the only thing no one could ever accuse you of being, Cahill," Random said to the skinny little man in miner's jeans and flannel shirt who was standing in the doorway grinning at him with a handful of crooked yellow teeth. The newcomer had a fleshy nose a size or two too large, jug-handle ears, a bantam-cock's manner, and a coxcomb of grizzled red hair to go with it.

"You need have no fear for my son's welfare," the elder Jordan said smugly. "I've engaged professionals to see that he remains safe on the trail."

At the word "professionals" Cahill's shadow stirred in the door behind him. For such a tiny man Cahill cast a big shadow: upward of six three, in fact, and wide enough to crowd the doorframe. The shadow's name was Obadiah Sutter. His face was mostly shaded by the broadbrimmed slouch hat he wore, but Random caught the impression of black-bearded jaws working on a plug of tobacco the size of a normal man's fist, and of eyes staring from the gloom beneath the hatbrim, insensate and yellow as a lynx's.

"Does your son have any gold teeth, Mr. Jordan?" Random asked. Jordan blinked. "Why, no. His teeth are perfect."

Random nodded. "Good. Then you won't have to inventory them when he returns—if he returns. But I'd suggest you hold his watch, money, and anything else these two jackals might fancy they could peddle for a mouthful of Taos lightning, while he's gone."

"Now just a goddamned minute." That shrill child's voice was unnerving, coming as it did from the cavernous depths of Sutter's body, whistling through the two-finger-wide gap in his upper front teeth.

"These men come to me with the highest recommendation, Mr. Random," Jordan said. "They're well versed in the ways of this harsh land."

"I'll say. Did you ever hear of the Camp Grant Massacre, Mr. Jordan? *That* was awfully harsh, especially on the hundred thirty-six women and children out of a hundred forty-four killed. Not to mention the twenty-seven kids sold into slavery in Mexico. These two heroes both took part in that escapade, and brag of it whenever they have a good load aboard, which is most of the time."

"No jury ever found evidence of wrongdoing at Grant!" Jordan bellowed.

"A jury composed of rapists, murderers, and swine, passing

judgment on men accused of rape, murder, and swinery is the best definition I can think of for a travesty of justice, Mr. Jordan."

"I won't stand here and listen to you slander the decent and honorable citizens of the Arizona Territory!"

"Then go stand outside." Random spun round to lean on the desk with both hands. "Colonel, what are you doing to me? I'm supposed to be running down Nducho and Aguilar before they start a fresh war, and you're asking me to drag along Beau Brummell and his pair of pet wolverines. Do I have to take a mountain gun and a brass band with me too?"

Sinclair spread his hands. "I'm afraid I don't have any choice, Mr. Random. Mr. Jordan insists that his son go along, and his two . . . bodyguards, as well."

"If I am to acquiesce in this furtive and, I think, insanely risky response to the Aguilar crisis," said Jordan, "I must at least have a representative in the party to make sure my interests—that is to say, the interests of the Bureau which I so proudly represent—are given due consideration."

Jordan looked out the window and coughed experimentally. "I'd accompany you myself were my health not so impaired by the rigorous schedule I am forced to adhere to in discharging my duties. As it is, I think you'll find my son a most worthwhile companion. He's clever and quite fit: a real man's man."

Random resisted the desire to massage his throbbing temples. "It doesn't appear I have any choice."

Young Jordan beamed. "Bully! I'm an excellent rider, Mr. Random. I shan't slow you down." Random's agreement to his coming along, however grudging, seemed to erase the mercenary's earlier slights against the boy's alma mater.

"That's good," Random said. "Because if you do, I'll leave you behind."

The conciliatory smile slipped from Brent Jordan's lips. Sinclair cleared his throat and rose. "The troops are waiting," he said. "I really must go and inspect them. If you'd care to accompany me, Mr. Jordan? And you, Brent?"

Brent bobbed his head in happy acceptance. The colonel gravely placed his chapeau on his head, buckled on his saber, and walked out while Lieutenant Mayhew held the door for him and the Jordans.

Outside, the men were drawn up in ranks, the cavalry with their yellow plumes to the left, spiked-helmet infantry to the right, all looking rather wilted by the hot sun. They were starting to grumble and fidget with heat and boredom, impatient to get to the weekly baseball game that, since the Army had abolished flogging, was the only thing to do on Sundays after parade. As the post commander strode forth with his rolling horse-soldier's gate, the small band broke into a lilting, asthmatic air.

Carrington grinned. " 'Garryowen.' The Sioux national anthem."

Random barked laughter. Carrington scooped his chapeau off the table and studied it. "Ridiculous hats. Never could stand the things. Make you look like a Russian admiral." He put it on a finger and twirled it. The plume slapped him in the face. He tossed the hat back on the table.

"It seems our lords and masters delight in tricking us out in silly costumes. Sometimes I wish the damned French had won at Sedan."

"I knew a few men back at Sidi-bel-Abbès who felt the same way," Random said dryly.

"I'm sure." Carrington pointed out the flyspecked window. At the end of the infantry rank nearest the sycamore-shaded headquarters, the fort's eight Apache scouts stood to attention. They looked even more ridiculous in their comic-opera Prussian uniforms than their white comrades, or Brown's black infantrymen, for that matter. "I'll bet some rising young quartermaster won a promotion for them. Imagine, facing the scouts' uniforms in white piped with red to symbolize the cooperation of the races."

"I'm trying not to."

Carrington turned on a heel. "You need a drink."

"You're right."

Carrington crossed to behind Sinclair's desk. "Fortunately, the colonel offered me free use of his sideboard. Preferences?" Random shrugged. When opportunity offered, he had quite a palate for wine. Otherwise his was a Legionnaire's sensibility as to drink: all he cared was whether it was alcoholic and whether it would cause him to go blind.

He sat down as his friend started to pour and picked up the latest number of *Military Information* from Sinclair's desk. It offered articles on the use of "electric projectors"—searchlights—in modern war, and on the design of Prussian kite-balloons, as well as promising a report on the Austro-Hungarian Empire's spring maneuvers in the next issue. Random tossed the magazine aside.

Carrington studied his friend as he handed him a tumbler of the colonel's most expensive whiskey. Usually Random read anything he could get his hands on, particularly if it pertained to military matters.

Random thanked him, sipped, stood up, and walked to the window. He looked out without seeing the men drawn up like toy soldiers on display, the lifeless flag drooping from the pole, the sprawling rectangle of adobe and warped whitewashed frame structures that was Fort Apache. He looked beyond, past the hunchbacked scrub pine and juniper that marked the boundary of the low mesa on which the fort was built, past the White River that flowed by below, past the red caprock of Sevenmile Rim to the high, dry, broken lands of the Natanes Plateau that separated the Fort Apache Reservation from the San Carlos.

Slowly his gaze swung northward. He had to crane to see the rugged profile of the White Mountains, which were actually blue-green and inviting at this distance.

Carrington's gaze followed his. "It's a lot cooler up there."

Random sipped at the whiskey. "Not for long."

"What do you think?"

Random laughed bitterly. "What do *you* think? Bad. The Territory's aching to see the last of the Apache. The wolves of Sonora are running loose and, if word gets out, the Indian-haters will have themselves a jubilee." He took a drink and grimaced as if the smooth whiskey had been dosed with alkali. "And I'm supposed to head it all off with a gaggle of greenhorns and backshooters."

"That sergeant seems pretty solid," Carrington said.

"I'm going to be putting a lot of stock in him," Random said. "But I don't think he cares much for me."

"Do you blame him?" Carrington asked. "He wears the Blue for thirty years and what does he get? Some jackass at Leavenworth decides it's funny to send the niggers on a snipe hunt to the most desolate post in the Union."

He shook his head in disgust and waved his arm at the soldiers out on the parade ground, who had obviously been dismissed and were milling around, eager to get out of the stiff, hot dress blues and into sensibly tan southwestern fatigues. "And what does he get here? You know as well as I do what a line of bull Sinclair was handing out about not entering the Negroes on the post rolls because of 'irregularity.'"

Random nodded deliberately. "I do. If he entered them on the rolls he'd have a mutiny on his hands."

"And just look at those Seventh Cav bastards. Too proud to serve beside Negroes—inheritors of the proud tradition of the Army's worst defeat since Second Bull Run."

"Manassas," corrected Random automatically, and laughed at himself. At once he grew serious again. "You sound bitter, Tom."

"And you don't?" Carrington seated himself on the colonel's desk and looked earnestly at his friend. "You've changed, Random."

Random took a deliberate drink.

"What's chewing you, old friend?"

The hardpacked dirt of the parade grounds was almost devoid of life. Colonel Sinclair and his guests had shown no sign of returning to the office. Either they had decided to go for a ride in the hills, perhaps to look at the old Indian ruins up on the East Fork of the White, or had repaired for tea and cookies in the house Mrs. Sinclair maintained for her husband behind a phalanx of flowerbeds. Random gazed sightlessly out at the deserted compound for a time before answering.

"Two sorts of things," he said. "Personal. And philosophical."

Carrington cocked his head. "Personal?"

"I killed somebody, Tom. Back in New York."

"With all due respect, that's nothing new."

"This was," Random said tautly. "May we leave it?"

Carrington spread his hands before him. "Of course."

Random nodded thanks. "As to the other, it's simple enough. I've been fighting for damned near twenty years, mostly in colonial wars. I never believed in it much; I believe in it a whole lot less now. But there's always been some overriding reason to keep fighting. At first, in North Africa, it was self-defense. Then I got promoted and went off to fight the Tuareg, and I could tell myself that the reason was to protect the Chaamba tribesmen from their neighbors' depredations, and not to spread Western civilization at the point of a gun.

"It was the same here in Arizona in the eighties. The Apaches I fought were raiders and killers who were as inclined to prey on their own people as whites and Mexicans. By the time I got here, most of the real patriot chiefs were dead, leaving mainly opportunists of the stripe of Geronimo. It was the *heshkées* I fought, the wild killers, not men like Nana or Chihuahua. Sometimes good men like Naiche and Mangas, who were too conscious that they could never measure up to their fathers and so fell under the sway of the Yawner." He shook his head. "But what it came down to was that basically the men I fought were men trying to keep their homes, even their lives. Hell, even a man such as Geronimo, who was as sympathetic to the plight of his kindred as, say, Little Phil Sheridan, saw his family butchered by Mexican cavalry." He shook his head and drained his glass. "And when the victory I'd helped work for finally came, what happened?

The whites broke faith again, shipped all the Chiricahua off to a stinking swamp guaranteed to kill them off by the dozens—those who'd fought for us as well as those who fought against us. And I helped bring it about. Even though Miles fired me, with Sieber and the rest, *I'd helped the bastards work their treachery*.

"I rationalized it neatly, saying to myself that my interest was to protect the Apache from the savagery of the raiders and the vengeance of the white-eyes. But all I actually did was take part in a campaign of murder, theft, and treachery that differed from those of the worst Apache marauders only in that it took place on one hell of a larger scale."

"I'm surprised you agreed to take this job," Carrington said softly.

"No, you're not."

Carrington smiled and sat back. "No. I suppose I'm not. I suppose I'm also the only white-eyes in the Territory who knows your real reasons."

"It's quite an experience to be on your way to visit old friends, only to find they've been murdered just before you arrived," Random said bleakly. "Let me promise you."

Carrington chewed his lower lip. "Why didn't you take after them yourself?"

Random laughed shortly. "I speak the Apache language and respect Apache ways, but that doesn't make me Nndé. Trying to track a band of *bronco* Chiricahua down a trail two days cold is not my idea of a profitable pursuit. Especially when every redneck on the Rio Grande has been riding up and down the valley for that two days muddying tracks and trying to beat confessions out of stray Pueblos. In a way it's fortunate Nducho kidnapped both Tse'e and Mariana. Those cowboys were ready for a real full-dress lynching bee—and they all knew for a positive fact that the 'red devils' the LaMontagnes had been sheltering against the good advice of neighbors had finally turned on them like captive wolf-cubs.

"Of course, that won't stop me from killing the Mountain Lion when I catch up with him."

"What would you have done if we hadn't called you in, then?"

"Why, I knew you'd call me." He laughed less brittlely than before at his friend's expression. "No, the spirits didn't whisper it in my ear. It was simple, straightforward Conan Doyle-style deduction. Northern New Mexico hasn't exactly been plagued with Apache raids the last few years; the fact that one struck the very ranch where Juanito and Mariana lived strained coincidence too much for me to accept. So that meant Nducho. With the Mexicans and the Yaquis slaughtering each other the Lion could run wild through northern Mexico as long as he wished with little actual danger. What brought him back to the States? And what made him scoop up his brother, who always refused the warpath, to go along?" He shook his head. "It had to be something big. Sooner or later the United States Army was going to have a crying need for someone who knew something about the Apache. And that meant they'd be getting in touch with me."

"What do you make of the Mountain Lion's springing his father from Sill?" Carrington hesitated slightly before speaking Nducho's English name; the Apache was too much for him. He grinned in envy of his friend's incredible talent for languages. Carrington had spent years in the Southwest and all he could boast was a half-dozen words of *coyote* Spanish.

"All I can read from that is that Nducho has a truly grandiose scheme in mind." He stroked his jaw pensively. "In fact, the evidence seems to point to the Mountain Lion's intending to raise the tribes against the whites."

"But the hard-line Cherry Cow don't love the White Mountains much more than they do the white-eyes."

Random nodded. That was no news. "But why else make the effort, to say nothing of taking the risk, of freeing Aguilar? If it was mere filial sentiment, why didn't Nducho move when the Chiricahua came to Sill two years ago?"

"Maybe he was biding his time."

"Nducho?"

"I withdraw the suggestion."

"Try this: Nducho is still no more than a raggedy-ass bandit leader. Haastįį 'Ítsá is a chief, by birth and by proven ability. If Nducho wanted to mount a war against the white-eyes, people would take the idea more seriously if the Old Eagle was behind it. Apaches aren't slaves to authority, like whites. A leader can only lead if he's got prestige. There are damned few Chiricahua who had more prestige than Aguilar, and most of them are dead."

"Why grab Juanito, then?" The words were spoken quietly, but Random did not miss the challenge in them.

"I don't know. Nducho's crazy enough to want to take the whole family with him in case he failed—real death-or-glory *Götterdämmerung*, right out of Wagner."

Carrington crossed one leg over the other and propped his chin in one hand. "You don't sound convinced."

*"What's that supposed to mean?"*

Carrington uncrossed his legs again. "Don't kill me for asking," he said carefully, "but don't you think the Mountain Lion may have had another reason for wanting his brother along? That special talent Juanito had, that was so helpful to us on our little junket to Mexico?"

"Then why did they take Mariana along?" Random snapped. "To skin out and dress his kills for him?" His face was white. "Juanito hates his brother's ways. You know that, damn it!"

"People change in ten years," Carrington said softly.

Abruptly the tension left Random's features. He laughed, but his eyes looked old and tired. "You've changed a lot, yourself," he said. "Sure you have. But you're still an honest man—and how you ever managed to get on McCook's staff with a handicap like that mystifies me."

Carrington laughed relievedly. "You haven't changed much either, I see. You're still an idealist—and you still care a damn lot more than you like to let show through that hardbitten mercenary facade."

"In this case I'm glad to admit it," Random said. "It's my only justification for getting involved. I'm happy to do my part in saving what's left of the Apache in the Territory, but at the same time I'm uneasy about the morality of trying to save people from themselves. But avenging one pair of friends, and rescuing another—that's plenty of reason to get involved."

This time Carrington's laughter was full-throated and long. "And you get to soak the Army for two hundred fifty ounces of gold into the bargain!" he roared. "And that means more to you than the gain itself."

"In this case, yes."

"You're the finest soldier I'll ever know. But you're a lousy mercenary."

"It's been said before. Usually with a different inflection. What about another drink?"

Carrington pushed off the table and went to the sideboard. Random gazed out the window. His attention was drawn by a flight of birds lazy-winging down toward the reeds that grew along the stream. Blackbirds, starlings, he thought at first. Then one landed on the mesa and he saw it was too big: crows. *This is the time the crows come back*, he thought.

Suddenly a premonition swept over him and chilled him through like a late winter wind from the treeless heights of the peak the whites called Mount Thomas, or sometimes Baldy, and which was known to the Apache by the holy name of Dził łigai si'áń, White Mountain. He sensed a movement of powers vastly greater than himself, unseen and ponderous and malevolent, and felt somehow that the stakes were greater than his life, or Tse'e's or Mariana's, or Nducho's; greater perhaps than the fate of the last Apaches in Arizona. He sensed that there would be no victory to this confrontation, that whatever the outcome, it would be gall upon his tongue.

When Carrington handed him a fresh glass, the earlier laughter was forgotten. And not even the whiskey could touch the chill that was upon him.

# CHAPTER FIVE

The moon's swollen face beamed down on the western mountains. Up on the Sevenmile Rim the coyotes tried to sing it the rest of the way from the sky. As their many-voiced chant died to a single lonely howl, Random raised his bottle in salute to the unseen chorus.

He sat with heels propped on railing that was peeling like a week-old sunburn. It ran around the swaybacked porch of the derelict officers' quarters that he had all to himself for the two nights he would be staying in Apache. Off behind him, across the parade ground, soldiers sang and joked and squabbled in their barracks. The sound had a lonely, desolate quality, like a small group of people conversing in hushed tones at the end of some great hall that echoed with emptiness. Fort Apache had been built to house a regiment. At the moment it held a handful of understrength companies, a hair over two hundred men—a malnurtured battalion at best. Most of the buildings stood empty, but for shadows and wind and lizards and the omnipresent dust.

The single coyote gave voice again, and the others answered, Greek-chorus fashion. Taking a mouthful of whiskey and rolling it over his tongue, Random smiled an autumnal smile. They fit his mood, these lonely sounds.

He was almost thirty-five—not old, by any means. Just arrived at that cold time of life when it came home to him that he'd never be young again. He wondered, not for the first time, if he ever had been young, and took another drink in wry celebration of the banality of the thought. He wondered if he would come back alive from the harsh task ahead, and wondered if he had finally reached the point where it didn't matter to him one way or the other. A chill came down from Mount Thomas, or the nearer mountain the Indians called Crown Dancer, and he was glad for the whiskey and the threadbare Legionnaire's capote he wore.

A small sound snapped his body and senses taut. He kept his boots propped and the whiskey bottle in hand, but ever so casually slipped his left hand across his body and into his coat. He heard steps approach around the corner of the clapboard building. Slowly he withdrew his hand.

"Mr. Random?" a voice asked from the darkness.

He saw the tall, heavyset figure standing on the path between the building and the steep cut of the east. "Mr. Jordan," Random said quietly.

The man started at hearing his name. "Why, yes. I hope I'm not intruding."

Random shrugged. Jordan was, but he had no urge to tell him so. The whiskey was mellowing him.

A heavy foot thumped the stoop. Jordan froze as he noticed moonlight glinting off the long barrel of a Colt. Random showed his teeth and gently let the hammer down. "I hope your son has better sense than you," he said.

Jordan licked his lips. "That's not funny."

"No, indeed," Random said agreeably. "If he comes sneaking up unannounced the way you just did when we're on the trail, he's likely to find himself buried among the roots of a mesquite bush."

He slid the gun back into its holster. "Have a seat. There's no porch swing, but there is an extra chair. Drink?"

Lowering his bulk into the chair, Jordan shook his head. Random upended the bottle and watched starlight dance in glass and liquid amber. "I thought you were dining with the colonel and his lady tonight."

"I excused myself," the superintendent said. "My son's still there, I believe. He's made quite a hit with the ladies."

Random smiled to himself. He had not been invited to dine with the Sinclairs and the post's other officers, one or two of whom also had wives at Apache. It didn't matter. Had he wanted to turn up, in no time at all he could have had Mrs. Sinclair and her cohorts begging him to stay; he had a boyish face that women favored, and considerable Continental charm where he chose to display it. But he had better things to do than seduce bored memsahibs.

Like sitting on the porch alone, listening to the coyotes and drinking down the moon.

Small cricket-creaks came from the chair as Jordan shifted uncomfortably in the silence. He cleared his throat. "I must leave Fort Apache early tomorrow on urgent business," he said. "Bureau matters. I've come one last time to try to persuade you to give up this madness."

"Tell me something, Superintendent. If this chase is so hopeless, why are you so eager for your son to come along?"

"I—that is, the boy needs a chance to prove himself."

"That's very strange. You're afraid for *me*, but you're willing to risk your son, just to put him through a rite of passage?"

"No, no, no!" Jordan's jowls shook in ponderous negation. "I see a certain risk entailed in this expedition for those party to it; but that's what a young man needs, the feeling of danger, bracing as a dash of cold water in the face. Good for the body, good for the mind." He held up his hand. "No. The danger I see is the danger to the citizens of Arizona, if these savages are allowed to rampage freely through the Territory."

"But they're not being 'allowed' to do it, Mr. Jordan," Random said. "That's why the Army hired me."

Jordan forced out a sarcastic laugh. "Do you imagine that you and a handful of men can actually track down a party of bloodthirsty renegades?"

"Yes. No other way to do it. Miles and his battalions never got near the hostiles, back in the eighties. Only small, swift parties led by experienced men and guided by Apache scouts ever had a prayer of tracking the Chiricahua down—or, better yet, intercepting and ambushing *them*, Apache-fashion."

"But these men you have with you! They're, ah, green. Wholly inexperienced."

"How experienced are Colonel Sinclair's troops? They've been out here for several years, certainly, but they've seen no serious action." He dropped his heels ringingly to the floorboards and sat up. "I can assure you, Mr. Jordan, I'd rather have a party of raw recruits who *know* they don't know what they're doing, than a troop of monkey-drill beauties from the Seventh who think they *do*."

"But what if you *fail*?" Jordan persisted.

Random fixed him with a piercing gaze. "If I fail," he said softly, "then it seems to me the Apaches still in Arizona will bear a lot more of the brunt of it than the white settlers. Shouldn't *that* be your main concern, Mr. Jordan?"

The superintendent looked away. "You are a mercenary, Mr. Random," he remarked. "You fight for pay."

"True enough. As far as it goes."

Jordan looked back to him, sidelong. "How much will you take not to fight?"

The bottle halted halfway to Random's lips. "I made a deal, Mr. Jordan," he said. "I keep my compacts."

A beefy hand waved the objection contemptuously away. "I'm offering you a better deal, Mr. Random. I have . . . connections. I—we—are prepared to make vast fiscal sacrifices to see that the right thing is done." He leaned forward. "You can name your own price."

"You're trying to buy me off for the Indian Ring?" Random asked. A dangerous tone had come into his voice. The Indian Ring of government contractors had assiduously kept the war-fires burning, even to running guns and liquor to the hostiles, so that federal procurement dollars would keep flooding into the Territory.

Jordan jerked, then threw his head back and laughed, high and edgy, so that for a moment Random thought the superintendent's mind had snapped. "No, Mr. Random," Jordan said, dabbing at his eyes with his handkerchief. "I can assure you, I'm not acting at the behest of the Indian Ring."

"I don't care who's behind you, Jordan. The answer's no." He tipped his head back. "Now tell me one more time why you're so set on your son accompanying me?"

Jordan came to his feet with surprising alacrity. "So there will be someone along with a responsible outlook—who might undo whatever damage you do. You're mad, Mr. Random. I should have seen it at once. Your resistance to authority, your preference for savages over civilized men: *mad*." His heels cascaded down the steps. He stopped at the foot of the stoop and turned back. "Good evening, Mr. Random. I hope you don't find the price of your folly too high."

He crunched off into the night. Random hefted the whiskey bottle, considering. A few ounces of Colonel Sinclair's best whiskey still sloshed in the bottom. Jordan had destroyed his mood of gently intoxicated reverie. The expedition did not set forth till day after tomorrow, but there was much preparation to be done. Now was as good a time as any to embark on his unvarying trail discipline of no alcohol.

He had an Indian's respect for the southwestern land. Now he acted with an Apache's contempt of the white-eyes' fort. He drew back his arm and flung the three-quarters-empty bottle after Jordan. It shattered musically against a rock, and he laughed at Jordan's startled yip.

"But, Theodore," the small, slim black-haired man protested. "*Savages?*"

Head drawn down between massive shoulders, eyes blinking

incessantly in the afternoon light, his friend plowed through the crowds along Canal Street like a minotaur. He seemed to pay no attention to the other, who though not much shorter in the leg had to practically race along to keep pace. "But where's the advantage?" he persisted.

"Elihu, let me ask you something," Theodore Roosevelt said. "What are the issues going to be in the presidential election this fall? Eh?" An Italian smiled at them through the clouds of steam rising from the tubs of his oyster cart, and waved at the popular president of the New York City Police Board. Roosevelt gave him back a toothy grin and a fencer's salute from his ebony walking stick. "Greasy Mediterranean immigrants," he muttered sidelong to his companion. "Can't abide 'em. Never could."

Still waltzing along a bit desperately at Roosevelt's side, Elihu Root pondered the question. He had a sharp, sallow face and slanted eyes peering out from beneath brilliantined black hair. A stranger looking at him would guess he had an admixture of Chinese blood. Which would have offended him mightily.

He shrugged. "Economics, Theodore. Free silver versus the gold standard, and the compromisers holding out for bimetallism." He glanced nervously upward. Concrete-colored clouds brushed the tops of the soot-streaked brownstones that lined Canal. As if in reply the heavens spit a few raindrops at the pavement. Root grimaced, concerned for the sanctity of the pleats in his black three-piece. Trust Theodore to disdain carrying an umbrella on such a day as this. "I didn't think you were interested in such things."

Roosevelt stabbed air with his cane. "Pree-*cise*ly! I am *not* interested in such issues, and neither is any true red-blooded American. They smack of money-grubbing."

"That may be, Theodore." Root showed how close he really was to Roosevelt by the address he used. Reporters called the bull-chested man with the elliptical pince-nez, bushy moustache, and startling flamboyant manner TR; the public called him Teddy. The inner circle called him Theodore, and knew those who didn't for rabble. "But just the same, there are many who feel such matters are vital."

The stick slashed the objection to ribbons. "I am sure there are plenty of so-called men who can think of nothing loftier than the pursuit of money. The fat bankers on Wall Street, the Reds waving transparencies on street-corners and booming for Bryan. But for the real American—these matters have no real meaning, don'tcha see?"

"Not altogether."

Roosevelt started a frown at his friend's obtuseness. Elihu Root was a good man, of good stock, a fine lawyer and well connected in Washington, where his practice was. He was also devoted to Theodore Roosevelt. But he didn't have the grasp of things, of issues and principles, that Roosevelt did. That was why he was follower and Roosevelt leader.

With that thought he softened and recalled the frown from his features. "Feel the pulse of America, Elihu," he urged. "It's all around you."

The cane became an artist's brush, painting a panorama of noonday crowded streets, throngs of working men and children and women bound for market, prosperous businessmen in striped suits and Negroes wearing shabby caps, overflowing the sidewalks, dodging the horse-drawn carts and wagons trying to avoid the wholly impassable crush of nearby Broadway. There was an almost Mediterranean contrast implicit in the scene. Canal was comfortably middle-class, lined with colorful awnings and cheery shopfronts offering sundries, tobacco, women's garments. Turn one corner and you came to the stately iron railings and lush lawn of City Hall park or the elegant world of Broadway. Turn another and you stepped into Little Italy or Five Points, slums that festered like an open wound. And everywhere the air almost thick enough to see with the smell of sweat, damp clothes, and horse manure by the pile.

"America's depressed, Elihu. Let the short-sighted prattle in terms of economics. America is in peril because she has turned her tread from the glory road. Her eyes have turned inward from imperial visions; all they see are visions of petty gain."

"But the frontier was closed years ago. The nation stretches from coast to coast. There's no more room for Manifest Destiny."

"Manifest Destiny?" Roosevelt snorted. "Reactionary doctrine, Elihu. Reactionary!" Elihu stared. Roosevelt laughed a high boyish laugh. "Manifest Destiny sought to bind America's greatness within the paltry confines of a continent. Men of vision see further than that. Much, much further."

Root gazed at him in awe. Enthusiasm was alien to his nature, but when Roosevelt soared to heights of exuberant ambition Root's spirit could not remain wholly earthbound.

But his lawyer's mind didn't altogether abdicate to his emotions, either. "I still don't see what some Indian's escaping from Oklahoma has to do with all this."

"It's my ticket to the White House." Roosevelt laughed uproariously at the look on Root's face.

"This country needs a strong man, Elihu. A robust hand on the reins of power. But she doesn't perceive that need. Not yet.

"The world waits, Elihu. With our cousins the British and the Germans we face the holy task of spreading the blessings of Western civilization across the globe. But our eyes are closed." He shook his head in massive disgust at the blindness of his countrymen. "A perfect opportunity awaits us in the Caribbean, where the Cubans and Puerto Ricans strain under the feudal yoke of Spain. But we cannot be troubled to liberate them, and free the New World from the last vestiges of degenerate Mediterranean domination."

"But, Theodore," Elihu yelped, totally bewildered. "Indians—?"

"The country doesn't need a Gold party or a Silver party," Roosevelt said, bulldozing the other's objections aside. "It needs a War party. Since America won't go out in search of adventure, she must be thrust into one. And since she will not look beyond her borders, she must have a war *within* those borders."

Elihu gasped at the impact of understanding. But he was still analyzing as they turned left onto the Bowery to the clanging rumble of a distant elevated train thrusting into the heart of the city. He picked for flaws in his friend's argument, attorney-fashion. "Do you seriously believe this lone renegade actually threatens the country, Theodore?"

"Of course not!" Theodore barked. His face shone with the Olympian amusement the thought gave him. "But this chief will succeed in raising the tribes against the white settlers, just like the old days. The Indians are easily excitable; a childish, simple folk. We did them a favor by taking their land away, Elihu. They have no concept of prudent, responsible stewardship. I know them well. I've spent some time in the West, Elihu, as you no doubt recall."

Elihu could not forgo a sardonic grin. Of course he did recall that Roosevelt had spent some time in the West. Theodore talked about it incessantly.

"So this chief will cause an uprising. The press will blow the menace out of all proportion to reality. The public will begin to clamor for a war of extermination against the red savages. And at about that time the Republican party will convene in St. Louis to select its presidential candidate for this year. The delegates will not give a fiddle for gold or silver at that point, Elihu; they'll be clamoring for a strong man, a man to *lead*. In short, they'll be clamoring for *me*."

Root was shaking his head as if something had come loose inside and he was trying to shake it out of one ear. Keeping up with Theodore in conversation could be even more difficult than keeping up with him on the sidewalk. "But if there's an actual uprising, Theodore, won't lives be lost?"

Roosevelt stopped. The jostling Bowery mob parted on both sides of him like a stream around a rock. He brought the cane to the en garde. Root stared nervously at its ivory tip. "Even you, Elihu? Has the rot gone so deep? There is no greatness without sacrifice. You can't make an omelette without breaking eggs." He whipped the stick down and paced away, as if not caring whether the other followed or not. "The small amount of blood shed in the crisis will harden the public to the greater sacrifices that must be made if this country is to pursue her destiny."

"You're right." Root puffed at his heels. "Forgive me, Theodore." Even with Roosevelt's bulk as a prow to break water, it was harder to breast the current on the Bowery than it had been on Canal. The crowds were more listless, less driven, though curses and laughter both flew more freely here. The looks Roosevelt received from passersby were not all admiration. Here he was known as the man who closed the saloons and beer halls on Sunday.

"There is one problem," Roosevelt admitted in an uncharacteristically muted voice as Root finally caught him up. "The Army intends covering this up. Squelching this renegade surreptitiously, without ever admitting publicly it's taken place. They fear the repercussions if it's found out they cannot protect American lives and property against a race of primitives who surrendered a decade ago."

Root smiled contemptuously. "If the Army plans to deal with this renegade itself, Theodore, I doubt we've much to worry about."

"But they don't. The Army's afraid its own official involvement will spill the secret. They've hired a civilian, a man who scouted for General Crook, to hunt down and disperse the Indians."

"How good a man could they get?"

Roosevelt's face assumed the aspect of the lowering clouds above. "A very good one. I've met him myself, in fact. Just this winter." He grimaced, slapped his cane into the palm of his hand. "I daresay he got the better of me. He's a wicked man, a confounded anarchist into the bargain. But he is very, very good."

Root drew back in amazement. Theodore rarely talked about men who got the better of him—because men rarely did. *I must ask him about this sometime.* "But what if this man succeeds in defeating the renegade before a war breaks out?"

Swollen beyond endurance, the clouds finally burst and let go a torrent of rain. As the downpour glazed his broad face and plastered his moustache to his upper lip, Theodore smiled. "You know I've contacts in the Navy and the Army, Elihu," he said, oblivious to the rain. "I have them in other branches of government as well.

"And one of them, I'm pleased to say, is on the very scene . . ."

" 'Lord, what fools these mortals be,' " said Captain John Raker (retired) of the Texas Rangers, as he gazed out the window at the crowd assembling up the red dirt street.

Behind him J. Ramsey Jordan, superintendent of District Seven of the Bureau of Indian Affairs, slumped in a beige and gold brocade chair savoring the coolness of the room and the cooler beer in his hand. Normally Jordan would scorn such a plebeian drink as beer, but at the Imperial Saloon it was the coolest beverage on hand. Jordan assuaged his class sentiment by ordering expensive Budweiser—brought by the Gila Valley, Globe & Northern Railroad to their railhead a few miles up the Gila from Fort Thomas, and then dragged laboriously to Globe across the San Carlos Reservation to the heart of the Pinals—in preference to Bohee or Silver King, or some other locally produced brew. Globe, Arizona, in 1896 lacked the common modern amenities of a gas, water, or electric works, but she had several breweries. And an ice house, thank God.

In Jordan's present state the need for a cool drink superseded the need to keep up appearances. The mining town of Globe squatted on Pinal Creek some fifty miles southwest of Fort Apache, not far as the crow flies. Not being crows, Jordan and his cavalry escort had to ride across the dreary parched waste of the San Carlos, and then deep into the rough, inhospitable Pinal Mountains to reach Globe. They had made Globe in just over two days, and justifiably considered they had achieved something.

Sergeant Mahaffey and his bay-horse troopers were off celebrating their achievement in a certain house that languished behind a twelve-foot-high fence a few blocks away from the Imperial on Broad Street, Globe's main drag. Being a man of serious intent, Jordan had settled straight to matters of urgent import. Which brought him to this second-story room, tastefully done up in red-flocked gold wallpaper, above the main drinking-and-gambling area of the Imperial. He was trying to discuss weighty matters above the din of drinking and gambling, as abetted by a gramophone endlessly grinding out "Daisy Bell"—the hit song of 1892—from a cylinder that sounded as if it had been used in a locomotive's pneumatic brake, and the hubbub of a crowd of miners, lumberjacks, cowhands, and drifters waving transparencies and booming for Bryan off in front of the Skating Rink two blocks away.

"Watch those Chinamen skitter," Raker said, still watching the Populist rally. "Wise of them. A crowd gets in a frame of mind like that, it generally goes out looking for a nigger or two to burn. Since there aren't many of that persuasion hereabouts, it might just occur to them to make a substitution." He spoke in a cultured East Texas drawl, with more of Louisiana in it than twanging West Texas.

Jordan was examining his linen traveling suit. It was desperately rumpled from two days on the trail, and smudged here and there with green and brown smears whose nature Jordan did not care to guess at. Likely the suit was ruined. *The sacrifices one is called upon to make,* he thought dolefully.

"Ah, yes, the lynching epidemic," he said in tones of pious disapproval. "A national disgrace. One more evidence that this country needs a strongman in the saddle."

Raker shrugged, as if to say lynchings and strongmen alike were of small concern to him. "You have a job for me, Mr. Jordan? 'Gather ye rosebuds while ye may,' the Bard advises us. There are other things I could be doing, sir."

Jordan forced a smile. "Nothing so profitable as listening to my proposal, Mr. Raker. After all, who am I to contradict Shakespeare?"

The ex-Ranger nodded. A misty look came into his eyes. They were not well suited to sentimental expressions. They had the dull gray luster of steel shot: shark's eyes. "Ah, yes. As my mentor and fellow treader of the boards, the lamented Mr. John Wilkes Booth, used to say, you can't beat Shakespeare, in life or on the stage."

Setting his drink on a gilded wooden stand beside him, Jordan removed his handkerchief from his pocket, folded it into a square, and carefully patted his forehead dry. The action diverted him, kept him from moaning aloud. It was not enough that he must rub elbows with Negroes and mercenaries of radical convictions: he had to deal with a stone-crazy gunslinger who constantly spouted Shakespeare and claimed to have acted beside John Wilkes Booth. Maybe he had. What Jordan had heard was that Raker had ridden with Quantrill in the war, which hardly seemed to square with his Thespian pretensions, though it didn't necessarily preclude their being true.

But for what Jordan had in mind, John Raker was the best. If the superintendent could endure the ride here to meet with the man, he could endure his eccentricities as well.

Jordan lit a cigar and told the story of Aguilar's escape from Fort Sill and its aftermath, while Raker sat on the sill glancing out the window from time to time. Then he told Raker what it was he wanted him to do.

"Now, let me get this straight, Mr. Jordan. You want me to help start a new Apache war?"

*Daisy, Daisy, give me your answer, dooo,* the gramophone implored.

"It ought to start of itself, Mr. Raker, given half a chance. I merely need you to ensure that it gets that chance." He blew out smoke. "You don't object?"

Gallows-tree shoulders shrugged response. " 'Nothing's good nor bad, but thinking makes it so,' " he quoted. "Money can make me think well of just about anything, provided there's enough of it."

"There will be."

Raker boosted his lean butt off the sill and dusted the seat of his trousers. "Then I'm your man." He smoothed back graying brown hair at his temples and reached for his hat.

"Just one thing more," Jordan said. "There is a certain complication."

"What's that?" Raker paused with the Stetson halfway to his head.

"This man the Army has hired. His name is Random, and my principal has specified . . ."

He stopped. "Why are you looking at me like that?" he demanded.

"Random? You said the man's name was *Random*?"

"Yes, yes. Now, my principal—"

Raker cut him off. "My price just went up one hundred percent, Mr. Jordan. One thousand dollars."

Jordan opened his mouth, shut it, took his handkerchief from his vest pocket, dabbed his sweat-shiny brow, and replaced the handkerchief. "Out of the question."

"Take it or leave it."

"Now wait, wait." Jordan's hands fluttered like fat pink birds. "There's a great deal at stake here. Don't you care about the future of your country? Don't you want to see America take her rightful place as a power among nations?"

"I don't give diddly for power or nations, Mr. Jordan." It was strong language for Raker. "Money's what interests me. And since there's quite a chance I won't be around to spend any of it, it will take a sight more than five hundred dollars to interest me in squaring off with Mr. Random."

A sneer lifted Jordan's heavy upper lip. "Don't tell me you're afraid of him."

Immediately he knew it was a mistake. Raker's face went taut as stretched rawhide, and his tanned skin turned gray-pale. The metallic eyes went dead. Not hot with anger or cool with indignation. Just dead.

They frightened J. Ramsey Jordan worse than anything he'd seen in over fifty years of life.

Raker sighed and set the dove-gray Stetson back on the windowsill. "Be glad you-all aren't wearing a gun, Mr. Jordan," he said quietly. When he saw the words strike home, he nodded and settled back against the heavy scarlet drapes.

"Have you ever wondered why none of the old-time gun-handlers ever went up against each other, Mr. Jordan? They made their reputations killing crazy kids and cowboys who thought drinking enough whiskey would make them bulletproof, and they stayed out of each other's way. Look at Abilene, back in the seventies. My good friend Ben Thompson and that Yankee nancy-boy Bill Hickok snarled at each other like tomcats on a fence for months on end. But they never threw down on one another. Fact is, they made each other so nervous that Hickok gunned down his own best friend, thinking he was Thompson rushing at him through a crowd. And they were the best in the business.

"That's the way Random and I are, Mr. Jordan. I don't say he's better than I am. But the two of us, we're the best." He chewed a corner of his moustache. "I didn't know he was back in the Territory."

"He just returned from the East, I understand." Jordan started to raise his glass, but his hand trembled so badly he gave up the effort. He could barely conceive of the impertinence—a cashiered Texas Ranger threatening *him*, a full superintendent of the BIA.

Outside, the Populists shouted "Down with capital and immigrants." *I'm half craa-zy, all for the love of yooou,* croaked the infernal device downstairs. Whether because of deterioration of the gramophone, record, or Jordan's temper, it was becoming progressively harder to tell whether the vocalist was male or female, or, for that matter, human.

"I don't believe it." Jordan rapped out the words as though beating them on a drum, hiding his trepidation behind Rooseveltian vigor. "I met Random myself at Fort Apache. I was certainly unimpressed. He's soft. A weak-kneed sentimentalist and an Indian-lover."

Raker did not remark on a superintendent of Indian Affairs castigating another as an Indian-lover, since in 1896 it wasn't that remarkable. As a rule, a man didn't join the Bureau out of love for his red brothers. He joined to share in the booty from short-weighting the Indians' rations, which was considerable, and sometimes to escape the repercussions of some political blunder back East. Raker knew that Jordan was at Flagstaff for the first reason, and guessed at the second as well.

"Our definitions of softness seem to differ, Mr. Jordan. I've heard Random's killed more men than cholera." He turned his eyes on Jordan and smiled with his mouth. "Doubtless that's an exaggeration."

"Very well," said Jordan, deflated. "A thousand dollars." Who knew? If Random really was that good, hard as it was to believe, perhaps Captain John A. Raker would not be on hand to collect his second payment. "I'll have the money to you by nightfall."

"Half," Raker reminded him.

Jordan nodded. "Oh, and one more thing. My son Brentwood will be with Random on this fool's errand. You are of course to make sure no harm comes to him."

"He's in on it?"

"Not at all. But I do have agents with the party who, ah, know the score." He raised his glass of beer, which had gone flat. "The boy's young. He doesn't understand the realities yet."

"Ah, the realities. 'For oaths are straws, men's faiths are wafer-cakes.'"

"Er—indeed." The quotation made Jordan uneasy, somehow. "Well, then, it's settled."

"Not quite."

"What do you mean?"

"What was it you were starting to tell me about Random?"

"Oh. Oh, yes." He smiled. "My principal gave specific instructions concerning him. If, in the course of this adventure, Mr. Random should meet with a fatal mishap—" He knit his fingers before his face. *On a bicycle built for two!* the gramophone. "—you may expect a certain, shall we say, additional emolument?"

* * *

Like a ghost, the wind wailed around the foot of the mesa. Mariana hunched over the small fire of dried grass, hiding its glow. It was unlikely anyone would see the tiny weak light way up here on the table-rock, tucked away under rearing tablets of sandstone. But she was Apache, and took no chances.

She breathed deeply, inhaling the aroma of a winter-fat doe rabbit roasting on a cottonwood spit. The smell went through her like a knife. She had nearly been caught by a party of Navajos following the war party's trail across their land in western New Mexico, and had had to ride hard two days to catch up to the raiders. Only today, after she had tracked the band to the desert above the Tonto Rim, almost within sight of the White Mountain where she had been born, had she allowed herself to hunt for food. The scant supplies she'd rescued from the house she had shared with Tse'e were long since gone.

*Tse'e.* The name stabbed deeper even than her hunger. She made herself concentrate on the rabbit as fat bubbled from the carcass and dropped sizzling into the fire. The rich aroma almost sickened her.

After a moment she was able to consider the situation in the cold light of Apache rationality. Two days' ride back toward New Mexico several new riders had joined the group, including one whose horse left strange tracks, as if always threatening to go lame but never doing so. The party had come straight here, and passed on into the White Mountains themselves. Mariana had held back. She could go to her father for help. His clan, and the other bands camped around Dził łigai si'áń, would surely take up arms at once to aid her in getting her husband back. And therein lay the problem. The hatred between White Mountain and Chiricahua was too recent and too raw. If the White Mountains openly confronted their old foes, there would be fighting. Should Mariana's attempts to get Tse'e back only result in his death, she could not live with herself—and suicide was an option no Apache took lightly.

So she would have to do it on her own. That in itself was a fearful thing. The people of the White Mountains were gregarious folk who loved company to ease the long hours on the trail and share laughter over the campfire at night—and to keep the ghosts who took the form of owls at bay. A White Mountain was almost never alone throughout life, and would not travel alone if there was any help for it.

But alone was precisely the way Mariana had come the hundreds of miles from the Española Valley to this wind-haunted mesa. And alone was the way she would have to walk if she ever hoped to see her beloved Tse'e again.

The rabbit done, she plucked it from the fire and ate it, pulling the steaming-soft meat apart with her fingers. She made herself eat with deliberation. She would not be reduced to indecorous behavior, even here on the mesa with no company but the waving shoots of grass, and the furtive black shapes that winged beyond the fire's reach. As she ate she pondered ways of freeing her husband, once she caught up with his brother's band. It would not be a matter of slipping into camp and slipping back out with Tse'e. She doubted anyone could sneak into the *broncos'* camp without being challenged, captured, and killed. She didn't fear death, but her getting killed by one of Nducho's *heshkéés* wouldn't help her husband one bit.

The rabbit tasted good. Once it was gone she felt better. She scooped dirt over the fire, dousing it and eradicating all sign of its existence. Then she drew her blanket over her and curled up under a mesquite with her carbine in her arms.

She would have to continue as she had, doggedly following the raiders, hiding from the whites and Mexicans and non-Apache Indians as carefully as they, for any lone Indian woman found wandering the desert was liable to be treated as property to be claimed by whatever man—or men—came along. She would endure the hunger, and the heat, and the loneliness, and worst of all the doubt that she would ever be reunited with the man she loved.

She did not know why Nducho had kidnapped his brother after so many years. She did not know why Tse'e followed, though she knew it was not of his accord. But she knew that she would follow him, and trust in the goodness of Yusn and her own Apache resourcefulness to make the chance to rescue him.

Mournfully the wind sang, and danced soft through spring-green grama. An owl hooted far away. She shuddered. It was a bad omen. It was also the loneliest sound she'd ever heard.

A few clouds drifted between her and the stars. *I will not cry.* In time she fell asleep.

# THE RAIDERS

The San Carlos Indian Reservation
Arizona Territory
April 13, 1896

# CHAPTER SIX

Dawn was just bleaching the eastern sky when Tse'e and his father rode upward out of the mist.

For a moment they sat silent, their ponies patiently standing, blowing out clouds of warm moist breath. It was one of those rare spring mornings when mist fills the valleys and canyons like cotton in a bowl. Men and animals stood isolated on a red stone island in a paling sky, with the smell of damp earth strong and sweet in their nostrils. The silence rang like trumpets on every side.

"It is a good day," Aguilar said.

Tse'e nodded. *At least I'm still Apache enough to see the beauty of the dawn.*

Aguilar nudged his horse with his knees. It plodded upward along the ribbon of trail. Its slow hoof-falls made sharp sounds, as though the world above the clouds were all the world there was, and this a sound to fill it. Tse'e followed his father, letting beauty ease the turmoil within.

The old man's chestnut reached the top of the butte called The Way Out in the tongue of the People just as the sun spilled between the twin prominences of White Against the Mountain. Tse'e caught a breath and held it. The mist lay all around, in fat slow eddies around the peaks and ridges, shining like silver in the first light of day.

His blacklegged mare let out a sigh and dropped her head to crop at the green shoots of a tuft of grama. Without thinking, Tse'e took an oily rag from the back pocket of his jeans and began to rub condensation from the barrel and receiver of the long rifle that lay across the pommel of his saddle. His father smiled.

"It's good that you care for your weapon so, my son," the old man said. "Many Indians don't. Do you still have rifle Power, then?"

The aged eyes were still bright, intent as a hawk's as Tse'e looked into them. He knew this was a leading question; knew that behind it lay the reason Nducho had kidnapped him from the serene life of the Española Valley.

Most Apaches were poor shots. Not just bad, but truly horrible. It had been a constant source of frustration to Aguilar's cousin Victorio, during his last fierce struggle with the white-eyes and the Nakaiyé sixteen years ago, to catch American or Mexican horse-soldiers in a perfect ambush, so that the muzzle-flashes all but singed the skirts of the enemy saddles—only to have the troopers turn and ride off, tails high and unscratched. A keen student of Victorio, Tse'e's friend Random always claimed the Chíhéne leader's brilliant campaigns would have kept his foes chasing him for years but for Apache marksmanship.

Tse'e was different. He was a superb shot, so good that Pierre LaMontagne had taken special delight in showing off Tse'e's skill to his friends. They were always astonished that the soft-spoken, frail-looking Apache shot with such fantastic precision.

A whiteman would say he had an eye for it. Apache called it Power. And Power was a fragile thing. It could flee at any time.

*And if I say I've lost my Power, will they let me go back to Mariana?* Instantly self-disgust filled him at the thought. Wishful thinking was a whiteman affliction. Maybe his brother was right. Maybe he wasn't Apache anymore.

Nor could he lie to his father. Not with those eyes gripping him like talons.

"I think so," he said.

*"Nzhóó."* Good.

The Old Eagle walked his horse across the rock-jumbled top of the butte. Stuffing the rag back in his pocket, Tse'e clucked his horse to a slow trot, to catch up with his father. "It is good that you choose to walk with me now, my son," Aguilar said. "I'm near the end of my time. Your company makes these days happy for me."

Tse'e's eyes stung. *What would he say if he knew how I longed to escape?*

He kept his face averted from Aguilar's. During his years among the whitemen he had learned to question the beliefs of his people, of White Mountain and Chiricahua. Not deny—but no longer to credit fully. Yet he had always believed his father had the ability to look through his eyes and know the center of him, the thoughts that dwelt there. Whether or not that was Power as Nndé knew it, he still believed his father had it.

But Aguilar gazed off across that broken mountain land, at the rocky promontories rising as though from a sea as the sun burned back the mists. "You were my favorite son," he said, still looking outward. A pang stabbed through Tse'e, and his fingers tightened on dew-wet reins. "My firstborn. I remember waiting in my wickiup, nervous as a *dikǫǫhé* the night before his first raid, fearing for your mother. She was a slight woman, like yourself and that pretty White Mountain girl you married, whose name I don't recall. But soon she came from the brush, holding you wrapped in a blanket. You looked at me with those black, black eyes and uttered a single cry."

The old man laughed. " '*¡Qué aguilucho!*' cried the Nakaiyé woman who was your mother's slave. 'What an eaglet—truly, an eagle's son.' And that cry was the only one you made. You were already Apache."

Pleased with the memories, he nodded to himself. A look was in his eyes that had occupied them often on the ride, an inward look of one who sees the past to the exclusion of the present. Seeing that look so much, Tse'e had realized why his father chose to join this last futile defiance against the white-eyes: he longed to relive the glorious days when he rode with his kinsmen against the pale invader.

Now Aguilar's eyes changed, grew troubled. "Your brother cried a lot when he was born," he said. "His birth was less auspicious than yours."

For a moment he seemed about to say more. A horned lark sang somewhere. Aguilar's eyes turned in again and he rode eastward, unspeaking.

The image of his mother appeared in Tse'e's mind. She had died when he was very young. He remembered the comforting warmth of her—most Apaches loved children, so that the youngsters were everybody's pets, but his mother had always meant a special kindness, a bit of sweet baked mescal perhaps, warm enfolding arms when the night sounds frightened him. She had died when he was a few summers old, and still he remembered his uncomprehending pain.

But he could not recall her face, and that saddened him. All he could see of her was her hair, long and black, and the way it shone in the sunlight when her Mexican slave-woman stood behind her and groomed it with a yucca brush.

The mare turned briefly from her path. Roused from his reverie, Tse'e saw that she was avoiding a jagged outcrop of feldspar and milky quartz. Tiny motes gleamed within the stone, sparks cast by the risen sun. Such outcrops, he knew, were taken by the whitemen as a sign that silver was near. He said as much to his father.

"You know Mother Earth forbids us to delve in her belly for the yellow metal and the white," said Aguilar with a touch of reproof.

"I didn't mean that, Father. But this is a rich land, as the whitemen see it. Their government lets them come into it and take out the precious metals, but many of them resent having Indians nearby. They'd welcome an excuse to move the White Mountains and the San Carlos away to Oklahoma. Or make an end of them.''

"So much the more reason to follow Yusn's bidding and drive them forth. If the White Mountains realize the truth of what you say, they will surely open their ears to Owl and join us against the white-eyes, as Yusn commands.''

He shook his head gravely. "I often fought the White Mountains in the past. They're good enemies, brave and clever. It grieves me that they turned away from Owl when he told them they must rise and join our cause. It's almost as if they were more loyal to the white-eyes than to Yusn.''

"You heard what they said when we met them at White Mountain, Father. They don't believe Niishdzhaa is the messenger of Yusn. And they don't believe we can win.''

Somewhat taken aback by his son's using the prophet's true name Owl, instead of the euphemistic Nndé, Man or Apache, by which members of the war party usually referred to him, Aguilar said, "With Yusn's aid we will win.''

"But what if you're wrong? What if Owl doesn't speak for God? What will it cost the White Mountains and the San Carlos?'' *What will it cost us all?* he thought but could not say.

"I believe in Owl,'' said Aguilar in a voice as soft as the last wisps of mist that clung to the valleys and the shadowed base of the butte. "You're young and headstrong, son. Perhaps when you're my age you'll learn the value of belief.''

They had reached the eastern rim of the butte now. To the east the Mogollon Mountains bit at the sky like teeth. Southward the butte began to buckle, becoming part of the Natanes range. Below them ran the Black River, hidden still in gloom.

"This butte we stand on, Father,'' Tse'e said, picking each word carefully. "We call it Ch'ígó'á, The Way Out, because long ago soldiers escaped over it from a band of People. But that's not its name.''

Aguilar turned to him in surprise.

"No. Its name is Chiricahua Butte. So it's written on the whiteman's maps. So it will be remembered, when we are dust.''

He pointed to the east. "And White Against the Mountain. To the whites it's the Poker Peaks. And *there*.'' He swung his arm north to where the White Mountain's bare top glinted in the sun. "That is not

Dził łigai si'án. It's Mount Thomas, named after a whiteman general who fought the People. Sometimes it's called Baldy Peak. Strange names, Father, are they not?"

"Strange and unpleasant to the ear," Aguilar agreed.

"They're the whiteman's names. The whiteman names the land upon his maps and so makes it his. That's the whiteman's magic."

Aguilar smiled. "Then our magic will have to be stronger. Do you still have the deer Power also, my son?"

Tse'e slumped in his saddle. For a time he had felt a closeness to his father that said that all the years of separation were a lie. Now it was as if Haastįį 'Ítsá was back in Oklahoma. Tse'e had spoken, but his father did not hear.

Resigned, he turned to his father's question. Even as a boy he'd always had extraordinary luck on the hunt, particularly when the quarry were deer. His fortune went beyond his marksmanship, for even the youngest child knew you couldn't shoot what you couldn't find. One animal more than any other he seemed to have success with—or Power over: the white-tailed deer, Tse'e.

But as to Power, he didn't know. On the other hand, Pierre LaMontagne never went—used to go—deer hunting without him, and seldom returned empty-handed. "I believe I still have that, also."

Aguilar sighed. "You make me proud. Such a young man, and you possess two Powers already." His face darkened. "Your brother hasn't yet been called by any Power, as you know. It worries me for him. I think it turns his heart bad."

Tse'e did not know. It surprised him; Nducho had always been the epitome of the Apache warrior, cunning, ferocious, and strong, destined to equal their father's exploits as a leader on the warpath. But if Nducho lacked Power, his ambitions could prove futile; no warband would ride without a shaman along. Which might account for Nducho's falling in with the hunchbacked prophet Niishdzhaa, down in the Sierra Madre.

"Will you call a deer now, son?" Aguilar asked, smiling.

Tse'e took a deep breath and swung from the saddle, tying the reins to the flat-topped Mexican-style horn. He knelt in the red dust, gazing across a land red and black and muted green, colors that seemed to glow in the newborn day. He'd washed that morning in the stream by the camp they had made on the western flank of Chiricahua Butte, as was Apache custom, though you weren't supposed to do so before a hunt. And he had eaten a bit of tortilla, though you were supposed to hunt with an empty stomach so that Yusn might pity you and send a fat deer across your sights. He'd made none of the ritual prepartions to hunt the deer, but then he never had.

Though he could scarcely believe it, his father accepted him as still being a true Apache. But his brother's gibes were true to some extent. Tse'e had been around the whites enough to be self-conscious about what he did now. He shut his eyes and forced himself to concentrate on the sunlight warming his face, the wind cool and sharp on his skin, the steamy smell of a fresh pile of dung his mare had dropped nearby, and to reach out of himself, beyond. . . .

He did not know how long it was before he felt his father stiffen. His eyes opened. A small nipple of volcanic rock jutted from the pine woods across the Black. From the trees an animal had emerged, head held high to test the wind. It was a prime young buck, its antlers, half grown out after being shed in the fall, already displaying the distinctive forward sweep of the white-tail.

A thrill went through Tse'e. *At least there's one way I can please my father.* He raised the Sharps. Stillness settled over him. The kick would hurt his shoulder, but Nndé did not dread pain. The deer was three hundred yards away, no distance at all for him. He drew back the big hammer and sighted down the long barrel.

He fired. The recoil tossed him back onto the caprock. At the instant of firing the buck leaped high and long. At the top of its arc the bullet caught it and hurled it to earth in a flurry of dust and kicking, dying legs. The thump of its body falling chased the echoes of the shot back to the ears of the father and son.

Screaming wildly, the captive doubled violently, trying to jerk his head free of the searing caress of the flames. For a moment he held his body bent, the cords standing out like cables on his brown neck. Then his belly muscles gave way and he fell back with a desperate wail.

The *heshkées* gathered around the lightning-blasted fir laughed. They laughed at the way the Nakaiyé's eyes bugged out as he fought to hold himself above the flames, rolling up in his head so that the dark irises almost disappeared to stare in horror at the smoke curling from his blackened scalp. They laughed at the way he jerked from side to side in a mad attempt to avoid the fire, and the staccato trapped-rabbit shrieks he uttered in time to his struggles.

Nducho laughed loudest of all. He was pleased, better pleased than he had been since the night of the raid on the LaMontagne ranch. He' been unwilling to stop here, on the fringe of the lunar waste of the San Carlos. But Aguilar said it might be wise to wait, to send a few men ahead to sound out the San Carlos Apaches. To Nducho's surprise Owl had agreed. The recalcitrance of the White Mountains had made the prophet wary. Both the White Mountains and the San Carlos had fought on the American side against the Chiricahua, but it had been to the San Carlos Reservation that the federal government had tried to confine the three branches of the Chiricahua, Cochise's Chókánéń, Victorio's Chíhéne, and such of the Mexican Ndé'indaaí of Juh as they could corral. So there existed more enmity between Chiricahua and San Carlos, by reason of increased friction. If anyone would betray the war party to the white-eyes, it would be the San Carlos.

So the bulk of the party settled in a narrow valley beside The Way Out, at a spring whose location Owl's Power had told him of, which neither Aguilar nor Chi', the two most seasoned campaigners, knew of beforehand. García, whose father had belonged to the Cotton-woods-Extending-to-the-Water-People clan of San Carlos before marrying a Chókánéń woman, had gone ahead to sound out his father's kinfolk.

That left the bulk of the war party, a good two dozen warriors including the two who had been with Owl when he met the main band in eastern Arizona, and more dubiously the two chubby White Mountain youths whose enlistment had been the sole positive result of the prophet's impassioned oratory before that people, to cool their heels in camp. Since yesterday they had sat around talking, gambling, or fiddling with their weapons. Some went hunting, as Nducho's father and brother had done this morning. Ever wary, Wears-Red-in-the-Storm had gone to scout out the war party's backtrail, in case the White Mountains thought of tracking them, or setting soldiers from Fort Apache after them. Nducho had been left to fret in camp—until a hunting party returned with a semiconscious Mexican.

It hadn't been that long since Nducho had enjoyed this sport. In Mexico it was a frequent diversion of Apache and Mexican alike. But torture was always a welcome pastime for the Mountain Lion. Yusn's generosity in sending him this victim with no womanish brother or overly moral father on hand to spoil his fun did much to wash the bitter taste of White Mountain rejection from his mouth.

The captive jackknifed out of the flames again. His mouth was a round black hole through which a keening ululation emerged. The men by the fire laughed and slapped bare thighs. The entertainment had just begun; the Nakaiyé had not yet been over the small fire long enough to feel its full effect, nor had he yet plumbed the depths of horror that he would reach with the realization that this was his whole future: mutilation and ghastly, unbearable pain. Later, when his brain began to bake and the blood to turn to steam inside his skull, he would thrash mindlessly like a snake with a broken back. That would be the funniest of all.

Holding his kettle belly in glee, Boca Negra turned and shouted a taunt at the larger group clumped around the spring, fifty yards up the tree-lined valley. "What are you, women? Afraid to see a Nakaiyé get what's coming to him?" As a half-breed, he always seemed to take special delight in the torture of Mexicans, as if to deny that half of his heritage. The men of that other group scowled; like the majority of Apaches they had no taste for this sort of thing.

At Boca Negra's side squatted Eskinyá, his whole lean body quivering with his excitement, running his tongue over and over bloodless lips. Eye sat next to him, and beside the one-eyed warrior one of the White Mountain recruits fidgeted, unsure whether he liked this sport and terrified of letting his uncertainty show. Finally there was Ha'aa, a slow-witted boy of fifteen, who sat on plump hams staring at the tormented man intently, the tip of his tongue protruding from his mouth. Ha'aa was an Apache who had been captured as a baby and raised a slave in Janos, in the Mexican state of Chihuahua. His skin was soft and pink and his body was well-padded with baby fat. Yet half his life had been spent at the grueling chore of making adobe bricks, with a blacksnake whip to keep his dim mind fixed on the task at hand. His back looked like a wicker screen from scars; yet he felt no animosity toward his captors, and seemed bewildered when a lightning raid by the war party en route to the United States burned the *hacienda* where he was enslaved and freed him.

Now he watched the torture, not because he enjoyed it, but because he did not comprehend it. It was a game, but the plump Mexican didn't seem to be enjoying it. He knew *he* wouldn't, and so he wondered why the others were playing this trick. Whenever anyone said anything he bobbed his head and said, "*Ha'aa, ha'aa.* Yes, yes," his eyes never leaving the perplexing scene.

Eskinyá picked up a stick and poked the prisoner, turning him to get a better look at his contorted features. "Don't worry," he told the man in Spanish. "I'll keep turning you till you're done on all sides."

The fresh outbreak of hilarity this brought on was interrupted by three shots cracking out nearby. The first flung burning brush into the air. Boca Negra yelped and fell backward as the second plowed a scarlet furrow slantwise across one thigh. The third shot struck the prisoner in the chest. He grunted, doubled, then hung loose, turning slowly, eyes still turned downward to the fire, but no longer heeding its sting.

Silence was absolute, but for the chatter of the frustrated chittering of the flames and the hiss-hiss-hiss of blood dripping into the fire. The Apaches by the spring stood with weapons in hand, staring at the single figure riding up the valley toward them.

The click of a rifle lever broke the quiet. "Come out of that bush, Nducho," called Wears-Red-in-the-Storm. "I won't hurt you." His pony tossed its ugly jug head and curled back its upper lip at the reek of burning hair and flesh.

Nducho bounded out of the patch of scrub oak where he'd taken cover, his own repeater in his hands. "You stinking son of a Pima whore! He was our captive. Why did you kill him?"

"I don't approve of your disgusting games. That sort of shit is worthy of Mexicans, not men. Victorio wouldn't have put up with it. I doubt your father would, either."

"Don't dare tell me what my father would do!" Nducho screeched. His hands shook so badly that the nickel-plated barrel of his Winchester made figure eights in the air. He looked for support to Owl, sitting on a rock by the trees midway between the two groups. The prophet had his hat pulled low over his eyes and seemed oblivious to what went on around him.

"I'd point that carbine somewhere else," Chi' said evenly.

On the wooded mountainside a quarter mile to the north and west of the camp, Aguilar shook himself at the sound of the gunshot. "Trouble," he said, and booted his pony to a gallop along a twisting dry streambed. Tse'e called after him to be careful. Cursing in English, the young man fumbled a huge Sharps cartridge from his pocket, cracked the chamber, and drove the round home. With a slash of his knife he cut the lashings that held the dead buck across his horse's rump. Then he sent the mare scrambling in his father's wake.

A remarkable tableau awaited as he loped out of the woods. Across the valley his brother and Chi' faced each other down the lengths of their Winchesters. The hideous shaman Owl sat aloof from the confrontation as Aguilar looked reprovingly from one antagonist to the other.

The corpse cooking slowly above a dying fire told its own tale.

"We're Nndé, not animals," Old Eagle said. "Who has done this thing?"

Nducho paled. He lowered his gun, then pivoted sharply and struck Ha'aa over the ear with its butt. The boy cried out shrilly and fell over,

clutching his head. "Ha'aa, you pig!" Nducho yelled. "We shoul[d]
have killed the Nakaiyé decently, as I said all along. Our honor i[s]
smirched, and all because I gave in to your lust for torture!"

The warriors looked at one another. Tears streamed down th[e]
accused's face. With only his guilt-born horror of causing his fathe[r]
pain preventing him from shouldering the Sharps and blowing hi[s]
brother's head off, Tse'e saw to his sick dismay that Aguilar believe[d]
Nducho. Had nobody else been on hand to see who instigated th[e]
torture, still no one else would have believed it was poor foolish Yes[?]
The whole band, almost, had seen Nducho light the fire with his ow[n]
hands. But no one would tell the Old Eagle so. Not even Tse'e.

The old man nodded. "You must learn to lead, my son," he tol[d]
Nducho, who stood before him with bowed head. "While no Apach[e]
can command another, you might have told Ha'aa he must leave th[e]
band if he persisted in his desire for torture. I know you would neve[r]
do any evil thing like this."

"No, Father."

"You permitted this because you feared to cause division in ou[r]
party. Fear no more. Yusn will not permit us to fail."

The others turned away. His face unreadable, Chi' laid his rifl[e]
across his saddlebow and turned to ride off down the valle[y]
Helplessly, Tse'e sat on his horse, wondering how much more of thi[s]
madness he could endure. Wondering if he could escape any mor[e]
than the poor devil hanging from his feet above the fire.

And above it all sat Owl, unmoving as an idol.

# CHAPTER SEVEN

"I believe Theodore Roosevelt makes the case most persuasively in his great work *The Winning of the West*," Brentwood Jordan announced. "Irrespective of the true motives of the participants, those who expanded American civilization into the western reaches of the continent were acting under a moral imperative to bring light to a benighted land."

Letting his scrubby little half-mustang gelding make his own way up the broad valley cut into the skirts of Mount Thomas, Random did his best to ignore the youngster's earnest words. He had too much on his mind to let his blood be raised by a juvenile's Ivy League chauvinism—or its source.

He glanced back. The replacement squad of Company G, 25th Infantry, was lined out behind him like beads on a rather crooked string. In the lead came Private Edward Jones, a heavyset man in his thirties who'd served with the 25th before and had reenlisted in January because the economy had little room for blacks in the wake of the latest slump. South Carolina-born, he sat the mule as if grafted to it, though he didn't seem to have accustomed himself to the McClellan saddle. After him, in tan fatigues, slouch hats, and varying degrees of rapport with their temperamental beasts, came the recruits. Last of all, riding his shaggy shavetail with the big U.S. brand, came Sergeant Brown. His hat was fresh off the block, with its crown squeezed into the natty Montana pinch that was becoming fashionable with the military after a dozen years of civilian popularity.

The sergeant's fatigues were tan too, though Army regs specified that noncoms' fatigues should be *bleached* muslin. But on a sunny day—and most were—an outfit like that would heliograph the party's position to roughly everybody in the Territory. At Fort Apache the day before, Brown had been resplendent in regulation whites. Aware of the prickly pride and resentment just beneath his hard outer coat of noncom brusqueness, Random forbore to bring the matter up. And this morning, as if by magic, Brown had appeared at the QM's corral in spotless tans, complete with appropriate patches, eliciting an

admiring nod from Random. Professionalism, that was the word for
it.

Now he swiveled his gaze alertly this way and that, which made it
perfectly reasonable that his eyes not meet Random's. Random knew
better. Brown resented being asked to bring up the rear; he was a man
accustomed to being the first into danger and the last out. But that was
the way it had to be. Random needed him to keep the flock from
straying, and to shepherd them if—when—they came under fire.
Random took it for granted at least one would fall off the first time a
shot was fired, though only two of the greenies had never actually
ridden before. In a way, that was all right, since they weren't meant to
fight from muleback. But it would be Sergeant Brown's task to see
none fell too hard or got dragged, and to make sure the rest got off and
into cover with dispatch.

In effect, Brown was riding drag on his inexperienced crew—the
toughest, most demanding position in a cattle drive. Random didn't
see fit to put that point to him. Were he to do so, he'd be comparing
the recruits to cattle, though in fact that was generous. In his
experience untried soldiers more closely resembled sheep.

But what Brown would have heard was a southerner comparing
*blacks* to cattle. So Random let matters lie. Uncomfortably.

Turning back, Random's face hardened momentarily at the sight of
the two riders up by the valley rim, paralleling the party like wolves
shadowing a herd and hoping for stragglers. He could hear them
talking, Cahill in his whiskey tenor and Sutter in his boys' choir alto.
Random couldn't make out the words, but he judged they were
discussing the lineage, habits, and other deficiencies of niggers. It
seemed their sole topic of conversation, except when the Cibicu
Apache scout Sinclair had lent him was in earshot. Then they threw in
a few good words about Indians, just to be fair.

Sensing his rider's preoccupation, Random's mount made a grab at
a juicy clump of grama, to be rewarded by a swift slap on the neck.
He bobbed his head in amusement. He was a wiry little bay, an early
product of Pierre LaMontagne's breeding program. His sire had been
a saddlebred, but his dam was an Apache-caught mustang. Apache-
fashion, he belonged to his mother's people. He was devoted to
Random, which didn't prevent his living up to his name: Malcriado—
the Misbehaver.

The valley rounded to a head a quarter mile ahead. As Random
turned forward he saw the scout, Doroteo, bring his gray and white

pinto out of the trees and wave his carbine over his head. Random waved back and kicked his mustang into a jolting lope.

"We're being watched," the scout said in Apache as Random rode up.

The scout was a square, sturdy man with a round paunch pushing out the front of the heavy blue woolen cavalry blouse, issue of 1872, which he proudly wore in addition to a white kiltlike Apache loincloth and hightopped *kéban*. He had anthracite eyes and a round face, ageless but seamed as the White Mountain country. The shoulder-length hair bound at the temples by the red scalpband of the scout was raven-black, untouched by gray. Yet Random knew that back at Fort Apache his favorite daughter had just presented him with a black-eyed granddaughter that was the pride of his age, whatever it was.

"See anyone?" Random asked in Chiricahua, a different language from that spoken by the western Apaches of White Mountain and San Carlos, but understandable to them.

"No," was the tentative reply. "Just a feeling."

"Remember what the white-eyes used to say. 'If you see Apache sign, watch out. If you don't see it, get out.' "

The arroyos etched in the man's face deepened appreciatively, and white teeth flashed in a sudden smile. Doroteo had never met Random before, but he'd heard of him from other Apaches. Still he had been wary; who knew what a white-eyes would do? Not Doroteo, even after years of working alongside them.

He'd been afraid when he had no more than a "feeling" to put forth that he'd be rebuffed for a superstitious savage. But Random knew Apache "feelings" were based on keen senses, experience, and maybe an unnamed extra factor: fallible, but not to be laughed at. So now Doroteo judged it safe to abandon the frozen-faced impassivity that was usually the prudent course around the whites. He grinned.

Random grinned back, relieved to have broken through the scout's reserve. Doroteo's eyes slid past him. He turned to see Jordan thundering up on his outsized chestnut stud, its three white stockings flashing like silver in the late-morning sun. It was a handsome animal. The glossiness of its coat told of solicitous porters brushing it and coddling it on the ride out from the East Coast, and assiduous currycombing by troopers at Apache. Back East it would have been a splendid mount. Out here the animal was a liability. It ate and drank three times what Random's scrub pony did, and if the war party ever actually cut loose and *moved* in the approved Nana style, Random judged the big stud would run itself to death in two days trying to follow, while his horse and the mules kept indefatigably on.

"What's going on?" Jordan demanded breathlessly. "What's he saying?"

"He says we're being watched, Mr. Jordan."

The youth peered at the trees, as if he might discern the unseen watchers by force of will alone. "You mean the red devils are all around us?" he asked, half anxious, half expectant.

"For God's sake, Mr. Jordan. They're not devils. They're men keeping an eye on intruders until they know their intentions."

Looking doubtful, Jordan straightened in the saddle and threw out his chest, to show his contempt for this furtive scrutiny, and to impress the hidden Apache with his lack of fear. He was impressive, all right. He wore a tan whipcord shirt and matching trousers, tightly cut, with leather reinforcing in the seat, tucked into high boots and cinched around his narrow waist by a pistol belt. The ensemble was topped off by an item of Army headgear that traditionally occasioned more gripes than the Prussian helmets: a pith helmet, gleaming white. The Army had given up on trying to make the squaddies wear the things. Jordan sported his as proudly as a new father. From the boot at his right stirrup jutted the butt and mirror-bright goldplated receiver of a One-in-One-Hundred Winchester 94 in .30-30 caliber.

In his heart Random knew this picture of robust American youth deeply impressed the White Mountains. They probably hadn't seen anything funnier in weeks.

Right now the important thing to do was appear calm. The watchers would know from this conference that they'd been detected, as they probably intended they be. Now the party had to show that it was not worried by their surveillance. So Random sat waiting for the rest to catch up, while Jordan jutted his chin at Baldy Peak and Malcriado munched grass.

Cahill and Sutter came trotting up ahead of the blacks. "Got bored back amongst them niggers," piped Sutter. "Thought we'd come up an' see what ol' Dorothy had to say."

"Now you oughtn't say a thing like that, Di," Cahill said, frowning in mock disapproval. "Admit it. Ain't never a dull moment with this-here traveling circus."

"There shouldn't be," Random remarked, "with a monkey and a trained bear to keep us all amused." As the pair frowned and dug at their ears, vaguely suspecting they'd been insulted, Random spoke past them to Brown, informing him of Doroteo's news.

A gangly, skin-and-bones kid who rode just behind Jones in the line turned in his saddle. "Y'hear that. Tass? They's out there. Gon' lift yo' wooly scalp *for sure.*" The youngster next after him went gray and scrunched down in his saddle. "Better get on the line to Jesus, Sky Pilot, put in a good word for us li'l lost sheep." A third youth bit his lip.

"Shut it, Garrison," Brown snapped.

Garrison said, *"Yes, Sergeant,"* and shut it. He was seventeen and the troublemaker of the squad. Though he was northern-born, like quiet Private Charles Harmony, whom he always called Sky Pilot because of the latter's religiousness, he delighted in talking in a Mr. Bones nigger-minstrel accent. He ragged Harmony and Tass Monroe, who were both the same age he was, without mercy. Random made a mental note to suggest Brown separate him from the other two and turned his horse to the uphill trail from which Doroteo had emerged.

"Just a minute," Sutter squeaked. "What if this Dorothy's leadin' us into a trap?"

Random turned to him and smiled. "Afraid, Mr. Sutter?"

Sutter's face went dough-pale beneath his beard. Random headed Malcriado up the mountainside. He heard a flurry of hoofbeats behind and tensed. But it was only Brent Jordan, glowing with righteous indignation. "Is it necessary to keep casting aspersions on Mr. Sutter's character?" the boy demanded.

"It shouldn't be."

Jordan blinked. "What's that supposed to mean?"

"It means *Mister* Sutter's character should be plain enough that I shouldn't have to continue pointing it out. Even to a sheltered Yale boy with his head full of Manifest Destiny."

Leaving the boy to simmer in his own outrage, Random rode on, keeping Malcriado's nose a safe distance from the tail of Doroteo's mount, to save the little bay from temptation. The pinto uttered a shrill whinny and danced sideways, nearly falling off the trail. A dry nervous rattle shivered in the cool air.

Patting the horse's neck and crooning to it, Doroteo urged it past the clump of rocks where a big rattler with the unmistakable dark lozenges of a diamondback raised a white-striped snout and shook a peremptory warning with its tail. "It's pretty high for rattlesnakes," Random said.

"I've seen them higher," Doroteo replied.

Random turned back to warn the others to steer wide of the rocks. It was early in the year, and the snake was full of poison and liable to be cranky. As Random turned a shot crashed from behind. The rattler's head went flying in a gout of dark blood. The dying snake rolled off the rock and thrashed among fallen spruce-needles as Random whipped the twin-barreled stage gun from the carbine loop at his saddlehorn and trained the weapon down the trail, thumbing back the hammers.

Thirty feet behind him Sutter smirked at him past a smoking Colt. The Peacemaker looked like a derringer in his paw. "Ol' Di's jes' having him some target practice," called Cahill. "Likes to shoot snakes, Di do."

Random eyed him coldly. "The snake was no danger."

"I thought it a capital shot!" Jordan's cheeks were flushed and his blue eyes bright. "Have you no sporting blood, Mr. Random?"

"None."

A commotion came from downhill. As Random foresaw, one of the recruits had fallen off his mule. It was Monroe, who though scared into a trembling fit by the experience was unhurt, thanks to the carpet of fallen needles. Harmony and Jones dismounted to help him.

"I don't think killing is a sport. Unless it's from need, it's butchery," said Random, turning his attention back to Jordan.

"Di was jes' practicin' his snake-shooting."

"I was aware of the purpose of the demonstration, Mr. Cahill."

The fifth recruit dropped from his mule and trotted up to poke through the debris around the rocks where the snake had lain, ignoring a shout from Brown. He didn't know one word of English. A lean coal-black hand shot out to seize something. "*Bon*," he said to himself, and headed back for his mule.

"What you got there, Tomtom?" asked Garrison.

The tall black thrust out his hand. Garrison screamed and fell off his mule as the severed snakehead wagged in his face. Brown cursed in disgust.

Having watched this vignette with keen interest, Doroteo turned back to Random and young Jordan. "Bad thing, bad thing," he muttered in English.

This struck a chord somewhere deep in Jordan's western lore: "He's upset because the snake is the Indian's friend. That's it, isn't it?"

"He's upset because the White Mountains aren't going to be too reassured of our friendliness if we ride in shooting up the whole forest," Random said.

Outraged, Doroteo glared at Jordan. "No damn snake *my* friend," he said.

\* \* \*

An hour later they stopped for lunch in a small clearing dotted with small blue wild flowers. They had quit climbing to cut across the mountain's flank so as to bypass the lower villages and come to the camp of Random's old friend, Thunder Knife. There was no need to rush, not yet, so Random gave the men an hour to rest and walk out the cramps in their inner thighs from the unfamiliar exercise of riding.

After they dismounted and broke out their cold biscuit and beans Jordan wandered close to Malcriado. The horse flattened his ears without raising his head from a bunch of fescue. "Careful," warned Random. "He bites."

The youth drew back. "I was just looking at your rifle."

"Vetterli, model 1878. Swiss-made." Random cracked off a piece of hardtack with his teeth. "Bolt-action, forty-one-caliber. Vernier sights, adjustable to fifteen hundred meters, though I wouldn't swear to be able to hit anything at that range."

Jordan turned his head sideways for a better look. He obviously couldn't work up the gumption to ask if he could pull the meticulously cared for weapon from its boot and chance being refused. "Have you considered getting something more modern?"

Random shrugged. "I've heard good things about the Mauser. The Krag's underpowered. Their only real advantage as far as I can see is that they fire smokeless, and don't pinpoint your position with an enormous cloud whenever you fire."

"I equipped myself with the most modern weapon available," the boy said smugly.

"No you didn't. You got a shiny toy with essentially a Civil War-era action, gold plating, and an octagonal barrel. It does fire smokeless, but it's still got little more range and accuracy than that Peacemaker you're wearing."

Jordan's cheeks and ears went pink. Not even he was brash enough to call Random on the subject of tools of the mercenary's trade. He looked around for a new subject of conversation.

Doroteo hunkered down beside the tall, rail-lean black soldier who'd retrieved the rattler's head. He'd been introduced to Random at Apache the day before as "Tomtom MacHoot." The name had a suspiciously familiar ring to it. Random had fired a question at him in French. The man's face lit with a smile and he returned a stream of syllables, part French, part incomprehensible except for a few words of Wolof and various other West African languages, of which Random had picked up a smattering in Algerian bazaars.

His name, as Random had guessed, was Tonton Macoute. He was a Haitian itinerant witch doctor, a cross between a sorcerer and a traveling salesman. For some reason he'd found it expedient to quit the island, and had wangled his way aboard a steamer, ending up in New York. A local black family befriended him, communicating with him the way Doroteo was now, by signs. Since times were no better for them than anybody else, they had not been able to offer him long standing hospitality, so they'd pointed him in the direction of the Army. You were supposed to know English before they'd let you in, but they'd taken him anyway.

It somewhat startled Random that the Apache took such an interest in him. Apaches hated snakes. After Macoute collected the rattler's head for a *gris-gris* or talisman, Random would have guessed Doroteo would want no part of him. It turned out, however, that Doroteo was interested in acquiring snake Power. The two, by God, were talking shop.

When he wasn't gesturing, Doroteo fiddled with the two thin chains strung about his neck. "What's that?" Jordan asked him.

Doroteo fished a tarnished silver crucifix out of his blouse. "Me Christian," he said with a grin. "*Inashood dilhiłń.*"

"Black Christian," Random translated. "He means he's Catholic."

Jordan was scandalized. "How can he traffic in such heathen mumbo jumbo, then?"

"Most Apaches don't see much contradiction between their ways and the Christian ones, at least not those who've converted." Random looked at him sideways. "Didn't you say you were in Jonathan Edwards?" he asked, referring to one of Yale's residential colleges. "And wasn't he the revivalist who loved to crib that line of Calvin's likening sinners to spiders in the hands of an angry God? If there's room for spiders in Christianity, why not diamondbacks?"

Jordan cleared his throat. He was losing his grip on the conversation again. "Er, what about that other chain?" he asked.

Doroteo's smile went away. He let the crucifix fall back out of sight and produced a small metal tab with a letter and number engraved on it.

"That's his tag," said Random. There was an edge in his voice.

"His what?"

"Tag." Random finished off his biscuit and brushed crumbs away. "Every Apache band is given a letter. Each married male in the band is given a number, starting with one for the 'tag chief,' who's appointed by the kind and loving government. Every married male has to wear his tag at all times or risk being picked up like a stray dog. Your dad's Bureau has a wonderful way of showing its respect for its charges, wouldn't you say?''

Young Jordan recoiled. In a moment he recovered and stammered something about the Indians bringing it on themselves with their wildness and irresponsibility. Random sneered and turned away.

For just a moment, though, the mercenary thought he'd seen doubt flicker in those blue eyes. *Maybe there's hope for him yet,* he thought.

He wasn't going to count on it.

With a big cat's lazy poise, John Raker sat his big Roman-nosed black and wondered how on God's green earth he'd managed to wind up with thirteen men.

It had been no trouble to round up a party. He had taken some expense money that J. Ramsey Jordan had given him as willingly as if it came out of the superintendent's arm instead of his pocket, and hired a well-sprung wagon and four stout mules. Then he'd hied over to McNelly's Champion Billiard Hall and Saloon on Broad Street and bought a dozen twelve-bottle cases of whiskey. Cheap, by reason of quantity and his own indifference as to its pedigree. He'd taken the Pledge, himself.

Having loaded up on fuel for the endeavor, he parked the wagon on a side street, gave a nearby loafer a dollar, and told him what would happen to him if anybody so much as cracked the seal on one of the bottles. Then he headed off for the rally with his deceptively easy ground-eating stride. He knew the whiskey was safe. The bum knew who he was.

A few earnest, low-voiced words, and he drifted from the rally with half a dozen men at his heels. Several stops in a smattering of Globe's many saloons and Raker had himself a respectable little force. He waited while they collected their mounts and traps, put old Jake LeDoux, a whiskered, peppery old Civil War vet from Gulfport, in the box of the wagon, and then headed east through the mountains toward San Carlos.

All without stopping to reckon exactly how many men he had.

*I must be getting old,* he thought. Thirteen men—that was careless, and carelessness wasn't like him.

They were good men, though. He surveyed them beneath a glowing evening sky. Tall, sallow hatchet-faced Deuce Lewis and his stubby pal Black Jack Hutchinson, for example. They were cowhands, gamblers, and sometime road agents, to Raker's certain knowledge,

handy men with six-shooters, and ones who knew how to keep their
mouths shut. Ideal recruits for Raker's Rangers, as he already thought
of his brave little band, sworn to protect white Arizona from the red
menace. There was Russian Nick, a ginger-bearded giant who made
up for his limited English by mostly letting his maullike fists
communicate for him, recently let go from a turpentine camp up at
Sixshooter Canyon for pulverizing the foreman's jaw in a dispute over
a bottle of whiskey, rather like the one he had upended at the moment.
There was Hodie Powell, a large man with thin pale hair and almost
invisible eyebrows, who'd been a foreman for the Graham brothers
over in Pleasant Valley, and scar-faced Lew Anderson, Lazy Ray
Gunther, a busted-knuckle miner named Frank Blair, and loose-lipped
orange-haired Sam McDowell, who everybody said was crazy
because he once beat his live-in woman friend so badly she lost one
eye. There was Big Bill Lewis, and shy, good-looking young Stu
Hamill, son of a local rancher, who seemed out of place in this rough-
riding crew but had insisted on going along to fight the wicked
redskins.

Best of all there was Jug Larrabee, who'd been a Waco lawman
back in Raker's Texas Ranger days. Those had been good days, the
high, wide old days when all you had to do to bust a difficult case was
lasso the nearest Mexican and beat a confession out of him. It had
been just such an incident that led to Raker's parting company with the
Rangers. A trivial matter of a greaser named Sánchez hanged for
murder in El Paso at just about the time a cowhand named Cottrell
was confessing to the crime in Austin. Unreasonably, Raker's
superiors refused to overlook it as the natural sort of mistake any man
might make, or even that the victim was a Mexican and not worth
kicking up dust about. The faux pas had made the Rangers look
dumb. *That* was Raker's real error.

Throughout all this, Larrabee had faithfully stood by his friend.
Moreover, in later days Larrabee did a stint as a scalphunter, selling
Apache hair to the governor of Chihuahua during the wars of the
1880s, and bore Random a personal grudge for forcing him out of
business.

Good men and true were Raker's Rangers, hard men, with neither a
Republican nor an Indian-lover among them. But one too many, all
the same.

"Where's these damn Cherry Cow we's supposed to be hunting
anyway?" a wheezy bass voice demanded. Raker's lips set in a hard
line beneath his gray moustache. "All that's out thisaway is San

arlos, and them Injuns don't squat to pee without the agent gives 'em
ave."

"Easy, Big Bill," Jug said. "You know all these redskins are the
ame." Good old Jug.

"I've been informed that the *broncos* are trying to raise the
eservation Indians against the white man," Raker said in his soft yet
arrying voice. "And we all know what fires of hatred burn within red
reasts for the white settlers of Arizona."

"The fires won't just be in their breasts if the damn Chiricahua get
old of any of us," Hodie Powell said. He took a pull at the bottle,
essed it to Stu Hamill, who caught it with both hands and almost
umbled it. The cowhand laughed and rubbed his hands on his leather
ants.

Low clumps of brush cast distended shadows across a landscape
oftened by the setting sun. Bold bands of orange, pink, and indigo
lazed in the western sky. Given one of these gorgeous firesplashed
unsets even the godforsaken fringes of the San Carlos could show a
ertain beauty, Raker reflected.

He drank a deep breath of evening-cool air. "The white man has
lways been a friend to the San Carlos," he said, "but they can't be
rusted to keep faith with us. It's been too long since we taught them a
harp lesson. 'The world is grown so bad/That wrens make prey
vhere eagles dare not perch.' *Richard the Third.*"

The bottle had come around to Big Bill Lewis, who was no relation
o Deuce the gambler. He swigged, then snorted derision. "Christ.
We're not gonna have to listen to that sorry old line of crap about how
ou and Wilkes Booth was pals, are we? Got a bellyful of that the
ime we ran them horses down to Mexico."

Raker frowned. Best ignore him, he decided. He raised his voice.
"We must be ever alert, and conscious of our responsibility to shield
he innocent from the wrath of the savages."

"An' who said that?" asked Lewis, hoisting the half-empty bottle
while the others scowled and wished he'd pass it on. "Was that ol'
Shakespeare too? A-haw-haw-haw!" Guffawing at his own wit, he
ipped the bottle back.

Without changing expression Raker drew his Colt and shot him out
from behind it.

The mules squealed and danced in their harness. Old Jake almost
fell out of the box. The others stared at Raker, their faces pale blurs in
the dusk.

"'Wine is a mocker, strong drink is raging,'" quoted Raker,

holstering his .44. Nobody asked him if Shakespeare wrote that too. "I make a point not to preach the virtue of teetotaling. But this should serve as an example of how otherwise good men can be led to ruin by the demon rum."

"It ain't no rum, demon or otherwise," a miner named Ame Cutcheon said. "It's Pinal Lightning, which Billy Saunders makes up on the Poison Springs Wash." He took off his hat and scratched his bald spot. "Seems to be all spilt. Pity."

Feeling Raker's gray glare upon him, he subsided, though muttering something under his breath to the effect of "waste not, want not." The ex-Ranger cleared his throat. "The whiskey's there for you to drink, boys," he said, "but by God, you'd best be able to hold it."

"Don't worry, Johnny," Jug Larrabee said. "We're all behind you Big Bill brung it on himself."

Raker rubbed his jaw. He was grateful to his old saddlemate for speaking up for him, but he could see some of the others were unconvinced. Young Stu Hamill looked positively green. He sighed.

*Maybe I shouldn't have acted so precipitately,* he thought. *Now I' have to give them something to get them solidly behind me again*

Nighthawks zigzagged through the gathering dark. The horses' tail swished rhythmically, warding off the same evening profusion of flie the birds were feasting on. Raker nodded to the corpse that lay on i back, belly rising like a hill in a striped cotton shirt from the dirt b the road. "Bury him," he ordered.

Then it occurred to him there were only twelve men with him now He felt much better.

"You move in strange company these days, my friend."

Squatting on his heels in the gloom of the wickiup, Random laughed grimly. "Not altogether by choice."

Random's host sat by the far wall of the brushwood-and-blanket shelter. The temperature was dropping with the sun, and he clutched coral-snake-colored Hudson's Bay blanket around him to keep warm Even through its bulky folds Random could see the way the flesh ha wasted from the man's once-powerful body.

This was Bésh Idi'dii, the great Thunder Knife. Once he had bee one of the premier White Mountain leaders, second only to Alchis to whom the whites had given their Medal of Honor. Now he wa W-2, in the parlance of the Bureau of Indian Affairs. For all his yea of loyal and courageous aid to the Americans, they had made him th second man in his band by the stroke of a pen. Whether it wa deliberate malice or just the blind, arbitrary working of the state that set him aside in favor of a fat and shiftless man who had adopted the whiteman name of Frank Russel, no one knew. But unlike other Apache leaders so displaced, Thunder Knife carried on with undiminished influence. He was a better man than the so-called Russel, and no matter how strong the white-eyes' government thought itself, it could not change *that*. He bore up under the insult with grace and strength. Just as he bore up under the disease that was killing him.

He leaned forward, picked up a brass pot and poured tea made from the Thelesperma plant into a coffee cup with a broken handle and handed it to Random. "It's good to see you again, old friend. You look well."

Random hesitated, sipped the brew. "It's good to see you," he said through rising steam.

Thunder Knife laughed. It was a big laugh to emerge from a man who scarcely came to Random's shoulder. "Ah, Green Eyes, my friend! With the white-eyes you are a white-eye, full of the indirectness they call courtesy. But with me, you are Apache—and you don't lie by telling me I look well."

He broke off into a coughing jag. It was a wet cough that made his whole body jerk. Random looked away, so as not to embarrass his friend by calling attention to his weakness. Just as he reflexively shut his nostrils and mind to the all-too-familiar stink within the *koogha*.

When the fit had passed, Thunder Knife sat up straight again and took a gulp of the scalding tea. From outside came the camp sounds, as the people came back from the fields, from hunting and gathering food, and the women lit the cooking fires. Random heard his men conversing, their voices oddly flat and lusterless against the rising and falling speech of the Apache. Cahill and Sutter were telling stupid-redskin jokes, judging by the way one would talk briefly and then both would laugh. Random wondered if they knew just how much English Thunder Knife's people understood. Few spoke the language—but understanding was a different matter.

"Nducho's been here," Random said.

"Yes."

"Will your people follow him?"

Silence ensued. It wasn't the Plains Indian manner of long stillnesses interspersed with bouts of grandiloquence. Generally Apaches spoke bluntly among themselves, having little patience with flowery phrases; even their songs were spare, though to Random at

least, no less beautiful for that. Thunder Knife's hesitation meant he
was giving the question special thought.

"Not him," he answered at last, after hawking and spitting into the
dirt. "But the prophet, Owl—some of the younger men are receptive
to what he says. Two youths disappeared the day after the East Folk
spoke here."

Random raised an eyebrow. "Owl?"

"Well-named, that one. A shaman, self-proclaimed prophet. Yusn
speaks to him, and has appointed him to raise all Apache in a war of
extermination against the white-eyes."

"That's not what Yusn told the Cibicu prophet." He referred to
Nochéé Dokliñi, who had been killed by soldiers in 1881. Following
Apache custom, he did not speak the dead man's true name, so as not
to disturb his spirit.

"No. That one preached that the Apache should live in peace, and
that Yusn would deal with the white-eyes in His own time. The
Chiricahua didn't listen then." He produced a wintry smile, which
turned the hollow places under his cheekbones to pits of shadow.
"Now Yusn has changed his mind to accommodate Ha'i'ąhá desires,
it seems." He spit into the fire. "The ill-named one will unite all
Apache, all right—in disaster. No good can come from taking Yusn's
name in vain."

"So it's this Owl who's the leader."

"No. Supposedly Aguilar leads. But from the talk I've heard, the
Eagle daydreams, Nducho struts about and froths at the mouth, and
whatever Owl wishes is done. Not an unfamiliar pattern, is it?"

"Unfortunately not. Sounds like Go'łika in his prime."

"A man who would lead without Power is pretty much at the mercy
of a man who has Power, especially if he has a smooth tongue." He
coughed. "You've been east to where they keep the Chiricahua. How
is the Yawner? Is he dead yet?"

"No. I'm afraid he's indestructible. He has all the other chiefs
convinced they let him down by not fighting on. He could charm a
baby from the breast, that one." Random shook his head. "If he were
white, he'd have been President years ago. The terrible thing is,
we've had worse ones."

"You'd know better than I. But Geronimo's an evil man. He'll be
reborn as a bear."

They sat awhile in the comfortable silence old friends find, even
when years have dropped like a handful of pebbles in a stream
between the times they've seen each other. Random was at ease in this

dome-shaped shelter clinging to a clearing on the western face of Mount Thomas. He did not deceive himself that he was somehow more Indian than white, though he'd often been accused of it. In the long run he could be no more comfortable here than in the teeming streets of New York, or the cafés of Paris, or the jungles of Costa Rica and Yucatán. It was his special talent to adapt to any surroundings in which he found himself, from the docks of Hamburg to the western Canadian plains to the mountains and deserts of the American Southwest. To absorb languages and outlooks and ways as though through his skin. But it was part of that ability that he could never be completely of one people, of one place. Apartness, aloneness: these were the prices he paid for survival. But sometimes there were respites, such as this time. He treasured them more than anything else.

"Can you stop your people from joining the raiders?" he finally asked, after watching the western sky deepen toward indigo.

Thunder Knife smiled. "I can't forbid them, surely. It isn't our way to be slaves to the word of another."

"Excuse it. I've been among the white-eyes too long."

Thunder Knife gathered the striped blanket more closely around him. "It rankles many of the young men that the only chance for battle and glory is to don the red headband of the *naabaahí*. Even before Owl came, some said that to be a scout for the Army is to be no better than the white-eyes' dog." He shook his head. "They can't know of the old days, of the burning homes, stolen women and murdered men the Chiricahua strewed across White Mountain land. Those who know, those who saw—they do not forget."

His eyes were obsidian-hard, giving back dancing flecks of firelight. For all his serenity and gentle speech, he had been a noted warrior, and he still had a warrior's eyes. Even the tuberculosis that would kill him in a year, two at the outside, could not dim them short of death.

"But the young ones—how can you tell them? If you speak of the old days, the wars with the Chiricahua, they grow bored and accuse you of dwelling in the past. All they know is the weight of the white-eyes' boots on our necks, and believe their elders craven for having aided their enemies."

He studied Random across the pale flames leaping around the kettle. "Perhaps you should talk to them."

"Do you think that would help?"

"Maybe they'll listen to a new voice telling them the same old thing. You're almost as persuasive as Geronimo, and you speak our tongue as though you were born to it—even if you do have a damned East People accent."

Random laughed. "It was the Chiricahua I learned it from. Small wonder I sound like one."

Thunder Knife picked up a stick and prodded the fire. "You'll kill Nducho, of course," he said, knowing the Mountain Lion had murdered two of Random's friends. "What of Aguilar?"

"I don't know. As long as I stop this"—he paused, having almost said *jihad*—"this holy war, it doesn't matter. I'd just as soon let him go." He grimaced. "Damned if I'll send him back to rot at Sill."

"He's too good a man for that," Thunder Knife agreed.

"What about Tse'e and Mariana? Did any of your people see them?"

Thunder Knife frowned and peered intently into the fire. "Tse'e was there," he said with a shade of reluctance. "He had a rifle in his hands."

Random drew back. "You mean he wasn't a prisoner?"

Once more his friend chose careful words. "There are more ways to bind a man than with rawhide thongs or chains," he said. "Tse'e carried a guilt around inside him from the day he saw his father shipped off to exile and imprisonment, while he remained free. The guilt gnawed at him like a rat." He raised his eyes to Random's. "It would kill him to disappoint his father again."

"Would he fight beside Nducho, then?" The thought stunned him.

"I don't think so." Thunder Knife dropped his eyes again. "But if the rat gnawed at him enough, who knows?"

"What about Mariana?"

"Nobody saw her." It was almost a whisper. The skin of his face had a frail parchment look, ancient, as if it would crumble to the touch.

Random rocked back on his heels, sickened by the implication. Nducho would kill a White Mountain woman with as little emotion as he'd kill a bug. It might even give him a special pleasure to kill the woman his brother loved so single-mindedly. "She comes of good stock," he made himself say. "She can take care of herself."

Thunder Knife showed him the skeleton of a smile. "Which one of us are you trying to fool?"

Random rose. "I have to see to my men. I'll speak to your people after the sun goes all the way down."

"None could do more than you. I thank you, my friend."

As he left, Random heard once more the tearing sound of his friend's coughing, and the thin tinkling of the chain around his neck.

# CHAPTER EIGHT

To Tse'e it always seemed this land had died and rotted down to bare jagged bones. But late spring rains had softened its outlines somewhat, muting the red sandstone and black lava with a fine, fuzzy coat of pale green. Here and there were low clumps of blue grama and sideoats. In places, the downward-sloping land was dotted with chaparral, mostly scrub oak, but also sumac, and manzanita, whose berries would soon ripen and be gathered by the People for food. The chaparral reminded Tse'e of the piñon- and juniper-clad hills around Santa Fe. But that land was much less stark than this.

As the sun neared the top of the blue vault of the sky, they turned their horses into the headcut of a canyon that led from the White Mountain foothills to the flatter lands below. White sunlight echoed from steep cliff faces and became a cacophony of heat, beating against them from above, from the sides, rising in a shimmering haze from rocks where lizards lay and dispassionately watched them pass. They were passing through a portal to the San Carlos Tse'e remembered from his youth, and it was like the gates of the whiteman's hell.

García led the way, with Aguilar behind, and then Nducho. He had returned that morning with word that at least some of the San Carlos Apaches were ready to hear the gospel of Owl. The news cast Tse'e into a dark pool of depression.

He was desperately lonely, grieving for the LaMontagnes, fearing constantly for Mariana. Had she been captured by vengeful whites, eager to exact some payment for the murder of the rancher and his wife? He ached to break from the band, run and search for her and seize her as a drowning man seizes a floating scrap of driftwood. Yet he knew that to do so was to condemn her: he knew his brother could carry out his threat. And would.

The image of the captive rose behind his eyes, hanging, dead eyes staring from a slowly baking skull. It could be Mariana hanging there, with her long black hair burned to stubble. So he rode with these wild, mad men. And he feared and hated them.

But not all. He could not hate his father. He could only watch in love and helpless agony as the old man clung more and more to the past, like a child with its favorite toy. Nor could he hate the grave, skull-faced man, whom he had always known as Lightning-Strikes-Near, and who was now called Chi'.

He remembered the warrior well from his happy childhood days in the Mimbres, those New Mexican mountains so like the White range he had grown to love. Lightning was always grim, aloof, and yet he never appeared at the camp of Haastįį 'Ítsá without a carved deer or rifle of driftwood, for the warchief's adored elder son. Somehow he inevitably ended by bouncing the delighted Young Eagle on one knee, gravely, as though performing a solemn duty.

Something—perhaps no more than his own soul-deep desperation—told Tse'e he could talk to this man. He seemed even now to lack the bitterness that rode so many of the others, or the madness of the *heshkéé*. The yellow rump and black tail of Chi''s scrawny Mexican buckskin swayed to the irregular tempo of the descent just ahead of Tse'e. The trail was wide enough for two here, so Tse'e urged his mare into a brief trot, trusting her to keep her footing on the shifting red dirt.

Chi' greeted him with a nod as he drew alongside. Today the older man wore a scarlet Pima turban on top of his red outfit, which was rare for a *bronco*, since it suggested the red headband that was the mark of the hated Army scout. Chi' had never cared much for the opinion of others, which Tse'e knew made him dangerous in the eyes of some.

In fact his fierce integrity posed hazards to himself as well. He was renowned for the manner in which he split with Geronimo after that worthy broke his word to General Crook and took the warpath again. "All you care about is the white-eyes' Power, which is power over others," he had told the Yawner. "You're no better than a white-eyes yourself." And he rode away. Nor did Geronimo put a Springfield ball into the man's broad back, though such an act was well within his repertoire. While he never aspired to chieftainship himself, Lightning-Strikes-Near was widely known to be as deadly a warrior as the martial Chíhéne, the Red Paint People, had produced. Geronimo understood his own limitations; if his Apache marksmanship didn't drop the defector on the first shot, he would not get a second. But Lightning had taken a risk, just the same.

Now Tse'e asked him, "Why do you ride with my brother?"

A shadow of distaste passed over the badlands that were Chi''s face. "I ride with Niishdzhaa," he said. "That your brother's along is circumstantial."

"But why?" Tse'e persisted. "You've nothing in common with *heshkéés* like Boca Negra and Eskinyá. Why stay with them?"

The older man sighed. "I have reasons I don't like to talk about. But you're the son of a man I respect, and you seem to've grown into a good man yourself. So I'll tell you.

"You know I lost my Power, a long time ago."

Tse'e nodded. He felt a thrill of anticipation. Power was an intensely personal subject to an Apache.

"I was with Victorio on his last day, when the Nakaiyé trapped us at Tres Castillos, in Chihuahua. Lozen, his sister, had the Power of sensing enemies, but she and Nana and your father were elsewhere on a raid that day. So they caught us on that hill, and ringed us with steel and fire.

"Victorio knew he wouldn't live to see the sunset. 'You must hide yourself when the Nakaiyé come,' he told me. 'Hide well. One of us must live, to carry the word of what happened here and see that we are avenged.' He looked off to the east, where Lozen and the others had gone. 'I would have my sister know the manner of my passing,' he said softly.

"I argued and pleaded, but I couldn't move him. When the Mexicans attacked, I fired until my ammunition was gone. Then I felt my chief's eyes upon me, and I slunk off like a whipped dog to hide beneath a rock shelf. My Power spoke to me as I watched the final slaughter, urging me to fight as the Nakaiyé and their Tarahumare dogs passed among the wounded, cutting the throats of men, women, children. I saw the Tarahumare Mauricio Corredor shoot Victorio, just as the Mexicans say, though they lie about everything else. From behind, he shot him. Many People say Victorio killed himself. I don't think that story does him honor, to say he took his own life with strength he could have used killing Mexicans. But people like that version, and such fabrications are often stronger than truth, though why Yusn permits that I don't know.

"For three days I lay under the rock, stunned by the horror I'd seen. And when your father found me there, I'd lost more than the leader I loved: I'd lost my Power too."

"But why?" Tse'e asked.

"Lightning judged me a coward," Chi' said bleakly. "Justly, I see now. Sure, Victorio ordered me to save myself—but was I *'indaa* ligai or a Mexican, to obey another's command over my own conscience?

"Since then I've tried to call my Power back to me. I've fasted, and sweated in the sweat lodges, and gone up to the high places in the storm, wearing red to draw the lightning, that I might know its Power once again, or a good, clean death. In vain, always in vain.

"So now I follow Owl. Not only for the sake of Yusn or the People, but for myself as well. For he's promised me that by following him I will win what I most desire: my Power, or death."

For a few moments Tse'e watched a red-tailed hawk kiting on the thermals that rose from the canyon, and listened to the mare's chuffing as she picked her way down. He was moved by the warrior's story, and honored that Chi' had chosen to tell him. Perhaps this strange, lonely man had never told the story before.

He understood why Chi' told it now, he thought. Though he'd never taken the Jesus Road, Tse'e knew about Catholicism. The LaMontagnes had been Catholic, though they had never tried to convert him or Mariana. The rite of confession had in particular always fascinated Tse'e. He sensed that he was cast in the role of priest, doing as much for Chi' by listening to the story as Chi' had done for him by telling it.

The canyon widened here, the walls falling away to both sides of the dry watercourse. A flat rock lay tilted beside the trail. On it stood Owl's horse, a shaggy white Plains pony with a peculiar gait, so that it always seemed on the verge of going lame, and yet never did. Glittering reptilian eyes glared from within the shadow of the ancient prophet's hatbrim. Tse'e's stomach surged within him as he realized the shaman was waiting for him.

Owl was shorter than Haastjj 'Itsá and his sons, by virtue of the crookedness of his spine, which raised his left shoulder above the right so that he always appeared off balance, whether mounted or afoot. His face was weathered and wasted as the desert land itself, as if the years had eroded anything of softness from it, leaving only the unyielding starkness beneath. His bony legs, twisted as cypress limbs, disappeared into lowcut doeskin moccasins. He wore a typical long Apache blouse with a rope tied about the waist to bear his medicine bag. He was not armed. On his head he wore a curious hat, a bowler, ringed with yellow stripes, with owls painted at the cardinal points: black for the east, blue for south, white for the west, yellow representing north. On another the hat would have appeared ludicrous. On Owl it was infinitely sinister.

"You doubt me, Young Eagle." The words were a rattlesnake buzz.

A chill went through Tse'e, as if the furnace wind had turned into the breath of December. He made himself face the old man bravely. "I do."

"The time of judgment is at hand," came the stick-in-dead-leaves rattle. "Be wary, lest Yusn find you wanting."

The procession passed by in silence, the raiders swinging wide to avoid the rock beside which Tse'e had halted his mare. It was said Owl could give you the ghost-sickness with just a look, shooting the sickness into you with his eyes. Chi' had ridden on with a nod, leaving Tse'e to face the shaman alone.

"It's not enough that you are Aguilar's son," Owl said. "You must not think to defy Yusn."

"You talk like a whiteman preacher," said Tse'e with a courage he did not know he had. "They too speak of a judgment to come."

"Know that Yusn speaks of white-eyes as well as Apache. But they won't listen. That's why He means to punish them—and we're his chosen instrument." His eyes seized Tse'e's like an owl's claws gripping a mouse. "Give over your resistance, Tse'e. Surrender to the will of Yusn."

Tse'e could not look away. His defiance melted within him. In rising panic he felt himself slip, felt his lips prepare to speak the words of submission.

As it sometimes does in the desert, the wind reversed its course. Just for a moment the breeze blew sweat and cool from the White Mountains. It carried a fleeting scent of the highlands, of fir and wild flowers and grass growing lush by a nameless spring. It defied the desolation on every side.

With a shock Tse'e was free. "You will not have me," he said. He kicked the mare hard, went galloping headlong down the canyon, hiding himself in a cloud of red dust from those eyes that grasped like talons.

"My God," Brent Jordan breathed. "The *savages*."

Grimly Random looked at the charred and flyblown corpse. Behind him he heard strangling sounds as one of the recruits got sick. The dead man hanging from a weather-silvered treelimb was like a brutal culmination of the debate that Random and the young man had been holding as they rode that day.

Last night he'd spoken to the men of Thunder Knife's camp, and of several other *rancherías* on the slopes of Mount Thomas. Owl was bringing disaster, he told them; the time for armed confrontation with the whiteman was not now. His listeners had been impassive, their response guarded, but they heard him out. With the reputation he had among them they might even have believed him.

Certainly some of them had. After the meeting had dispersed, one of Thunder Knife's people had cautiously approached Random, with the result that as the first gray fronds of dawn sprouted above the horizon, the group rode south for the San Carlos. Their luck was good. In the flat country near Nash Creek, ten miles south of the Sevenmile Rim, they cut sign of the war party.

Kneeling in the dirt beside an algerita bush, Doroteo pointed to a scatter of hoofprints. "Look like horse going lame," he announced in English for all to hear. "Belong bad-name medicine man."

Skilled as he was at tracking, Random saw only prints much like any other. That was why Doroteo was along. "Follow them," the mercenary said.

Sutter and Cahill sneered. Jordan vacillated, on the one hand dubious about relying on a mere savage, and on the other hand thrilled to be witnessing a display of the "red man's" wilderness lore right out of Fenimore Cooper.

"You mustn't think I'm ignorant of southwestern matters, Mr. Random," he said, laying his mount alongside, though carefully out of range of Malcriado's teeth.

"Why would I think a thing like that?"

"My father has often written me about what it's like out here. And I read what General Miles wrote about his campaigns against the hostiles. In warfare the Apaches are a sneaky, underhanded race. They operate by stealth, subterfuge, and ambush." He shook his head. "They could not long hope to stand against the courageous Anglo-Saxon, with his forthright, headlong approach to war."

Random laughed. "They didn't stand for long. A mere four hundred years. First against the Spaniard, then the Mexicans, and then us. I've heard it theorized the Aztecs tried to push their borders this way and the Apaches talked them out of it. Not a bad performance for a people who never seem to've numbered much above three thousand."

Predictably, Jordan was scandalized. "Are you trying to tell me you approve of their furtive style of warfare? To skulk about the country like packs of coyotes, murdering isolated white men and stealing stock, and never standing up for an honest fight, man to man?"

"Yes," said Random, who wasn't in a mood to mince words this
morning.

"But that's dishonorable!"

Random looked at him hard. "What exactly do you call honor, Mr
Jordan? As few warriors as the Apaches could muster even in their
heyday, even armed better than they generally were, they would have
been wiped out in a set-piece battle with anything larger than a
battalion. They would have lost the war at a stroke."

Jordan pulled back his shoulders and swelled his chest. "That
would have been the *manly* way."

"They tried a head-to-head fight with the Army once," Random
said, "at Apache Pass during the Civil War. The federals turned a
mountain gun on them, and the Apaches never truly recovered from
the losses they took that day."

"They were honorable losses," Jordan declared. "They should
have fought on in that manner despite their setbacks. Death before
dishonor."

"A fine phrase, Mr. Jordan. But when you're talking about a man
defending his land, his wife and children, against a better-armed and
vastly more numerous foe, where exactly does the path of honor lie?
Is it more honorable to stand upright in front of a bullet, so you can
die knowing you died like a man? Or to fight in the way that gives you
the best chance to win, or at least delay defeat, to keep your wife from
being raped, your children from having their brains dashed against
a rock, or being sold into slavery?"

Cheeks flushed with exasperation, Jordan had flung, "You obviously have no concept of the meaning of honor!" and spurred his horse
ahead. Casting sharp looks at Random, Cahill and Sutter had ridden
after him and brought him back to the group. With *bronco* Apaches on
the loose, the forests of the southern fringes of the White Mountains
were not the place to go for a solitary ride.

Now young Jordan looked from the mutilated corpse to Random,
and his eyes burned with a terrible brightness.

"Deploy the men, Sergeant," Random told Brown. He had seen at
once that the campsite was several days cold, but it wouldn't do any
harm to give the soldiers a little practice. And with the Chiricahua, the
best chance to take was none at all.

Brown dismounted his squad and spread them out prone among the
flowers in a circle around the blasted tree. Pulling his stage gun from
the carbine loop, Random dismounted and walked to the tree. Dorotea
came along, and behind him Jordan, holding his fancy presentation

Winchester as though he couldn't wait to use it on somebody. He made Random uneasy. Buck fever had made many an untried soldier blast holes in his comrades.

Leery of contracting corpse-sickness, Doroteo examined the body from a respectful distance. "Cherry Cow do this. Cherry Cow bad ndin."

"The murderers!" Jordan said again. He was plainly at pains to keep from following the lead of Private Monroe in spewing that morning's beans, bacon, and biscuit all over the clearing. "How can you defend devils who make war like this?"

"I can't."

Jordan blinked, smiled, reached up to smooth back the corners of his moustache. "Then you admit the Apache's way is wrong."

"No." He gestured at the corpse with his shotgun. "I've seen white mobs do as much to blacks. This is *heshkéé* work. Not *Apache*."

"But—but those are rabble! Lynch mobs."

"You seem to recognize two classes of white men, Mr. Jordan. Why is there just one kind of red?"

He knelt, prodded the body gently with the twin muzzles of the Remington to turn it. "See this?" He pointed to where a round hole in the man's chest, rimmed with crusted blackness that was not char, could be seen through a milling mass of flies. "Someone shot him dead. Since there are no signs of a subsequent battle, it must have been one of the raiders. Even at the worst of times there were plenty of Apache who hated this sort of thing."

"It was probably just some elaboration of their horrid little game."

"No. He's not burned much. The fire was allowed to die quickly—and believe me, when the *heshkéés* do this sort of thing, they tend their fires lovingly."

"So you admit the—the animals make an art of torture! How can you doubt the civilizing mission of the white race?"

"Because I've seen too damn much of what the white race does!" Random's face had gone pale beneath its deep tan. A curlicue scar glowed pink on the curve of his left cheekbone, below the eye. "I was on Wounded Knee Creek when the Hotchkiss guns went to work. Have you any idea what a two-pound explosive shell does when it hits, say, a six-year-old girl? Is *that* civilizing, Mr. Jordan?"

"But that was war!" The youth took a step back.

"If you call opening fire on a crowd of people with no more than a few rusty carbines among them 'war.' If the Indians had done such a thing, it would have been called a massacre." He shook his head in disgust and started to walk away.

"I'm sure wrongs have been done the red man," Jordan told hi
back, with the air of one trying to be reasonable in the face
obdurate irrationality. "Americans are a vigorous people, an
sometimes overzealous. But whatever wrongs they've done have onl
been in response to such bestial acts of wanton cruelty as this."

Random turned back. "If you keep on the way you're going, M
Jordan, you'll end up just like your father."

Jordan beamed.

"A typical nineteenth-century horse's ass." He walked towar
Malcriado. He heard something thump to the ground, and steps.
hand on his shoulder spun him roughly round.

"Put down that shotgun," Brent Jordan said through clenche
teeth. His hands were empty. The Winchester lay gleaming among th
flowers a few paces behind him.

Random stared at the boy, not comprehending. "Put it down an
fight like a man!" Jordan insisted.

"You're crazy." Random turned away.

Jordan grabbed his shoulder, whirled him back around and hit hi
on the jaw. Random staggered back a step. Jordan yelped and clutche
the knuckles of his right hand.

"What in hell's name is wrong with you?" Random yelled at hir
"If the shotgun was cocked it would've gone off." He rubbed his ja
as he spoke. The scene was unreal; not even the bone-ache where he
been struck fully penetrated his conviction that this was too absurd
actually be happening.

The boy lunged at him, swinging wildly despite the inju
Random's jaw had done his fist. Random sidestepped. Jordan we
past in a bullmoose rush, and Random clipped him one-handed ov
the ear with the butt of his stage gun. Jordan sprawled facefirst in th
grass. Moaning, he rolled over and started to get up.

A small, solid sound by his ear stopped him. He turned his ey
right. His mouth slackened at the sight of the gleaming blade of a sl
Moorish knife sunk to the bone hilt in a tuft of mountain muhly not
inch from his face.

"I'm not a football dummy," Random said coldly, "nor do I fig
for recreation. You'd best keep that in mind from now on, M
Jordan."

"You—you struck foul," Jordan gasped. He kept rolling his ey
back to look at the knife, as if expecting it to spring from the grou
and gash his cheek.

Slowly his color returned. With it came a touch of bravado. "A tr

nglo-Saxon scorns a knife," he said, with only a slight tremolo to
ar the haughtiness of his words.

"I never gave much of a damn whether I was a true Anglo-Saxon or
ot." Random tipped the shotgun onto his shoulder. "Incidentally,
ere's a fine point of life in the West that you apparently never
arned from the writings of Mr. Roosevelt."

Jordan picked himself up, brushing grass and crushed flowers from
is clothes. "What's that?"

Random nodded at the heavy Colt still in its holster on the youth's
ght hip. "A man wearing a gun's presumed to be ready to use it. If
e attacks another armed man *without* using his gun, the customary
erdict is suicide." He smiled at Jordan, who had gone the color of
e feathery ashes that fluttered in the breeze beneath the corpse.
Your western Anglo-Saxon is a rough-and-ready breed, you see, Mr.
rdan."

Still smiling, Random pivoted to face Sutter and Cahill, who,
aving recovered from their initial astonishment, were starting
urposefully in Random's direction. He clicked back both hammers of
e shotgun with his thumb, though the weapon stayed on his
oulder. They stopped. "Good boys. You're Mr. Jordan's body-
ards: attend to his body. Sergeant Brown?"

"Sir?" The sergeant stood by the mules, watching with hooded
es.

"Your men have had a chance to see the stakes we're playing for,"
andom said, "and you're no longer beneath the gimlet eye of
olonel Sinclair. So I'm telling you again: you don't have to
company me. I appreciate your assistance, but I will not order you
follow."

The squad looked to Brown. "Yes, sir," he said, unmoving.

Random sighed. "Very well, Sergeant." He uncocked his shotgun
d returned it to its loop. "I'd be obliged if some of your men would
ve me a hand burying this poor son of a bitch."

A quail's cry from the scrub brought the camp alert. Tse'e glanced
from where he was squatting on his heels polishing the Sharps. His
other sprang to his feet, working the action of his Winchester with
urgent sound.

"It's Delzhee coming in," called Boca Negra from concealment
nong the rocks near the edge of the low mesa on which they'd
mped. "He has company."

Nducho screamed orders. Raiders scrambled for cover. Boca Negra laughed. "Don't get excited. It's not the horse soldiers. Just a coupl of ratty San Carlos. They're not wearing red headbands."

That meant they weren't scouts. "What if they're Agency police? Eskinyá asked.

"Only two of them?" The half-breed laughed derisively. "Yo know how they work. They run in packs."

His apprehension evaporated, Nducho rose from behind a manzani ta. "They're coming to tell us that San Carlos has joined us," h announced. "Our time of triumph is at hand!"

"*Nzhǫǫ*," said Owl. "You're a great leader, Mountain Lion."

But no sooner had Delzhee and the two San Carlos topped the ris than Tse'e began to doubt that Nducho's triumph had in fac materialized. They were both dressed in traditional manner, one in white Mexican straw hat, one in a Pima turban. Both were armed wit carbines, and both wore the same look of flat impassivity th Apaches usually adopted with whites.

"It's good to see you, my friends," called Nducho expansivel "How many of the brave San Carlos ride to join us?"

The taller and older of the newcomers looked at him. "None."

Nducho blinked. "What?" Owl screeched. "Are there no men o the San Carlos?"

Scowling, the round-faced youngster in the turban started to rais his gun. The elder held up a hand to stay him. "Contain yoursel Temerario." To the crookbacked shaman he said, "We've receive tidings that made us doubt your grand schemes can succeed."

Owl's face darkened. "What tidings are these? Whatever h happened my magic will set right."

Temerario uttered a yelp of laughter. "Your magic won't chang *this*," he said, husking his voice to mask an adolescent squeal "Green Eyes has returned!"

*Green Eyes!* Fear fled Tse'e. The raiders would surely be disperse now, and Mariana and he saved.

"We got the word from clansmen on White Mountain," the old San Carlos said. "He rides with some other whitemen, some blac whiteman troopers, and a Big Shit Cibicu scout."

"Who is this Green Eyes, to make your dung grow watery wit fear?" Owl demanded. "He cannot defy the will of Yusn!"

"Strange Yusn hasn't seen fit to mention him to you. He's a might warrior and magician, an Apache cursed by being reborn a whit eyes. The whitemen name him Random."

"A white-eyes?" cried Nducho, his voice trembling with passio "We're not afraid of them!"

The San Carlos shook his head patiently. "He's not *bináá ligai*, but *ináá dotl' izh*." Not white-eyes, but Green Eyes. He spoke in the odd hush-mouthed San Carlos dialect that made an *n* where a White Mountain would say *d*, and a Chiricahua *nd*. "You East People should fear him. He had a lot to do with making you give up."

Nducho bridled. "*I* never surrendered!"

"I did," Aguilar said gently. "And I've heard of this Green Eyes. He came to see us when we were held at Fort Marion, and men of repute spoke to him in a friendly way. Even Geronimo, who cares for no white-eyes."

The San Carlos with the hat nodded. "We know him too. That's why even young braves like Temerario here are reluctant to join you. Green Eyes beat you before. He can do it again."

Owl's spindly arms shot skyward in wrath. "Doubters! The power of Yusn is greater than any man's!"

"No one doubts that, ill-named one. What we doubt is whether you truly speak for him." The middle-aged man looked at Aguilar, and then at the Old Eagle's younger, fiercer son. "I'm against any joining you. The whiteman's hand lies heavy upon us, but not so heavy that we forget the days when you raided us as if we were Nakaiyé. Others can do as they will, as is Apache law. But I assure you of this: No one will stir from this reservation until you show you can do more than talk of great victories and the will of Yusn."

He turned his mare and sent her careering down the steep side of the mesa. After a defiant scowl at Owl and Nducho, Temerario did likewise, whooping as his mount slipped and stumbled down the rocky slope. Tse'e winced reflexively at his treatment of his mount, and knew wryly that this was the whiteman's way, to care so for a riding beast.

His heart filled to bursting with a wild, impossible hope. "You're finished, my brother!" he shouted to Nducho, who stood shaking with rage, watching the San Carlos drawing a dust-cloud across the desert. "Green Eyes will run you down like a coyote taking a rabbit."

"No! He's just a white-eyes. I'm not afraid of him."

His rifle cradled in the crook of one arm, Chi' stood by looking thoughtful. "I know this Green Eyes; I've fought him. You have too, Nducho. You should know he's a strong man, and brave, and doesn't say things he doesn't mean. And he speaks our tongue too well to have been 'indaa ligai always. Maybe it's true that he was Nndé in a former life."

"Then he's a traitor to the People, and will be reborn as a bear!"

screamed Nducho, flailing his rifle at the air. "I'm not afraid of him
*Don't try to make me say I'm afraid!*"

The raiders exchanged troubled looks. The killing frenzy was o
the Mountain Lion now, and it befit that those around him trea
warily. But the seriousness of the matter at hand outweighed commo
caution. "What about Green Eyes's Power?" asked one of the wa
party. "Didn't he kill the Tarahumare pig Mauricio?"

"He did," Tse'e affirmed proudly. "I saw it with my own eyes. H
shot the man who killed Victorio and the American soldier-*nant*
Crawford."

"Victorio was not *killed*," Aguilar said sternly. "He took his ow
life."

Studiously avoiding a glance at Chi', Tse'e said, "All the mor
reason to honor Green Eyes for killing Mauricio Corredor, for
Victorio killed himself, didn't Mauricio dishonor his spirit b
claiming to have sent it to the Happy Place?"

"Don't confuse us with your white-eyes talk," snarled Nducho. "
Green Eyes is such a great warrior, great will be *my* honor when I ki
him."

"You forget his Power," Chi' said.

Nducho's face went stiff as a corpse's. Only Chi' would dare pro
the Mountain Lion with talk of another's Power. Nducho coiled in o
himself, as if readying to leap on the older man and rend him with h
teeth. Chi' watched him, wholly relaxed.

Finally Nducho let his breath whistle out between clenched teetl
He turned to his brother. "Your Green Eyes uses his Power to tl
detriment of the People. He's a witch, and I personally will give hi
the punishment Nndé law demands for witches: burning alive."

Once more dread wrapped Tse'e like a blanket. It was not so muc
his brother's low-voiced threat, though that was horrible enough. Bi
as he looked out at the desert beyond his brother's hate-filled face, th
flat dry land, dappled with shadows of drifting clouds, seemed
waver and change. For a moment he saw as from a high place, a lii
of men, ant-tiny with distance, winding its way toward him throug
chaparral. The vision was gone as quickly as it came.

But in its wake he knew that, instead of salvation, the coming of h
friend would bring destruction. To himself, to Mariana, to Random—
or to all of them.

# CHAPTER NINE

Pungent smoke boiled into the cloud-gray sky of dawn. Orange flames flapped in sheets above burning wickiups and a thick, nose-clogging, throat-catching stink filled the air. The roaring of the flames almost masked the throaty buzz of thousands of flies, their bodies glistening pearly blue and green in the feeble daylight, gathered on the corpse that lay sprawled half inside the largest shelter.

Sitting in the wagon's box, John Raker dipped a scrap of cloth in a bucket filled with water taken from the burning *ranchería*'s well and fortified with lye soap, and rammed it down the muzzle of his .44. He wrinkled his nose fastidiously against the mingled reeks of death and burned powder, thinking that this might be the time to investigate smokeless gunpowder. The new version, cordite, reputedly lacked the earlier guncotton's unfortunate propensity for going off of its own accord. This damned black powder fouled a barrel so that after a few shots it was caked like the stacks of a Pittsburgh foundry, and a positive bitch-kitty to clean.

"Shee-it!" said Lazy Ray Gunther, emerging from a patch of saltbush buttoning up the fly of his jeans. "It's true what they say about these 'Paches. Ain't hardly human. Why, that li'l gal din't cry out one little bit. Just laid there glaring at me like she wanted to tear my throat out with her teeth."

"Good thing she wasn't Cherry Cow," Raker observed, switching to an oily patch. "She *would've* torn your throat out. Or worse. I've known those she-wolves to keep hideout dirks in the strangest places."

Strolling to collect a half-empty bottle from the wagon, the big man essayed a laugh at Raker's humor.

"Well, she was surely cherry, if not exactly Cherry Cow," he said. His own joke pleased him so much that he almost choked from laughing, and whiskey slopped down the front of his cotton shirt.

Raker looked up briskly. "Watch your tongue. I'll have no truck with foul language."

Gunther took the bottle from his lips with a comradely smile. It faded as his eyes met Raker's. "Sorry," he mumbled, and turned away.

The rest of the Rangers were beginning to emerge from the chaparral. Young Stu Hamill's baby face was flushed and sweaty, as if from a sudden onset of fever. The other men exchanged lazy grins and comments pitched low so that Raker wouldn't hear.

He heard them muttering, and guessed what they were saying. Their dirty humor didn't bother him much. It was "full of sound and fury, signifying nothing," as dear old Johnny Booth would have said. Come to that, this brand of idle talk was a marked improvement over the muttering that had taken place since Big Bill Lewis's mishap. *That* had bordered on rebellion.

Yesterday he'd scouted ahead of the party, which was held to a crawl by the wagon, on Hamlet, his strapping black stud. In late afternoon he spotted a thin wisp of brownish smoke drifting into the sky to the south and east. He had tied Hamlet to a mesquite and gone afoot to investigate.

He was some miles east of the San Carlos Agency proper. Here the land was fairly flat, sloping slowly to the east, dotted with dwarf oak. But its flatness was deceptive; the smoke appeared to rise from the very ground, and it wasn't until he was within thirty yards that he could actually see the brush huts clumped in a small fold in the land.

A stocky, big-bellied man in a red shirt and Apache leggings sat on a rock before the biggest wickiup, braiding a rope from long strips of rawhide. On the hard-trodden earth nearby burned a dried-grass fire, beside which squatted an old woman in a long skirt, roasting a rabbit on a green cottonwood withe. A slim girl, fifteen or so by the looks of her, was on her knees grinding Agency-issue cornmeal on a *metate*. Several naked children of both sexes ran loose among the huts, laughing happily at some game. Raker watched as the western sky became a yellow ocean in which the molten gold orb of the sun glowed fiercely, then nodded to himself and withdrew. The San Carlos obviously weren't expecting trouble. They probably wouldn't even bother to set lookouts around the camp. It was the ideal place, both to fulfill his mission from Jordan, and to ease his men's discontent.

The Rangers struck at dawn, just as the topmost rim of the sun showed behind the toothed jaw of the Gilas. The old woman was already up and about, fussing over the morning fire, as a younger, stocky woman hauled water in a battered old kettle to boil coffee. She was the one who saw the first bearded whiteman burst from the brush. She screamed and raced into the biggest wickiup. An instant later the man Raker had seen the day before appeared in the entry, working the action of an ancient Henry. A volley of bullets caught him and dropped him where he stood.

At the first shots the old woman darted into the chaparral. When the man fell the younger woman kicked a hole through the rear of the wickiup and fled with her children trailing after like baby quail. They were lost to view immediately.

In spite of a sharp warning from Raker, Deuce Lewis the faro dealer swaggered into one of the other wickiups as if planning to set up housekeeping. The others heard him scream. A moment later he reeled out, holding his face and moaning. A knife-slash had opened his cheek to the bone, barely missing his left eye.

Gun in hand, Raker went in, bent over and fast. The slender girl hissed and stabbed at him with a butcher's knife. He caught her wrist and cracked her smartly across the cheekbone with the barrel of his Colt.

After she was subdued, a quick search of the camp revealed pathetically little of value: some saddles, cracked and blackened with age, a few baskets traded from the Zuñis, a bolt of mildewed blue cloth from the Agency. As Jake LeDoux cursed the wagon-mules into camp, Raker ordered the wickiups torched.

A cry floated up from the chaparral. Amos Cutcheon lumbered into the camp holding a kicking, squalling girl wrapped in his thick hairy arms. "Found her in a ol' arroyo, over by the brush corral where their ponies is," he announced. "Ain't so much a looker as the one you caught, Johnny—she's younger, and a mite plumper." He grinned. "But hell, she'll do."

"'Tis enough; 'twill serve,'" Raker said, and nodded. She and her sister would do very well at keeping the men from brooding any more about the fate of Big Bill.

"What did you do with the women?" he asked now, as Jug Larrabee strutted up for a pull at the bottle, his elbows held out from his sides as though he were stepping out in his fancy duds.

"Left 'em hog-tied back in the weeds." His Adam's apple bobbed as he swallowed. "*Ahh.* Should we kill 'em, Johnny?" His lips gleamed moistly.

Raker shook his head. "We'll let them go when we're finished here. That way they can spread the word as to what happens to redskins who don't know their place."

He had pondered Jordan's instructions, and decided this was the best way to carry them out. The man was one thing. It was no crime to kill a buck Apache in Arizona. Maybe on the books. But not in fact, not when a man charged with killing one would be tried by a jury of just such good men and true as Raker had gathered around him. Besides, he'd had a gun. It was clearly a matter of self-defense.

If the girls complained of being manhandled, nobody would listen—or care if they did. Killing them was another matter. Wholesale slaughter, even of Apaches, was liable to involve the Army. And that was something Jordan said was not to happen. Not until the Apaches themselves forced the Army's hand.

Larrabee drank again, blew out a long wet breath like a sighing horse, and wiped his mouth with the back of his hand. "Ain't we finished here, Johnny? We left ever'thing in them lean-tos to burn. 'Twarn't worth ten pinches of dried mule shit, all found."

Raker's fine eyebrows rose to arches precisely drafted by hours spent before a mirror. "Aren't you forgetting something, old friend?"

"What's that?" The bristle-bearded little man asked the question warily. John Raker was his friend, but he knew the man's moods were unpredictable as a Kansas twister—and about as safe to trifle with.

"It's Sunday. We've been about the Lord's work." Raker raised his voice. "Now it's time to harken to the Lord's word. Gather round."

The Rangers stared at him. He stood up on the box. "On your knees, Christian soldiers. It's high time we gave thanks to God for our victory over the heathen."

He had produced an immense Bible with a busted black leather binding, which customarily rode in his saddlebags, and was thumbing through it, squinting in search of an appropriate text.

The men looked at one another.

The erstwhile Texas Ranger cleared his throat and posed dramatically above them. "Our text for today," he announced, projecting his voice as if to fill the whole vast beggar's bowl of the San Carlos, "is Ecclesiastes One: 'The words of the Preacher, the son of David, king in Jerusalem.

"'"Vanity of vanities," saith the Preacher, "vanity of vanities; all is vanity."'"

One by one the smartass smirks slipped from the upturned faces. It wasn't just the image of Big Bill Lewis springing belatedly to several minds. Raker's stage-trained voice rang like a bugle call, his words echoing in their ears, clear and compelling. Jug Larrabee solemnly removed his slouch hat. Frozen-faced, the others followed suit. The little ex-lawman went reverently to his knees on the hard bare dirt before the burning houses. The others did likewise.

" 'For in much wisdom is much grief: and he that increaseth knowledge increaseth sorrow.' " Raker closed the book with a hollow thump.

"Amen," said Larrabee, loudly.

"Hallelujah," cried the others, caught up in it all despite themselves.

And the flames boomed and crackled, and the flies sang their secret songs, and the smoke went up like an offering to heaven.

"Don't be reluctant, Sergeant," called Random from beside the campfire. "Come on and join us."

For a moment Brown hesitated, his eyes scanning Random's face. Holding his mess kit, full of steaming beans and salt pork, he came gingerly over to take a seat on a handy rock. Obadiah Sutter hawked and spit. "Cain't speak for nobody elst," he said in his strange high voice, "but the day I'm willin' to sit at meat with niggers is a long way from dawnin'."

Digging his spoon into his own kit, Ramdon smiled. "Don't let us keep you here against your will, Mr. Sutter." He waved a hand in a circle that took in hills and mesas covered by a canopy of sky. "You've over seven hundred fifty square miles of San Carlos Indian Reservation to choose from. Feel free to pick another spot. Maybe Nducho will invite you to dinner; *he's* not black."

Sutter scowled and turned his yellow eyes away. He made no move to relocate, but put his head down to converse with Tim Cahill in a surly fluting voice.

Random did not let the man's presence detract from his appreciation of the setting. This was one of those beautiful spots you find in the damnedest places out West—and San Carlos was among the most outstandingly damned. The campsite was between the sheer sandstone face of a bluff and a loop of small shallow stream running down out of the Gila Mountains. Cottonwoods flanked the pebbly streambed, and green reeds waded in the softly chirping water.

In spite of the tensions of pursuit Random was almost able to enjoy himself. Cicadas droned in the cottonwoods. Nighthawks flung themselves crazily around the sky in pursuit of the swarms of gnats and mosquitoes that boiled up out of the reeds like the smoke of a wildfire when dusk settled down. Random had learned to love the *bled*, the desert, in North Africa with the Legion. Paramount among its pleasures was to find such a cool, lovely spot as this, from which to observe its forbidding splendor.

At a second fire several yards away Private Harmony tended a bubbling pot of beans, salt pork, and brown sugar, the standard campaign fare of the Southwest. Presently the rations they'd packed with them from Fort Apache would run low, and Random would have to swing by some settlement for fresh provisions. Obviously he couldn't bring his whole ménage trooping into some hole-in-the-wall town or trading post, not without exciting just the sort of comment and suspicion he'd been commissioned to avoid. But he knew he could trust Sergeant Brown to keep the party out of trouble in his absence. Even if the man neither liked nor trusted him.

"Don't you think it demoralizing to permit lesser ranks to eat with their superiors?" Jordan asked, rearranging his food with his fork, as if that might make it more palatable.

Wincing at the boy's tactlessness, Random made himself respond in level tones. "First, I think the military caste system is nonsense. If a man is good enough to risk your life beside, he's good enough to eat beside." He took a bite, chewed, and swallowed. "Second, nobody here's an officer."

"You are."

"I *was*. I resigned my commission when I was twenty-one."

"But Colonel Sinclair said you were to be regarded as a captain for the duration of the emergency," Jordan said doggedly.

"That's so Sergeant Brown can legally accept my orders—though I don't intend to issue any, as I've tried to make clear. I'm a civilian, Mr. Jordan. I fully intend to remain one till I die."

He glanced up at the crackle of grama grass beneath a boot. It was Monroe bringing a plate of beans for Cahill, uneasily, as if it might explode at any moment. Had Random believed in giving orders, *that* was something he would have stopped: the black soldiers serving the whites. He helped himself to food, and preferred that the others did too. But the black soldiers seemed to expect to have to wait on the civilians, and he didn't see fit to make an issue of it.

"Besides," he continued to Jordan, "I'd think you'd be honored to break bread with Sergeant Brown. He's served his country for decades, to judge by the hashmarks on his arm. Whereas I, to whose presence you've yet to take exception, am nothing but a mercenary with no concept of duty—as you're so fond of pointing out."

Jordan blushed. "Well, of course I've no objection *personally* to the sergeant's taking his meals with us. It's only a matter of principle." He turned apologetically to Brown. "I—I've several good Negro friends, back East."

"No doubt," said Random.

He sipped his coffee. He knew he shouldn't be hard on the boy. Since yesterday's altercation young Jordan had gone out of his way to be civil to Random. One thing Random had to credit him for: He didn't hold a grudge. *I wonder where he got that? Not from his father, surely.*

Just as he started to say something more, Monroe, circling timorously behind Cahill so as not to pass between him and the fire, tripped on a root and spilled Cahill's beans in Sutter's lap.

Squalling like a wounded cat, Sutter came to his feet. "You clumsy, good-for-nothing nigger!" he screamed, backhanding the youth across the mouth. Monroe's head snapped back, his slouch hat sailing into the night. He sat down abruptly.

"I'll kill you!" Sutter raged, and pounced.

Random threw his beans in the big man's face. With a mad glare Sutter grabbed at him. Random kicked him in the belly, moved past him as he doubled, catching one treetrunk arm and twisting it hard up between Sutter's shoulderblades. Sutter moaned and went to his knees.

Cahill and Jordan were on their feet. Young Jordan was sheep-faced with amazement at Random's tackling the bearish gunman unarmed, in violation of the very point of western etiquette he'd so graphically illustrated for the boy the previous day. "You ain't gonna let him manhandle you like that, are you, Di?" asked Cahill, hopping from foot to foot.

"You bastard!" The words whistled horribly between the gap in Sutter's teeth. "I'll kill you! I'll break you in two!" He bucked, trying to throw his opponent off. Random wrenched his arm until the shoulder creaked.

Sutter screamed.

"I won't stop you from saying what you want," said Random through his teeth, "but my tolerance stops short of letting you pound on children who haven't done you any harm." He shoved the man's face into the dirt, released him, and stood back. "Make another move for him and I'll kill you, Sutter."

Ponderously Sutter drew himself up to his knees. Crumbs of black loam were caked in the sticky mess that covered his face and matted his beard. His eyes glowed like coals. His hand hovered by the butt of his pistol.

If Random had offered the slightest provocation, acted either belligerent or scared, the big man would have drawn, then and there.

But the mercenary simply stood over him, arms folded across his chest as if he hadn't a care in the world. After a moment Sutter deliberately moved his hand away from his weapon and let Cahill help him up.

Random extended a hand to Monroe, who sat where he had fallen, eyes wide, a trickle of blood running from the corner of his mouth. He stared up at Random for a moment. Then he took the hand and let Random help him to his feet.

Monroe bolted off to the cookfire, where the other soldiers sat staring. Random retrieved his mess kit, rinsed it in the stream, then walked over to ask for a new helping. Silently Harmony dished him out one.

As Random returned to his place, Doroteo glanced up from where he sat conversing in pantomime with Tonton Macoute. "That one's a bad man, my friend," the scout said in Apache. "You took a risk."

Random shrugged. "It's a risk having those two along," he replied in the same language.

"I think he'll try to kill you."

"Probably. But the other's worse. Sutter's more dumb than malevolent. He was orphaned when he was a boy, and had to go live with an uncle. The old man was a crazy blackstrap Methodist minister, who thought the way to save the boy from sin was to beat it out of him. As a rule he used an ax handle in his ministry, I understand, which is where Sutter's top incisors went. Poor bastard."

"It takes a good man to pity his enemies," Doroteo remarked. "Of course you won't hesitate to kill him if you have to."

"Of course. But it's Cahill I really have to watch."

"True." The scout showed white teeth and patted his carbine. "I had him covered, while you fought his friend."

Random smiled back. "Thanks."

He started to turn away. "Just a moment," Doroteo said, and made signs at the Haitian.

The dark goblin face split in a startling grin. "Good," he announced. "You good friend, me: *bon*." He spoke the words slowly and painfully, and looked immensely pleased when he'd got them out.

"I teach him English," Doroteo said in that tongue.

Random opened his mouth, shut it again. It seemed life still held some surprises for him. *"Très bien,"* he said to Macoute, and "Keep up the good work," to Doroteo, and went back to the fire to eat his beans before they congealed.

He nodded to Jordan. "You look as if you'd just found out your broker meant to vote for Bryan."

Jordan sniffed. "That was a disgraceful display."

"It most certainly was. A great brute of a man knocking a skinny scared kid about. Enough to make a man lose his appetite."

"That wasn't what I meant," Jordan said testily.

For a moment Random sat staring into the fire. Then he set his kit on the ground. He *had* lost his appetite.

"You know why Monroe's so damned self-conscious, don't you?" he asked. Jordan shook his head. "His name. His legal, Christian, baptized name is Potassium Nitrate Monroe."

Jordan managed to look disbelieving and appalled at the same time.

"Let me tell you how it is, my young friend," Random said, "among the landed gentry of the South. The first son gets the property—the plantation, in the old days, and now whatever's left. The second goes to VMI. The third winds up in medical school, whether or not he's got the brains to blow his own nose.

"So the South teems with doctors, many of whom would be better suited to bending iron around barrels or digging ditches. When a poor black family has a child, often as not they come to ask the advice of the great and noble healer as to what they should name it. The white doctor comes up with a name like Potassium Nitrate, say, or Expectoration, which sounds impressive as hell if you don't happen to know what it means. So the parents thank the witch doctor profusely and go off happy. And the kid spends his whole life being laughed at by woolhats."

His lip arched contemptuously. "That's what they call a *gentleman* in the South. So forgive me if I don't think much of the pretensions of Yankees." He shook his head. "I'd think the whole class equally worthless, but my father was of that stock, and he was one of the finest men I've known. He fought slavery and Lincoln with equal passion, and regretted to his dying day that he once passed up a chance to shoot Bedford Forrest."

Sutter lumbered back from washing most of the filth from his face and person in the stream. He glowered at Random and sat back out of the light, among the cottonwoods. Cahill hunkered by his side.

Brown returned from seeing Monroe tended to. The sergeant's face was thoughtful. Random felt for him. He knew Brown would have liked to treat Sutter as Random had. But he could not. The world didn't work that way in 1896.

"If your father had been serious about opposing slavery," Jordan said earnestly, "he would have heeded Lincoln's call and not turned traitor to his country."

Wishing he'd kept his mouth shut, Random met Jordan's gaze dead-on. He wondered how the boy would respond if Random spoke in such a way about *his* father. Probably there'd be another display of virile ferocity like yesterday's.

He sighed. His father was dust, and his honor secure enough that it didn't matter a whole hell of a lot what some wet-eared kid said about him. "He didn't see it as turning traitor. And he didn't see that Lincoln really cared about ending slavery. What mattered to Lincoln was laying the federal yoke on the necks of the people. Freeing the slaves was incidental—a means to an end."

"Surely you don't believe that cynical rubbish!" Jordan exclaimed.

"Mr. Lincoln never did anything for the good of the black man," a new voice said. Random and Jordan snapped their heads around. "He despised them as much as any southerner," Sergeant Brown added.

The sergeant's rugged, handsome face was hard. Random wondered what had jarred the man from his taciturnity, and put that angry shine in his eyes. "Mr. Lincoln said there must be a superior and an inferior in society," Brown said. "He was content to have the whites superior and the blacks inferior."

"Come, my good man," Jordan said with a smile. "He may have said such a thing, but you mustn't let that blind you to the great things he did for your people—"

*"He did nothing!"* Jordan recoiled at the sergeant's vehemence. A vein throbbed in Brown's forehead, and his face was a mask of beaten bronze in the flickering firelight. "I'll tell you what he did for my people—and I mean *my people,* sir.

"I was born on a plantation in Tennessee. When I was three my parents escaped to Illinois. They took me and my sister, who was three years older.

"We were hidden by sympathetic whites, but somebody informed. We were caught and imprisoned. The local abolitionists hired a good lawyer to prevent us being handed over to the slave-takers, since slavery was illegal in Illinois—this was before the Dred Scott decision, so we had a chance.

"But the slave-catchers hired a slick attorney, a very prominent man, to represent them. He maintained that the Fugitive Slave Act said we had to be returned. He made the jury believe it. They sent us back to Tennessee. My father was whipped until he could not stand, Mr. Jordan. I had to watch.

"After that our family was broken up. My sister and I were sold to a schoolmaster in Arkansas. My mother went to Georgia, my father to Mississippi. We never saw either of them again.

"The schoolmaster didn't treat us badly. We were lucky. He taught us to read and write, and talked of freeing us. He never did.

"My sister died of cholera when I was thirteen. That same year the war broke out. I ran away, went North. For a while I was held as a contraband—you might not know the term, Mr. Jordan. It means enemy property seized by the Army.

"Finally I heard the Union was forming black regiments, and volunteered. The North was in a bad way for men, and they took me. I fought the last two years of the war, then quit and went looking for my parents. I didn't find them. After a while I gave up and reenlisted.

"I've been in the Army ever since. I've fought Comanche, Cheyenne, Arapaho, and Sioux. I was in the Victorio campaign in New Mexico. My company guarded the Pine Ridge Agency during the Ghost Dance troubles, and I was wounded by a striker in 'ninety-four. I can't say the Army's a good life, Mr. Jordan. But it's all I know." His eyes had turned inward, now, and he spoke into the fire. "At least I can pretend I'm a free man."

"What has this got to do with Abraham Lincoln?" Jordan demanded, his voice strident in the quiet that had fallen on the camp.

"Oh. I guess I forgot to say." He raised his head and looked into the young man's eyes. "That was the name of the sharp attorney who got us shipped back into slavery. Mr. Abraham Lincoln, of Springfield, Illinois."

# CHAPTER TEN

From the brush that lined one bank of the shallow draw along which the war party traveled spilled a half-dozen horsemen, armed and painted as for war. In the lead, Boca Negra jumped from his horse and raised his rifle. Ignoring him, the newcomers stationed themselves across the arroyo, blocking the Chiricahuas' path.

Nducho reined his pony in behind the half-breed and glared savagely at the newcomers. "Why are you sniffing around us? Do you plan to go barking to the white-eyes that we're here?"

At a placid trot Owl brought his pony up even with Nducho's. "Wait," he said, holding up a hand as shriveled as a dead cactus branch. "I think the Dilzhé'é have something to say to us."

Aguilar rode by the two of them, sitting straight in his saddle. "Greetings, Temerario," he said to the round-faced youth in the middle of the line of horsemen.

Temerario nodded. His eyes were bright and eager. "We've come to join you," he said.

Tse'e's heart dropped into a pit that suddenly yawned inside him. *We've come to join you!* Sickened, he wondered what calamity had caused this abrupt turnaround by the men of San Carlos.

The question did not escape his father. "Two days ago you were unwilling to ride with us. Today you're eager to. Why have you changed your minds?"

"The white-eyes," an older rider said. "They've come out of Globe, just like the old days. They killed a man in his own *kową*, raped his two young daughters, ran off his horses, and burned his *ranchería*." The speaker turned a round face to spit in the sand. "We know better than to wait for the whiteman's justice to avenge him. Or protect us."

"So we've come to fight!" shouted Temerario. He seemed to Tse'e to be just as hot to join the war party as he had been to defy them two days ago. "Lead us to vengeance against these devils!"

Aguilar's aristocratic old face had gone long and thoughtful. "How many are they?" he asked.

"We counted the prints of eleven horses, a wagon, and four mules to draw it. One horse goes hitched to the tailgate of the wagon; we only found tracks for thirteen men. The wagon is heavily laden."

"No doubt it's filled with arms and ammunition." Aguilar nodded with youthful vigor. "*Nzhǫǫ!* This is good news indeed. We must capture this wagon. It's a pity Nana can't be here." He laughed with pleasure at the thought; his friend Nana was noted for his Power of finding weapons and ammunition. "Will you follow me?"

"No!" Everyone stared at Nducho as the word burst from him. "We—we're not ready yet. Too many of our men are untried. We can't attack so many, not if they're that well equipped. Not yet."

Astonished, Tse'e stared at his brother. Nducho the headlong, Nducho the *heshkéé* paragon, urging caution? It was incomprehensible.

His eyes glittering like obsidian, Owl peered intently at Nducho. "The Mountain Lion is right," he rasped. "Yusn doesn't will that we throw ourselves away. I smell a trap. Death sometimes rides the white-eyes' wagons, as we learned to our sorrow at Apache Pass. Who knows but that these white-eyes carry a cannon with them, in hopes of luring us to our destruction?"

To Tse'e this argument sounded ridiculous. Where would the whiteman get a cannon? The Army guarded theirs jealously, and there were no others in the Territory. Tse'e guessed that Chi' saw how ridiculous the idea was, but the warrior's face was unreadable as always.

Nducho licked his lips, smiled, and was wholly his brash feral self again. "We need still more men, and more experience for the ones we have. If we can win an easy battle with the white-eyes and show the People we mean business, we'll get both at once, *¿qué no?*"

"Where will we find *nnaa* so easy to defeat?" asked a thin youth, who wore boots, jeans, a yoked cotton shirt, and a slouch hat.

"There're lots of mining camps in the mountains around Globe," offered one of the raiders, a hardbitten, bow-legged Chókánéń named Todéédi who had been on several raids this far north since the surrender. "Since the Apache Kid disappeared they've grown careless. We could easily kill some of them."

Nducho nodded briskly. "Fine." He looked to Aguilar. "Shall we camp and lay our plans then, my father?"

When Owl seconded his son's objection to his plan, the fire and firmness had gone out of Aguilar, and his chin slumped wearily to his chest. "What? Oh, yes, yes. That's the thing to do."

Chi' pointed to pewter-hued clouds piling up over the mountains to the east. "If we're going to talk, let's get out of this damned arroyo. It won't help our cause if a flash flood washes us all to the Gila."

The San Carlos turned their horses and the raiders followed. Nducho gave his brother a wild gloating look. "Your Green Eyes's Power has failed him, *shikis*. His death is assured."

"Terrible the fate of him who defies Yusn," Owl intoned, and sent the half-lame white scrabbling up the bank.

"Freeze." Though Random didn't raise his voice, the word rapped out crisp and hard as an ax striking wood.

Supervising the saddling of the mules, Sergeant Brown turned to stone. The soldiers exchanged puzzled glances. Grinning, Garrison turned his head toward Monroe, who was shaking inside his fatigues. Brown's eyes froze the grin on his lips.

Perplexed, Jordan looked to Random, but stayed where he was, kneeling to roll his blanket. With a gap-toothed smile of derision Cahill turned to his friend, who stood sullenly by with arms folded across his huge chest.

Then Cahill gazed past the slope of Sutter's right shoulder, and paled. The smile slipped from his weasel face.

"What's going on?" Jordan asked.

Random jerked his head toward the cliff that loomed above their campsite. "Look for yourself."

A solitary scrub live-oak stood guard on the very lip of the promontory. Next to it stood an Apache, a rifle in his arms. His hair was bound by a scalpband, his face painted with blue and yellow stripes.

"Harmony's up there, sir," Brown said quietly.

"I know." The quiet boy from Albany had been sent up to the top of the rocky outcrop to keep watch. There was no sign of him now. "I think he'll be all right." He felt a white-hot stab of anger at himself. He or Doroteo should have been up on the bluff at all times. He'd been away too long—not that that was any excuse.

"What if he's not?" Jordan asked, his voice rising. He stood.

"Then we have enough to worry about ourselves."

As if sprouting from the wind-carved red rock, a half-dozen Apaches rose into view atop the butte, silent, watchful, ominous. Some wore Apache garb, others whiteman–cowboy-style clothes, which made the dark, painted faces even more menacing.

"Will they attack, sir?" Brown asked.

Laying his hand on Malcriado's rump, Random walked around from where he'd been cinching up the saddle to the animal's right side, which was nearer the cliff—and nearer the big Remington shotgun and the Vetterli in its boot attached to the saddle's right side. "If they were set on attacking, the first we'd have seen of them is the muzzle-flashes of their guns. They mean to talk. At least initially."

"Green Eyes," called the man at the butte's tip.

"I'm here."

"You haven't spoken truly to the People."

"Who says this thing?"

"Burning Sky." The warrior named himself. He looked to be Random's age, old enough to remember the exploits of Green Eyes. A bad sign, that even one such would doubt him. "But everybody says it now."

"They must feel they have a reason."

"They do. A party of white-eyes has come out of Bésh bagową, killing, raping, burning. They think to treat us as they and the Pima treated the Aravaipa years ago. We think otherwise. Some of us have already ridden to join Nducho and Aguilar and him whose name is bad luck to speak."

*Whites from Stone-Their-Houses*, Random thought. *Globe.* He wondered if it was coincidental that the settlers' taste for redskin-baiting had gotten the better of them at just this time. Coincidence or not, it was shattering news.

"Shit," he said in English.

"What's the red devil saying?" Jordan asked.

"Shut up." Then, in Apache: "This is evil business. All People now such white-eyes are my enemies as much as theirs."

"So you say. There are those who wonder if you say one thing with your mouth, and another in your heart."

"Bid them ask the wind and water, Coyote and the sun, where they can find the white-eyes who hunted Apaches for their scalps after I forbade it. The wind's scoured their bones, water tumbled them, the sun has bleached them and Coyote cracked them for their marrow."

"This is known," Burning Sky acknowledged gravely. "For this reason we warn you: Leave Apachería. The San Carlos have tried to keep the whiteman's peace. Now they themselves have broken that peace, and we will fight. I tell you, Green Eyes. *Go.*"

He turned away. "Wait," Random called. "What about the black whiteman?"

Without a further word Burning Sky disappeared. The sound of

Sergeant Brown unsnapping his holster flap rang loud as a shout. "Wait," Random said. The sergeant stayed where he was, but one hard brown hand rested on the hard-rubber grips of his service .38.

A minute went by, and another, marked by the swishing of the horses' tails, the shuffling of cottonwood leaves in the breeze, the manic chatter of the stream. There was a crackling among the gray-green bushes at the foot of the cliff. Two Apaches appeared, dragging an ashen-faced, bareheaded Private Harmony by the arms. They threw him in the dirt, and one contemptuously flung his slouch hat and Springfield down beside him. Then they vanished without a sound.

Jordan dashed for his saddle, lying on its nose by the buried remnants of the campfire. He yanked his Winchester from its scabbard and jacked a round into the chamber.

"Jordan, what in hell do you think you're doing with that?" Random snapped.

The boy turned his face toward him. Spots of color burned high on both cheeks. "Why, aren't we going to give battle to the red devils?"

"No."

Cahill yipped laughter. "What's the matter, Random? Afraid?"

"Absolutely."

Monroe and Tonton Macoute had helped Harmony to his feet and were dusting him off. "Sky Pilot," Garrison said shakily, "you surely are one dumb nigger."

Harmony pulled away from his comrades, came to attention before Random, and saluted crisply. "I—I'm sorry, sir. I tried to keep a good lookout." His underlip quivered.

"You don't have to salute me," Random said gently, and laid his hand on Harmony's shoulder. "Mr. Harmony, there are to my knowledge two non-Apaches in the Territory who might have had a chance *not* to be taken unaware up there: Iron Man Al Sieber and myself. Don't feel bad. Be glad you're alive."

Harmony bobbed his head. "I am, sir. I'm thanking Jesus right now."

Random quickly recited his conversation with Burning Sky in English. Jordan listened skeptically. "They're lying," he said when Random had finished. "White men wouldn't do such things."

"Really?" Random cocked an eyebrow at him. "Ask your two friends about it—they *did*. Camp Grant, Arizona, 1879. Out here it's no crime to kill an Apache, Mr. Jordan. Or rape one." He shook his head. "Strangely, the Apaches don't quite see it that way. Must be because they're savages."

Doroteo scratched his head. "This bad thing," he said. "Fuck me plenty."

Jordan jumped. "I thought Indians didn't curse!"

"They don't, as a rule," Random said, "in their own language. But English and Spanish are another matter. They're the languages best suited for cursing, anyway, except for Arabic. Which not many Apaches speak."

Jordan looked stricken. Apparently the West wasn't shaping up according to his expectations. Random mounted Malcriado. "Saddle your chestnut," he told the boy. "It's time we moved on."

"Where're we going?" piped Sutter.

"We're going to follow Mr. Jordan's red devils," Random said, "right back to their village."

"There are bad whitemen," Random told the circle of firelit faces. "There are bad Apaches too. Does the fact the former exist mean you have to join with the latter?"

The San Carlos considered the question in silence. Random glanced around at his own party, sitting in a semicircle on his side of the fire. Sutter and Cahill sat as far apart from the rest as they possibly could without leaving themselves in the dark in a village filled with none-too-friendly Apaches. For once they were subdued, confining their commentary to dark looks at Random and his audience of men from the nearby San Carlos camps. Jordan sat on one side of Random, Sergeant Brown and his squad on the other. Brown squatted impassively, Apache-style, elbows resting on his thighs. Garrison sat next to him, continually nudging the hapless Monroe in the ribs and ragging him in a whisper that the sergeant chose to ignore. Next sat Harmony, and finally old-soldier Jones, professionally stone-faced after his years in harness. Doroteo and Macoute huddled together, with the scout trying to convey the sense of what was being said by gestures and occasional English speech.

But underlying all their facades was fear—and wonderstruck relief that they were still alive. Random could feel it beating from them like heat from a stove.

Actually, their continued survival wasn't that astonishing. In early afternoon they had followed the Indians' tracks into the middle of a sizable *ranchería* on Hackberry Wash, perhaps five miles southeast of the Agency compound. The camp lay in the shadow of the three sandstone towers the whites called Mount Triplet, and which the Apaches, with similar literal-mindedness but different perspective, called Nothing-Grows-There. A posse of young boys playing war had seen them approach and gone racing into camp to spread the warning. The men of the camp stood watching with weapons in hand as they party rode in, but made no hostile move. It was simple solid Apache logic: Green Eyes was brave, but no fool. He wouldn't put himself at risk riding into the camp of men who had just warned him to vacate the premises without a compelling reason. Most likely he had something to say; if it was that urgent, most likely it was in their interests to hear it.

Of course, there was danger in Random's approach. But his gamble paid off. Burning Sky listened to Random's request for a parley, nodded, and sent young men galloping off to neighboring *rancherías* to spread the word.

The descent of afternoon into evening had been particularly exasperating for Brent Jordan. He wanted to know why Random didn't just go charging in and demand the Apaches listen to him, rather than politely requesting their presence. Random explained that one, it would be a breach of common courtesy, and two, Apaches were not people it was healthful to push around, given as they were to expressing resentment in terms of knives, guns, and similar implements. "They're just a robust, vigorous people," he said solicitously.

Next the youth had taken exception to Random's insistence they wait for full dark to talk to the San Carlos, though many arrived in the slanting yellow light of dusk. "Must wait for night, talk over campfire," Doroteo explained in tones that begged the young easterner to understand. "Snakes be angry, otherwise." Random nodded affirmation.

Jordan had sat down on a rock and put his head in his hands.

"'Tain't fitten for a white man to truckle to savages," Sutter declared.

At this crudely expressed but nonetheless salient point Jordan had perked up, only to wilt beneath Random's perversity. "No one's keeping you here," the mercenary pointed out. "If you're offended why don't you leave?"

Valiantly, Jordan sought to strike one final blow for sanity and the inherent superiority of the white race. "Just look at those simple happy Negroes," he said, pointing to privates Garrison, Harmony and Monroe. They were crouching by a buckthorn bush, slapping each other on the back and laughing at the antics of a gigantic three horned rhinoceros beetle they were pestering with a stick. "They're just like children."

"They *are* children," Random had replied. "Seventeen, the lot of them."

One corner of Jordan's moustache hiked up in what was meant for disdain, but came off as mostly petulance.

"We have to defend ourselves," a voice said through the fire.

"You do," Random answered. "I'd never deny anyone that right. But you're proposing to attack people who've never done you any harm."

The San Carlos laughed. He was a young man in traditional garb, his face vulpine, his eyes alert. "They mean us harm enough."

"Granted. But if the People start killing whites indiscriminately, they won't just mean you harm. They'll rub you out. They've been waiting for the chance for years."

"But their prophet says Yusn spoke to him, ordered him to war with the white-eyes," said an apple-cheeked young man in a red-checked shirt. "All the white-eyes in the world aren't mightier than Yusn."

"True. But does the Ha'i'ąhá prophet really speak for Yusn? You could claim to, just as easily—or I. Would you or I then be prophets too?"

"What if the Chiricahua's lying?" said a third. "What if we can't beat the white-eyes? Let's try, I say! We've lived as animals long enough. It's time we died like men."

*It's an Apache Brent Jordan, by damn.* "Do that," said Random with a wolf's grin. "Even if by a miracle you kill all the whitemen in Arizona, more will come, thousands more, and wash you away as a cloudburst washes out an anthill. And they'll laugh. 'At last,' they'll say. 'We're rid of the dirty redskins, and we've got their land.'

"What would futile struggle be now—*except a greater surrender?*"

The listening San Carlos sat back, murmuring "It is so" to themselves. But the fox-faced youth was still thinking fast. "You say the East Folk are all talk," he said. "What have *you* offered us but words?"

"You speak well," Random said. "All I can offer is my promise: the whitemen who have harmed you will be punished."

Mocking laughter answered him. "And since when does the white-eyes' justice extend to the People?"

Random's eyes narrowed to slits. "I'm not talking about the white-eyes' justice," he said, his words barely audible above the snarl of the flames. "I'm talking of the justice of Green Eyes."

# CHAPTER ELEVEN

They saw the smoke even before they heard the distinctive sharp popping of gunfire.

A dirty gray plume sprouted from the labyrinth of mesas and arroyos just to their west. The land's contours had kept the noise from them, or perhaps the shooting had just begun. "Sergeant, take your men and swing south," Random said. "Get as close as you can without being seen, then dismount and deploy in skirmish line. Use your judgment about engaging."

"Sir." Sergeant Brown called orders and the six mules went jogging away, the soldiers bouncing in their saddles, alternately clutching at their floppy hats and the butts of their rifles, which kept wanting to pound them in the kidneys. Random would give no orders, only suggestions—and the experienced Brown understood at once how sound the suggestions were.

So wrought up by the prospect of action that he almost dropped his rifle hauling it from its boot, Jordan asked, "What about me?"

"Come along. You too, Doroteo." He kicked Malcriado into a lope down the steep slope. Hoofbeats drummed behind him and he assumed the rest were following. Doroteo he was sure of. The rest he didn't care about. In fact he'd just as soon they made themselves scarce.

Heading south from the Mount Triplet camp, Doroteo had surprised them early in the morning by announcing that the war party's trail cut directly across their path, going west. Now they were southwest of the Agency, between it and the Gila River. Random intended to stay clear of the Agency if possible. The agent no doubt had instructions concerning Random—and since they'd originated with J. Ramsey Jordan, Random was not that eager to find out whether they were to help or hinder. He assumed the superintendent was cagey enough to know that if he sabotaged this mission and the Army found out about it, they'd be sure to drag Jordan with them into whatever morass ensued. But he couldn't be sure. Overestimating a man of Jordan's caliber could be as dangerous as underestimating him.

Head back, eyes rolling, Jordan's big chestnut pulled even with Malcriado as the homely little half-mustang bottomed out into a shaley draw. The boy swung his rifle overhead one-handed. "Tally-ho!" he cried. "What glorious fun!"

Without replying Random drew his own rifle from its scabbard. The smoke seemed to be coming from several hundred meters away. He elected to weave through the arroyos rather than spend his mount struggling up and down the steep rubble-strewn slopes. He had both the smoke pillar and the sporadic gunfire to guide him.

In a few minutes they pounded into a narrow gulch. "They're on the other side of this ridge," Random told Doroteo. "Head north and circle around. Cut them off if they break that way."

"What about me?" asked Jordan breathlessly as the scout galloped off.

"I'd rather you stayed out of the way." The boy's expression told him exactly how likely that was. "Very well. Come with me."

He started to swing off his horse. Briefly, incongruously, Random thought of his father. He had been generally free of the pretensions and prejudices of his class, but it would have given him genuine pain to know that his only son, not only by training but by preference, was an infantryman who never fought mounted if he could help it.

The scream arrested him before his boot hit ground. It was feminine, drawn-out, and filled with fear.

He'd assumed the battle was between Nducho's raiders and whites who'd strayed onto the reservation. Now he knew better. Anger burned inside him as he swung his leg back over Malcriado's back, turned the bay's shaggy nose up the slope, and kicked him hard.

They topped the rise, Jordan right behind him, carefree as though he were riding to the hounds. Two hundred yards away huddled an Apache *ranchería*. Two of the three wickiups were burning with flames almost invisible against the sky's glare. Several men rode among them, shooting into the chaparral and hooting to one another.

A girl ran through the scrub, stumbling, frantically fighting the thorns that clutched at her long skirt. Her black hair flowed unbound behind her. A man bore down on her on horseback, laughing through a thick brown beard.

Jordan hauled in on the reins so hard his chestnut reared and almost fell. "But they're white men!" he exclaimed in disbelief.

Malcriado's tail dug a furrow in the dirt in a real sliding stockman's halt. Random was off him in an instant, folding into a kneeling position, seating the steel buttplate against his shoulder. Two hundred meters was point-blank for the Vetterli. Random lined up the front blade and rear notch on an expanse of blue flannel and pulled the trigger.

"C'mon and git it, you li'l bush mare," cried the big-bellied man, leaning from his saddle to grab at the girl's streaming hair. "You'll like it—I promise."

Random's bullet caught him just under the collarbone. He gave a gurgling scream and went facefirst into a cholla.

"Jesus Christ!" came the cry from the flaming camp. "Head for timber, boys, it's the Cherry Cow!"

Two riders reined in to stare at the ridge. Calmly Random worked the bolt, ejecting the spent casing and driving a fresh round into the chamber. Brent Jordan just sat there stunned atop his mountain of a horse, a perfect target against the sky as he grappled with his horror and disbelief.

"Gaw *damn*!" one of the riders shouted. "They're white!"

"What the hell? They shot Amos!" His companion loosed several shots from his revolver.

"Get down, you idiot," Random said. At that range a man wasn't likely to hit anything smaller than a roundhouse with a pistol, especially shooting from horseback. But Jordan was asking to collect a lucky hit. Random drew a bead on the center of a gunman's chest.

An uneven volley rattled from a hill to the south. The marauders' horses danced and screamed. Whether one was hit or just scared Random couldn't tell, but his own shot flew wide of the rail-thin black-haired man he was shooting at. From the north came more shots, crack-crack-crack, the reports stumbling over each other like a firecracker string going off as Doroteo emptied his magazine in the general direction of the camp.

The white-skinned raiders turned tail and followed the example of their comrade who had first cried the warning. Random fired several more times, not hitting anything, not really trying. Wholesale bloodshed probably wouldn't help keep the Territory calm.

The marauders vanished. Random stooped to collect his brass, then walked over to Malcriado, who stood patiently, ears perked, munching grass and obviously enjoying the battle. He slid the Vetterli back in its boot, collected the reins, and mounted.

"But they were white men," repeated Jordan, in a devastated voice.

\* \* \*

"It weren't right, to treat a man like that." Cahill's eyes went for Random like daggers. "Turnin' a white man's body over to them savages—it ain't *hoomin*."

"Would you have preferred that he was still alive?" Random asked.

"Injun-lover." Sutter's voice rose to a pinnacle of contempt. "You oughta be hung."

Around the cookfire the younger soldiers chattered like jays, still in the grip of the day's excitement. Garrison insisted he had hit at least two of the riders. Harmony's reserve had loosened enough for him to speak admiringly of the way Random had shot the brown-bearded man right out of the saddle, and timid Monroe shook his head over the surprise on the faces of Burning Sky's San Carlos when Random rode into their camp that afternoon. He'd been leading a large splayfoot black and white paint with the body of its late owner draped across the saddle, tied at wrists and ankles with a rope passed below the horse's belly. "Here's a token for those who doubt the word of Green Eyes," Random said, and threw down the paint's reins. Then he'd turned and ridden straight out into the desert.

"Were you scared, Tass?" Harmony asked.

"N-no."

Random grimaced. *Poor kid.* He'd almost certainly been scared witless. But at least Monroe and his comrades had come through their first action intact, which was a milestone.

But then, no one had shot at them yet.

"Hey, horsecrap, 'Tassium Nitrate," Garrison said. "You was so scared you almost shit your pants. Man, you like to drop that old trapdoor."

"*Garrison,*" the sergeant growled.

They had camped in a draw where it was unlikely the fire would be seen from any distance. The older soldier, Jones, was on sentry duty. After consulting with Doroteo, Random had decided that he and the scout did not have to keep watch at all times after all. The Chiricahua didn't like to move around at night, for fear of ghosts, and the white intruders wouldn't either, for fear of Chiricahua. Random or the scout would have to keep watch during the danger times, when they made camp at dusk and before they broke it at dawn. The others could stand guard the rest of the time.

As usual, Doroteo and Tonton Macoute were engrossed in conversation. The Haitian was a quick study. There was enough

Spanish in Haitian Creole to give him and Doroteo a small but useful vocabulary in common. Now he and the Cibicu could converse at length in a bizarre admixture of Spanish, English, and White Mountain Apache, leavened with signs and a few words of French that Doroteo had picked up from Macoute. Now that their dialogue was largely spoken, Random could catch the drift of it. It seemed Macoute was thinking of setting up practice here in the Territory when he got out of the Army. Doroteo was enthusiastic; apparently Cibicu needed a sound practitioner of snake magic. Random thought about starting a collection to import *voudoun* missionaries to the Fort Apache Reservation. It would drive a whole spectrum of people he disliked wild.

When he had time he wanted to talk to Macoute at length. He knew little of Haiti and wanted to know more, and thought to pick up a little Creole into the bargain. But that would have to wait until this business was resolved.

Provided, of course, that he was alive then.

Brent Jordan sat on the ground with his knees drawn up, staring moodily into the fire. He'd only picked at his meal, which was hardly surprising. Even the heartiest Anglo-Saxon appetite must eventually quail at the prospect of one more meal of beans, brown sugar, and salt pork no amount of boiling could soften past the consistency of a latigo. The last cask of hardtack packed from Apache had been broken open yesterday, to reveal a large and thriving colony of maggots. Random opined that the post QM had thoughtfully provided them to give the men a little extra meat. Doroteo had offered to go hunt down a deer, but Random declined with thanks. Ammunition was too scarce for that.

But it wasn't the awful fare that accounted for Jordan's lack of hunger. From the pensive lines of his face Random judged he was asking himself a number of questions, and not liking the answers he came up with—or the lack thereof.

Nearby Random sat cleaning the Vetterli. It was a chilly night, and the fire had been built higher than usual. A few clouds drifted against the stars, and the moon was low in the sky.

"Why'd you quit the scouts?" Jordan asked, not looking up.

"I didn't quit. I was fired, along with all the rest of the scouts. Then General Miles and a third of the United States Army went thrashing all over Arizona and half of Sonora trying to find a few score hostiles." He stuck his thumbnail into the breech and held the rifle up to reflect firelight along the bore, so he could check how clean it was.

"In the end it was a couple of Chiricahua who'd broken with Geronimo who ended it. They talked Geronimo into surrendering. Mangas gave up a month later, and the war was over."

" 'Tweren't how I heard it," Cahill said. Sutter sat unspeaking at his side, a mountain of hostility.

"No," Random said. "What you heard was the self-serving nonsense Miles put out, about how he and his silly heliograph bested the savages, and how Geronimo marveled at the whiteman's magic, that could pass messages quickly over great distances." He laughed derisively. "Geronimo knew about heliographs when he was losing raiding parties in Chihuahua in the fifties. Besides, Miles's heliograph system was a joke. The message received almost never resembled what was sent. Once the unit I was guiding received urgent orders to dispatch five live fish to Fort Apache, forthwith." He fed the bolt carefully back into the receiver. "There was a trout stream nearby, and I tried to talk the lieutenant into complying. But he was afraid Nelson wouldn't see the humor in it."

"That's the General of the Army you're talking about," said Jordan.

*At least he's still got the sand to work up a little righteous indignation,* Random thought. "True, which will be unfortunate if your imperialists get us the war they want so badly." He threw the bolt home. "But he's also the man paying me handsomely to keep Owl from playing Saint Dominic to the settlers' Albigensians, so I probably shouldn't speak harshly of him."

"I'll say. He's a hero!"

"Not one of mine."

A queasy silence settled around the fire. A cricket tuned up briefly, but it was too cold for him to put much heart in it. The soldiers had quieted somewhat. Random suspected that after-battle depression had set in.

Off to the west sheet lightning flared above the Pinals, and thunder grumbled under its breath. Sutter stirred. Cahill fidgeted at his side, as if expecting something to happen.

"You're a murderer, Random," the big man said.

His face was very pale beneath the undergrowth of his beard. Before Random could reply, Cahill leaned forward and said, "Yeah, that's right. That's the gospel truth. You shot a man in cold blood today. Why don't you tell Mr. Jordan about those others you murdered, back in 'eighty-five?"

"What's he talking about?" Jordan asked.

Random drew a deep breath, let it slowly out. "In the late eighteen thirties, the governments of Sonora and Chihuahua offered a bounty for Apache scalps. Eventually it was discontinued, but when trouble broke out in 'eighty-five, that swine Terrazas, who was governor of Chihuahua—and still is, for that matter—revived it. So much for a man, so much for a woman—so much for a child. General Crook disapproved, but some enterprising individuals decided to cash in anyway."

"And you murdered four good men," Cahill hissed. "Maybe more."

Random laid the rifle aside, picked up a stick and poked at the fire. "Hunting Chiricahua scalps carried dangers quite beyond any I might have provided, Cahill. And I've never shot anyone who wasn't in the process of trying to hurt somebody. Customarily me."

"Don't try to talk out of it," Sutter shrilled. "You killed John Bryant and Ed Brooks and who knows who else!"

"What happened?" Jordan almost pleaded.

Random pulled himself to a squatting position. "Plenty of men stepped forward to take up the governor's generous offer. The problem was, one scalp covered in straight black hair looks much like another, whether it comes from an Apache, a Papago, or any other Indian. Most Mexicans' hair looks the same, and for that matter so does Chinese. There're even more Chinese in northern Mexico than in the Southwestern United States; they own most of the banks in Sonora and Chihuahua." He shrugged and tossed a driftwood log into the blaze. "So Terrazas wound up paying for a lot of scalps that were never attached to an Apache. That's neither here nor there. I didn't see that that trade ought to continue. So I passed the word to stop."

"I thought you believed in unrestricted trade," Jordan said.

Anger flared in Random's eyes. "I don't find that funny," he said curtly. "But you don't mean that as a joke, do you? For God's sake, Jordan, I believe in the freedom of voluntary transactions. You don't think anybody willingly parted with his scalp—or hers?"

The young man shook his head. "I don't know what to believe."

"Then there's some hope for you."

Jordan started to ask what he meant. Sutter lurched to his feet. "A man who'd turn on his own kind's no better than a rattler," he declared in his high whistling voice. "We know how to handle snakes in these parts."

Random began a flippant reply. Then he saw the big man's hand move. Firelight danced along the blued barrel of Sutter's Colt as it swung inexorably up. Fast as Random was, he had no chance to draw.

As the pistol roared, he threw himself into the fire.

# CHAPTER TWELVE

Three yellow flashes ruptured the dark. A burning piece of wood spun like a catherine wheel in the air, thrown upward by a bullet. Sutter squealed like a wild horse, surprised and disappointed that his intended victim eluded him.

The timbre of his cry turned to horror. An unearthly figure loomed beyond the fire, a blazing man, tall and terrible. With a pistol in his hand.

Sutter shrieked as two bullets ripped through his belly, a high plaintive sound like a wounded child. A third shot boomed, and a big dark hole appeared beside his nose, just beneath one glaring yellow eye. His head snapped back and he fell.

Random threw down his smoking pistol to beat at the flames that danced on his clothes and in his hair. Springing to his side, Doroteo snatched up a blanket and threw it over the mercenary's head.

Cahill looked up from beside the big man. "Murderer!" he howled, and clawed for his revolver.

The sound of hammers being drawn back turned him to a statue. Eyes wide, he stared at the faces that confronted him over the barrels of four Springfields. Naked terror shone on Monroe's face, and curious calm on Harmony's. Garrison's fear hid behind eagerness. Tonton Macoute just grinned his jack-o'-lantern grin. Slowly Cahill's eyes tracked from face to face. Nowhere did he see the slightest sign of what he longed for most: mercy.

Last of all he turned to Sergeant Brown. Brown's new-issue Colt was leveled at his chest. "Take your hand from your weapon, Mr. Cahill," the sergeant said softly. "I think you'd better take off your gunbelt and throw it over here."

Glaring like a penned wolf, Cahill did as he was told. "You niggers'll pay for this. You cain't do this to a white man."

As Random walked painfully around the fire, a nervous voice hailed him from the darkness. "It's all right, Mr. Jones. Go back to your post," he called back. He sniffed, reached up to pat out a smoldering spot in his hair. The skin of his face and hands glowed angry red and felt like a fresh sunburn. His clothes and hair were singed and stinking. But he was alive.

He was also shaking all over from reaction. *God, that was close.* He could not remember a nearer approach of death. Not when Anya Ehrenkranz had whipped a pistol from behind her skirt and shot him from a range of five feet, not when the shell from H.M.S. *Caligula* had struck the rocks almost on top of him and blasted a two-inch steel fragment into his thigh, not even in the Ahaggar Mountains, fourteen years ago, when he had watched in helpless horror as a black Tuareg lance bit into his chest like a serpent.

"Shall I place Mr. Cahill under arrest, sir?" Though Sergeant Brown's tone was businesslike, Random got the impression nothing would give him greater pleasure.

"You should put Random under arrest!" Brent Jordan almost screamed. Fists clenched in rage, he faced Random across Sutter's body. "Sutter was right. You're a murderer. I'll see you hanged for this."

Random looked him up and down with infuriating calm. "Very well," he rasped, hoarsened by inhaled smoke. "When we get back to Apache, *if* we're both alive, you can swear out a warrant on me if you still want to.

"For that matter, you can ride out of here right now if you want, go back to Globe and gather a posse. But I'm going to do the job I was hired to do. I'm going to track down the rest of the pack of two-legged animals we ran into today, and whip them back into whatever holes they crawled from. Then I'm going to find Nducho and kill him, and Owl too if I have to, and as many *broncos* as it takes to free Tse'e and Mariana and squelch this war before it begins."

Jordan opened his mouth. "I'm not done yet," Random said. "There's one thing more I have to say."

The youth moistened his lips. "What's that?" he asked, aiming at defiance and missing.

"When this job is finished, you can do what you like about me. But until that time anyone who tries to hinder me is my enemy."

"What do you mean?"

"What I mean, Mr. Jordan, is that if you get in my way, I'll kill you." He turned away. "I think I'd best get some water on these burns. My thanks, gentlemen. But you can let Mr. Cahill go. I think he'll behave himself."

In all his life he had never been more wrong.

But he couldn't know that. Yet.

* * *

"Temerario," a voice called from the cliff beyond the tank.

The war party jerked to a halt. Their parched mounts tossed their heads and whickered, tantalized by the brackish smell of water nearby. "Who is it?" shouted the chubby San Carlos, pointing his rifle at the red stone wall that overhung the small muddy pool. Tse'e saw the rest of the raiders do likewise. It worried them that they could not see the speaker, and they poised with rifles raised, ready to flee or fight as called for.

A whinny answered their thirsty horses, seemingly from the sandstone itself. A single horseman rode into view, and Tse'e realized that what appeared to be a solid rock face was in fact split by a crack, cutting transversely into the rock so that none of the raiders saw it before the rider emerged. With a start Tse'e recognized the spare middle-aged San Carlos who had been with Temerario when the news of Random's return was broken to the party.

"*Nzhǫǫ*," said Owl, raising a hand in greeting. "You've come to join us, then."

The other ignored him. "Temerario, I've come to bring you home."

Temerario laughed in disbelief. "Go home! I ride to glory with the Mountain Lion. Why should I go back?"

Contemptuously Nducho laid his carbine across his pommel. "What makes you think Temerario would go back with you, old man?"

The newcomer looked straight at Temerario. "Green Eyes brought the corpse of one of the white-eyes murderers to Burning Sky's *ranchería* yesterday. He killed the pig himself. Green Eyes is still Green Eyes, his word good and his Powers strong." His voice dropped. "So give up this doomed madness. Come back with me, my sister's son."

For a moment Temerario sat unmoving in his saddle. He looked at Nducho. Then he nudged his pony with his knees.

Point-blank, Nducho shot him in the belly.

Gray-faced, Temerario sagged. With a piercing cry of anguish his uncle whipped up his rifle. Boca Negra shot him in the shoulder. He reeled back, trying to bring his weapon to bear on Nducho one-handed. Baring his teeth Nducho swung up his own carbine and fired as quickly as he could work the action. The San Carlos's horse screamed and fell, struck in the neck and chest.

Temerario's horse bolted. The young man fell writhing and

moaning in the dust. His uncle, bleeding from a half-dozen wounds, struggled to free the leg trapped under his fallen mount. Bullets spattered around him like the first drops of a cloudburst as others in the war party cut loose. His face disappeared in a spray of bright blood and he collapsed.

Ringing silence followed the frenzy of gunfire. The only sound was Temerario's dwindling groans, and the spastic breathing of his uncle's mortally wounded mount. Then the war party fractured like a rock split by a hammer. The two White Mountain boys whipped their horses into the tank, churning the shallow water to a green and white froth and disappearing into the cleft in the rocks. At the same instant the handful of San Carlos volunteers scattered in all directions. Shrieking imprecations Nducho thumbed a cartridge into his Winchester and fired after them. A few of the raiders did likewise, but every man of them had burned a full magazine in butchering Temerario's uncle, and could only fire single shots at the deserters.

In a moment the Chiricahua were alone but for corpses. Three of the party had not fired a shot: Tse'e, his father, and Chi'. Now the middle-aged warrior urged his horse forward until he was knee to knee with Nducho. His face was bleak as bleached bone.

"You bloodthirsty young fool! You've started a blood feud with your *heshkéé* craziness. The San Carlos won't rest until they hunt us down!"

Nducho's face darkened. "Then we'll kill them as we killed those traitors!"

"No, we won't, Nducho," Delzhee said. "Not the whole tribe."

Tse'e bit his lip, almost daring to hope once more. This was the first sign of dissent. Perhaps the mad, bad times had run their course, and the war party would simply disintegrate here in the foothills of the Mescal Mountains.

"*It is good!*" Owl's sudden cry brought their heads snapping around. Tse'e's mare shied, and he wondered if the old man had lost whatever grip he'd had on sanity.

"Yusn has given us a sign!" the prophet declared, holding his arms high. "These White Mountains and San Carlos have grown soft from lapping up the white-eyes' urine. They are a weak reed, and Yusn has shown we cannot lean on them for strength."

"But what are we to do?" Chi''s tone was almost pleading.

"*Mexico.*" It was a whisper, but it blew like a zephyr through the hot dead air there by the tank. "The last free Apaches live there. True People, Enemy People and Chókánéń and Red Paints. *They* will have ears to hear the truth. *They* will follow—as did you, my brothers. And when we return at the head of an avenging host, the San Carlos and the rest will beg to be allowed to ride with us!" His voice rose to a peal, ringing out from the impassive red face of the cliff.

*What host?* Tse'e wanted to scream. *All that's left in Mexico is a handful of aging, hunted men even crazier than the ones you've already got!* But he knew it was no use. The others listened to Owl as to the voice of God. They were the ones who lacked ears to hear the truth, and this nightmare ride would continue to whatever disaster lay at its end.

What tortured Tse'e most was that Haastįį 'Ítsá, the wise, brave man whose counsel had been sought by men like Victorio and Mangas Coloradas, could not see what was happening. He was riding to his own destruction. In agony Tse'e knew he could not let his father ride that path alone.

Sadness dimmed the eagle keenness of the old man's eyes. "I thought we could bring all Apache together to fight the white-eyes. That's how it should be."

"This way we purge the weak and unworthy, to build a stronger People," Owl said. "*Mexico.* Our destiny lies in the land of the Ones Who Go About, the Nakaiyé. There live the strong men; there live the free."

Nducho swung his carbine over his head. "Mexico!"

"If Yusn wills it," Aguilar said. And Tse'e saw him slump, as if part of him died with his blasted vision of Apache unity.

So the war party turned their horses southeast, into the desert toward the Gila River Valley that would lead them most quickly to the south—toward Mexico and the bright vision spun by a prophet's words. And away, as Tse'e reflected, from the "avenging hosts" that would shortly be swarming from every *ranchería* on the reservation to track the raiders down.

Doroteo saw them coming, hard and fast out of the northeast. The approaching riders were far enough off that Random had time to dig his men in at the foot of a hill. He rode with Doroteo to meet the newcomers, leaving Brown in charge. The sergeant could handle the men, including Jordan. As for Cahill—if he objected to being bossed around by a nigger enough to wander out and collect a chunk or two of Apache lead, Random would lose little sleep.

Random and the Cibicu scout rode forth openly. If the newcomers proved hostile, the pair would turn about and lead them into the

others' fire, thereby turning a neat Apache trick themselves, as
Doroteo observed appreciatively. But instead of being attacked they
were hailed from a distance, and halted their horses to await events.

"Events" proved to be Burning Sky and about twenty-five San
Carlos, most unknown to Random. They were painted, armed, and
grim, but it was quickly apparent that Random and his men weren't
the occasion. "Everything you said was true," Burning Sky said.
"The Chiricahua have brought only sorrow to the Dilzhę́'é." He told
the tale the San Carlos deserters had brought of the murder of
Temerario and his uncle.

"Now we hunt the Mountain Lion. He'll pay a heavy blood-price
for my cousin and his nephew."

Random shook his head. "No. Go back to your camps. So many of
you will draw the whitemen's eyes. If word gets out about large
parties of armed Apache on the move, it could bring other *nnda* out to
join the ones who're troubling you already."

"But our clansmen must be avenged!" a warrior cried.

"I'll exact your vengeance on Nducho," Random said. "Along
with my own."

Burning Sky frowned. "Do you take too much upon yourself?"

"If I do, you can always take the vengeance trail again." Random
grinned abruptly.

"You can avenge me too."

"Which way do we go now, sir?" Sergeant Brown asked when
Random and Doroteo came back to the foot of the solitary hill.

Random stood a moment, rubbing the scar on his cheek and
considering. "They'll run," he said at length. A vagabond wind
skirled white dust about his knees. "Not even Nducho's crazy enough
to take on the entire San Carlos tribe. Even if he were, I doubt the rest
would put up with it. Come to that, I doubt Aguilar's senile enough to
go along with that kind of stupidity either."

"White Mountains chase too, those boys get home," Doroteo said,
referring to the two youths from the Fort Apache reservation who had
fled the war party after the murders by the tank. "Be plenty mad that
those Ha'i'ąhá killing Apache again."

"What about that medicine man, sir?" Brown asked.

Random nodded glumly. "Good question. Owl might just believe
that God will whip the western Apaches for him, and talk the others
into it too."

Doroteo frowned at this. "I've heard the self-proclaimed prophet with the unlucky name is old," he said in Apache. "He didn't get that way by being stupid. Crazy, maybe. Not stupid."

"You're right." He translated for the others, then started ticking off the raiders' options.

"North we can eliminate right away, unless they actually are insane enough to take on two whole tribes of Apaches, which we've agreed isn't likely. West are mountains, rough enough that they'd have a chance of eluding pursuit. On the other hand, that way you have reservations for Pima, Papago, and Maricopas, none of whom is liable to welcome them. Down in Mexico are the Sierras, but there's also a war going on, between the Mexicans and the Yaqui. Eastward lies the old Chíhéne country, in New Mexico. Aguilar might want to go there, to roll in the earth at the place where he was born."

Jordan shook his head, disapproving such primitive antics. Random ignored him. "I think Mexico," he said. "The Sierra Madre is the Chiricahua's traditional hideout when they're on the run from the States. And it's the Mountain Lion's lair."

"So you think they're running off to hide." Jordan's words wore open contempt. "Your job's done, isn't it? You can get your gold and go home."

"No, my job isn't done. For the Army I have to break up the war party. And for myself . . ." He shook his head. "They're not going to hide. Not long. I think they'll just wait for the San Carlos to cool off a bit and come back. The Yaqui war will probably help them; the *federales* will have other things to do than bother them.

"Also," he said, shaking a finger absently, "also, they've been trying frantically to recruit more men. They've lost their recruits from around here, and ruined their chances to get any more. But there should be other Chiricahua loose in Sonora and Chihuahua. Nducho could conceivably pick up some new hands there." He turned to Doroteo. "Does that make sense?"

"*Ha'aa.*"

"Then we assume they're bound for Mexico, and try to head them off."

"What if you're wrong?" Brent Jordan asked stiffly.

"Then it looks as if I'll have to give General Miles his money back."

But Random and Doroteo had not reasoned wrong. They were ten miles southeast of the meeting with Burning Sky, with the sun straining to reach noon overhead, when Doroteo stopped his horse a hundred yards in front of the column and dismounted.

Random signed the others to a halt, so there wouldn't be ten animals trampling through the ephemeral signs that betrayed the passage of the war party, and rode ahead by himself.

The Cibicu was squatting in the dust, nodding to himself. He uncapped his canteen, took a satisfied swallow, and passed it to Random. "They passed this way," he announced as Random tipped the canteen and drank. He reached for a single dusty ball of horse dung that bristled with galleta tufts, broke it in two. Inside, it was green and soft. "Two hours ago, maybe a bit more. But not much."

Random felt his heart beat fast. "Which way?" Doroteo pointed in a direction a point or two more easterly than their own course. "So we were right about that too. They're going to follow the Gila." That surmise had not been a particularly risky one to make. If the raiders wanted to get out of the Territory as rapidly as possible, they'd hardly want to struggle through the Mescals when they had a clear shot down the valley.

He turned back to Malcriado. "Here's something," Doroteo said.

At his urging, Random hunkered down by his side. "The party's smaller by the number Burning Sky told us it'd lost," the scout said. "But look here: Another horse has passed this way recently. It wings out in the offside-rear. None of the raiders' does that."

Random grimaced. "You mean somebody new has joined them?"

"No." A copper-colored finger pointed to a print. A spatulate silver stinkbug lay crushed, half in, half out of the semicircular depression. Doroteo brushed the bug with a finger, sniffed, held it out to Random. "These prints are even more recent. Smell."

"I'll take your word for it." Random straightened. "So somebody else is following them."

"So it seems."

"Who? A San Carlos out for his private revenge?" He shook himself. There was no point in speculating.

Excitement rose within him. Two hours behind the war party! The end of the chase might lie within their reach.

Random practically vaulted onto Malcriado's back. He slapped the little bay on the neck as it pinned its ears in protest. "We've found them," he called to the others, waving his hand in the air. "Gentlemen, the time has come to *move*."

* * *

Like the cry of a hawk the sentry's call drifted down the blunt face of the bluff. The raiders gathered up their weapons and stood. Tse'e looked up from the depths of his private hell to see Eskinyá standing high above them, waving furiously. An eyeblink later the skinny *heshkéé* had disappeared.

Shortly the lookout came slipping and sliding down a skirt of fallen earth and rock. He held Nducho's prized field glasses well above his head, though having to negotiate the slope with one free hand meant he sat down roughly several times on the trip down. But Nducho had let him know in highly descriptive terms what would happen to him if the glasses were damaged. Eskinyá reckoned a few scrapes and bruises on his rump and legs were small price to pay for ensuring the binoculars' safety.

"What did you see?" Nducho asked edgily.

They had crossed the Gila for the sake of having the river between them and the vengeful San Carlos. Aguilar had suggested a slight detour to take advantage of the high ground along the northern rampart of the Mescals, to spy out their backtrail. Now the wiry *heshkéé* looked past Nducho at the old man. "It's as your Power told you, Haastjį 'Ítsá. We're being followed. Three white-eyes, six buffalo soldiers, and a red-headband *naabaahí* dog."

"Green Eyes," somebody muttered.

Tse'e gave a shout of laughter. "You're doomed, Brother! Green Eyes's Power is stronger than yours, stronger than that of the false prophet Owl. Run to Mexico, brave Mountain Lion. Hide high and hide deep in the Mother Mountains. It can't save you now."

Shocked at his own rashness, he expected to see the wildfire blaze in his brother's eyes. But Nducho regarded him with perfect calm, his eyes searching his older brother's face, then flicking to the blackstocking mare, which was hobbled nearby cropping the crinkly black grama. He nodded his sharp chin decisively.

"Not so, *shikis*," he said. "Not so at all. The white-eyes will be stopped—*here*."

Lizard-quick he stepped to the mare's side and yanked the Sharps from its lashings one-handed.

"And you, my brother, are going to stop him!"

Tse'e's vision blackened. He staggered back. Nducho shook the long gun in his face. *"Take it!"*

*No!* he thought. It was too monstrous, he could not believe even his brother would be so cruel, as to demand this thing.

"Take the gun," Nducho hissed. "Climb up to the top of this bluff and stand off Green Eyes and his men. *Or your woman will pay the cost!"*

*I could take the gun, turn it on him,* Tse'e knew. *Nducho would die before the others could kill me. I could save Mariana, at least; surely the others wouldn't trouble to carry out his threat.*

But his father nodded and said, "I am proud of you, my son. Yusn has chosen you to ensure our great victory." A great sickness washed over Tse'e then, for he knew he had no choice.

Aguilar stepped forward to lay his hand on his son's shoulder. It was a strong, fine hand. The years had weathered it like the perdurable sandstone of Apachería, bringing out character, wearing away exteriors to reveal the hard-rock strength at the core. "Come with me, my son," he said.

It was as if the rest of the war party had been translated into a dream world. Tse'e saw them, felt them, staring as his father turned him and guided him into the rocks and chaparral at the foot of the cliff. But there was no connection between him and them. Owl raised a withered arm, so different from the lean muscle-corded arm of Aguilar, and began to exhort the raiders in his dead, dry voice. His words brought no sense to Tse'e's ears. The young man had passed beyond him now.

It was as if they were the only things that lived in that wilderness of red stone and aromatic scrub and blue, blue sky. "It's a good thing that you do," Aguilar said, and pride swelled his voice. "I must tell you again how full my heart becomes whenever I look at you. You are so strong, so brave."

He shook his head. "Father, I'm not."

Aguilar only smiled. "You're too young to recognize your own strength."

Side by side they walked unspeaking, their *kéban* crunching softly in the dry red dirt. "I've not told you how it was in captivity, in the place called Florida, where the air was always like a hot wet blanket, suffocating more than nourishing the lungs. You were fortunate to escape that, my son."

*I escaped because of the man you're asking me to kill!* He could not speak the words.

"It was hard in Florida. Many People died, some from fever, some from sorrow. The white-eyes are cruel, son, cruel beyond my capacity to understand. It's kinder to cut off an Apache's hand than to cut him off from the land whose rocks are his bones, whose soil formed his flesh.

"It was hard in Florida, and hard in Georgia when they moved us there. Things got better when we went to Fort Sill, to dwell among the Kiowa and Comanche and their strange allies who talk like Apache but dress and act like Kiowa. But Oklahoma is not our home."

"I should have stayed with you, Father," Tse'e said in a rush, his voice clumsy with suppressed tears. "I should have shared your captivity. I shouldn't have abandoned you."

"Don't talk foolishly, my son. I shouldn't dwell on those times; forgive an old man's rambling. Do you think my captivity would have been eased by my knowing my beloved son shared its hopelessness and hardship?" He shook his head. "Yusn blessed you by sparing you. Be thankful. It was ever a comfort, knowing my sons were free."

Had Tse'e truly let himself listen to his father's words, he would have known the old man was giving him a gift a second time: his life. Aguilar was absolving him of the guilt that had eaten at him for years. But that guilt had become a part of Tse'e, as much a part of him as his rifle Power and his abiding love for Mariana. Tse'e would not forgive himself; he could not hear his father forgiving him.

And the moment slipped by on the wind, and was gone.

Aguilar stopped, faced his son, laid both hands on his shoulders. "You've always been my favored son, Aguilucho." His warm breath feathered on Tse'e's face. "I'm afraid Nducho sensed it. It may have changed him in a bad way, as a rock lying atop a seedling will twist its growth." He shook his head, joy and sadness at once showing in his eyes. "You have always been the stronger and the straighter of my sons. I'm happy that you do this now for Nducho's sake more than mine. There are things . . . things he can't do."

"I understand," Tse'e lied. He was bewildered, he understood nothing of this. *I? Stronger and braver than the Mountain Lion?* His father was lost in dreams again.

Aguilar let his hands drop to his sides and turned away. "We must go back now. You must climb up on the cliff to be ready for our enemies. But I shall see you soon, my son, and I shall greet you with a song of joy and pride."

Tears streamed freely down Tse'e's cheeks, and the rifle weighed like lead in his hand. Aguilar's eyes seemed clearer now than at any time since their reunion in the fireshot night in the Española Valley. Yet their clarity was illusion. The old man still lied to himself.

Head bowed, Tse'e followed his father back to where the others waited.

* * *

The wind had risen. It sobbed and whispered among the rocks and brush at the top of the bluff. Calmly, Tse'e laid the rifle on the rock before him. He reached into the back pocket of his torn jeans and took out a tattered cardboard box. From it he removed twenty cartridges, each as big as his index finger, and arranged them in a small hollow on a buff-colored rock to his right where they would not roll away. Brass gleamed dully in the afternoon sun. The Sharps had no magazine, and would have to be reloaded each time it was fired.

He sat for a moment listening to the wind. He thought of Mariana, with sadness. She belonged to another life, a life that ended long ago.

He knew he was betraying her. Up here he was beyond Nducho's eyes. He could wait until the war party had passed on and then descend, take his sturdy gray mare and ride into the east to find his woman. Even if Nducho should realize what had happened—if Random didn't kill him—and came looking for Mariana to exact the price of her husband's disobedience, at least Tse'e would be there to defend her.

But that would mean abandoning his father yet again. He couldn't do that. Not even for Mariana.

*Forgive me, my love,* he thought. *At least the thing I do now secures you from Nducho's vengeance.*

He shook back his hair, which he had been letting grow since his brother kidnapped him, took a blue handkerchief from a pocket of his shirt, wound it expertly, and tied it about his temples. Squatting beside his rifle, he picked up a pinch of dust and rubbed it on his palms to keep them from growing slick with sweat. Then he lowered himself to his belly, picked up the rifle and looked out along the barrel.

Far to the north rose the White Mountains, blue below high-piled clouds. Nearer by bulked the three prominences of Nothing-Grows-There. Then the band of the Gila glinted like lead, and the land rolled upward from it to the mountains, dotted with scrub oak and manzanitas.

Choices surrounded him, all threatening. He could destroy Mariana; he could abandon his father; he could help the madness of Owl to spread like a disease until it wiped out his people; he could kill the man who was his best friend. They advanced on him, menacing, like the evil clowns of Apache legend. There was no way he could turn without running into one of them, or more.

His father wished him to come up here and delay the pursuit;

Nducho ordered him to, with Mariana's life forfeit if he refused. He knew what he had to do.

He would delay those who pursued—in his own way.

And he would escape the evil choices that hemmed him in.

He flipped the rear tang sight erect, adjusted it for a thousand yards. The big hammer cracked back beneath his thumb. He snugged the stock against his cheek, brought the globe front sight onto the target he had chosen, clicked the set trigger. The slightest pressure on the other trigger would now fire the rifle.

He drew in a deep breath. The smells were vivid in his nostrils, rock heated by the sun, the dusty scent of brittle-dry brush, gun oil thick and cloying. He had been here before, but never in the flesh.

He saw from a high place, a lonely place, a line of men, ant-tiny with distance, winding its way toward him through chaparral.

*Forgive me*, he thought, and squeezed the waiting trigger.

# THE WHITE-TAILED DEER

The San Carlos Indian Reservation
Arizona Territory
April 23, 1896

# CHAPTER THIRTEEN

A bullwhip crack split the sky.

Hard after it came a flat *thunk*! like an ax hitting green wood. And Private Charles Edward Harmony, the shy religious kid from upstate New York, spun backward over his mule, arms and legs flapping like empty sleeves.

Mules trumpeted alarm at the noise and the sudden bright smell of blood. Random was out of the saddle before Harmony hit the ground, the Vetterli in his hand, shouting, "Everybody down! Get into cover *now*!"

The men obeyed instantly.

Harmony lay spread-eagled on his back. His eyes were wide open. His chest looked caved-in beneath the blood-soaked breast of his shirt. He was immobile as a rock.

Random cursed to himself in Arabic. In his whole long and violent career he had seen no more than a handful of men killed instantly by a gunshot. The human body just didn't work that way. It could absorb incredible amounts of damage and still function, weakly, tenaciously, like a candle flame sputtering in melted wax and refusing to go out without a final defiance. But Harmony was dead and had been the moment he left the saddle. Had Random torn open the red-dyed shirt he would have seen the young soldier's whole chest discolored by a rapidly purpling bruise centered on a half-inch hole through the breastbone. Not even Random, seasoned as he was, felt inclined to turn Harmony over to see what the exiting bullet had done.

He got up on his hands and feet and darted across a brief stretch of sandy soil to the cover of a buckthorn. When he was halfway across he heard the thunderclap of a second bullet, and reflex shot him right into the middle of the bush, though the danger had passed by the time he heard anything. The black-tipped thorns ripped through his shirt and the skin beneath as he rolled free and grabbed his rifle.

He heard rustling in the brush nearby. "He's dead, Sergeant. Leave him." The sound stopped.

Off to the right a rifle fired. "Stop that! You'll only give your position away," Random called.

He lay behind the buckthorn and scanned the countryside. Ahead the land pitched up into foothills and then jagged mountains. A bluff thrust out toward him like the bastion of a fortress, red rock turned bronze by the slanting light. His muscles taut with tension, his stomach feeling scooped out with the knowledge of having lost a man, he fixed his vision on the salient of stone.

A ball of dirty-gray smoke puffed from the head of the bluff. A half second later the bullet thudded home. Random heard a shrill yelp, followed closely by the distance-faded boom of the report. "Anyone hit?" he called.

A pause. He tasted bile. Then, "N-no, sir." It was Garrison, and there was no cockiness in his voice.

Marveling at the youth's luck, Random said, "Stay low—he won't miss again if he sees you."

A thrashing came from the left and Random turned his head to see young Jordan crawling toward him on his elbows, holding his rifle high to preserve the shiny finish of the presentation piece. "Where is he? I want a shot at him!"

"Move off!" Random rapped. "Don't clump up and give him a better target than he's got already. And put that silly popgun away."

"Popgun!" Jordan sputtered. "This is the finest—"

"It doesn't have the *range,* you idiot. Look how far that bluff is."

Jordan squinted across land mottled by long afternoon shadows. "Don't be absurd. That rock's half a mile away. He couldn't possibly be . . ."

Jordan watched in awe as smoke rolled into the sky above the bluff. Then he shouted and rolled frantically as a bullet gouged a three-foot furrow by his side.

"Is that one of the war party?" he gasped, from the comforting shade of a dwarf live-oak. "I thought you said Apaches couldn't shoot."

"This one can," Random answered grimly.

From the second the thunderbolt struck down poor Harmony, Random had been fighting against the knowledge of who the unseen marksman was. One look at the wound in the private's chest and the struggle was over. Random knew only one weapon capable of making a wound like that at a range of a thousand yards: a long-barreled Sharps, caliber .50-140. It fired a ball weighing 950 grains, *two ounces,* four times the weight of a big .45 bullet. And the Sharps was fearfully accurate, consistently beating specially built British rifles at the exacting Creedmore matches; at a thousand yards, given reasonable conditions, a competent marksman could put *every shot* into a target the size of a man.

But the man behind the distant Sharps wasn't just a competent marksman. He was the best natural shot Random had ever seen.

There could be no question. The gun could only be LaMontagne's, the hands that held it only Tse'e's. And while the question *Why? Why? Why?* dinned in Random's brain he had no time to ponder it.

Knowing the futility of it, Random lined the Vetterli's sights onto the red headland. It was good luck bordering the miraculous that Tse'e had hit no one but Harmony. But not altogether surprising—fear had lent Random's men remarkable facility in hiding, and even the White-tailed Deer couldn't hit what he couldn't see. He had fired at the smoke of Garrison's Springfield, and the glint of Jordan's Winchester, and fortunately neither had betrayed a man exactly enough.

Now Random strained his senses to pick out his enemy, his friend, at the spot revealed by the Sharps's smoke. *There:* a tiny patch of darkness against blue sky. Random sighted, fired, knowing it would be miraculous if his puny response took effect. The Vetterli was an excellent rifle, and Random an excellent marksman. But the simple fact was that both were brutally outclassed.

The Sharps spat smoke. Random rolled hard to his right. The bullet plowed through the bush behind which he'd hidden, showering him with dirt and broken branches.

Grimly he rolled toward the cover of another bush.

Feeding a fat shell into the smoking breech, Tse'e prayed that his friend would choose to fire back. If he guessed who was facing him—and certainly he had—he might well decide the thing to do was to lie low and wait for darkness.

That would be too much delay.

If Green Eyes didn't return his fire soon, Tse'e decided to start picking off the horses and mules that were by now scattered over several acres of chaparral. Random would have to respond then, or risk having his party set afoot.

Then Tse'e saw the smoke of a rifle firing. Immediately he shot back, trusting his friend not to linger an instant in the spot from which he'd fired. Random did not disappoint him. As the Sharps roared and slammed Tse'e's shoulder with the force of a kicking mule he saw a flurry of motion and dust behind the far-off bush.

As the ringing in his ears receded Tse'e heard Random's shot moan close by, rising harmlessly into the sky. *"Nzhǫǫ!"* he exclaimed. He hadn't expected Random to come so near on his first try.

Reloading mechanically, he breathed deep and forced his mind to concentrate. The People said his rifle-skill was Power. Very well. He would summon that Power to him now.

To share.

For a moment his vision hovered, unfocused, in the space behind his eyes. Then it leaped forward with breathtaking suddenness. He saw the whole sweep of the San Carlos, from the Mescals across the Gila to the far White Mountains, from the Pinals in the west to the Natanes Plateau in the east, and all that lay within. He saw a bitch coyote slipping from her den along Sevenmile Wash, and an eagle wheeling above The Way Out, breast feathers flaming in the setting sun. He saw the geckoes and chuckwallas settling in for the night, and the small furred creatures beginning to stir; saw the trembling of leaves and knew where the wind walked. And he saw the men cowering in covert among the stunted trees, and knew their lives were his to take.

But he did not want them. Instead he reached out with all the strength he had, seeking the familiar presence of the friend who sought to kill him.

Random fired. As soon as the recoil passed, he was in motion again. He didn't bother watching for the shot to hit. Hit or miss, he'd never see it.

Evening came down fast. The light was going trickish.

*Why?* he asked himself again. Had Tse'e been twisted by Owl's words? Had he become another Nducho, avid for the sight of white-eyes' blood? Random couldn't believe that. More likely it was for Aguilar's sake that Tse'e did this thing. The rat of guilt Tse'e carried always within had finally gnawed its way free. Nor could Random blame him, for choosing the bonds of blood over those of friendship.

But he would kill him. If he could. And that wasn't likely.

A curious calm possessed him as he drew bead again. Some freak of the dying light touched the bluff, brought it leaping out in bold relief. He could clearly see Tse'e's head and shoulders outlined against the sky as the Sharps belched smoke.

Random fired.

\* \* \*

Tse'e's shoulder felt broken from the savage pounding of the Sharps. He paid it no mind. Filled with his Power, he was as remote from his own pain as if it had been another's.

He could not chance Nducho taking vengeance on Mariana. He could not defy the wishes of his father. But neither could he help the war party start a war that could have but one end: the final destruction of the People. Nor could he kill his best friend.

His brother and father had demanded he delay the pursuit; he had. And now he saw the smoke of Random's rifle, and felt with his expanded senses that the bullet's path was true. Along that path he would escape from the choices that surrounded him.

He looked down upon his friend. *It is a great burden I lay upon you, Green Eyes,* he thought. *I hope you can forgive me.*

He sat up.

Scarcely daring to believe that the time of reunion was at hand, Mariana made her way swiftly yet silently down the rocky spine of the bluff. She imagined the look on his face when she called to him, and almost giggled. Then, knowing herself near madness, she clamped her self-control tighter.

Caught on the south bank of the Gila between the war party and the men who rode in pursuit of it, it had taken all Mariana's Apache skill to evade detection. But evade it she had. She had watched from an arroyo fifty yards away as Nducho sent Tse'e clambering up onto the top of the bluff that grew out of the Mescals, and knew that Yusn had answered her prayers at last. While Tse'e had ridden with the war party she had no chance to rescue him, nor even to communicate with him. Now for some reason the party was leaving him behind. In her fierce all-consuming joy she had not stopped to ask herself *why* they were letting her husband go.

She dared not call up to her husband, lest one of the raiders have remained behind to keep an eye on him. The war party had ridden into the mountains along the southern flank of the bluff. She hid her pony in a brushy draw on the north side and began to climb.

Holding her carbine carefully in one hand, she picked her way across a jumble of sandstone slabs. Then she heard the thunder of Tse'e's rifle, and the question she had not dared ask herself was answered.

For a moment she stood, frozen. Flinging caution away, she ran, slipping on loose rock, dodging hunchbacked trees. It seemed that the thunder had been going on for hours when she burst through a screen

of brush to see her husband lying on his stomach less than a hundred
feet away, firing the gigantic rifle out across the lowlands.

For all the noise she'd made, he gave no sign of knowing she was
near. She drew breath to call her greeting to the man she loved. As
though sensing her, he sat up abruptly.

And was knocked with terrible suddenness back from the lip of the
cliff. Mariana screamed. Tse'e landed on his back, arms outflung, the
rifle by his side. For the first time since that night in the Española
Valley his eyes met those of his wife.

But there was no life in them.

Several miles to the south, leading the war party on a winding trail
high up a mountainside, Aguilar stopped his horse and turned. The
men behind were startled to see tears on his weathered cheeks,
gleaming in the last amber light spilling through the pines atop the
peak to their west.

"Daa'itsaa," he said. "My son is dead."

The crunch of steps mounting the side of the abutment was loud in
Mariana's ears. She nestled down a little farther behind the algerita,
making sure of her cover. Automatically she noted that it was a big
man coming, a whiteman by the size and the fact that he wore boots,
though something in the cadence of his steps put Mariana in mind of
an Apache who was making no effort to climb quietly.

She felt no curiosity as to why that should be so. The man who
showed his pale face above the red rim of the cliff would be the man
who murdered her husband; that was all that mattered. She eased the
Winchester's hammer back. She could hear others coming, below the
first man. It was the first man she wanted, and she would have time to
deal with him, even escape before his companions arrived.

She didn't know if she wanted to escape. All there was in living for
her was avenging her husband. Tse'e, whom she had loved and
cherished and held in the dark night when nameless fears preyed upon
him; Tse'e so strong and gentle and unheeding of his own strength.
Tse'e whom she had followed alone through an enemy land. Tse'e
gone.

Stone cracked under a boot. A black hat, flat on top, appeared
above the cliff's edge. She drew the carbine's stock snugly against her
shoulder and slid her finger inside the trigger guard. She had been
schooled in shooting by the White-tailed Deer. She would not miss.

The face below the hatbrim lay in shadow. Unconsciously Mariana bared her teeth. Then the face lifted. Her finger went slack on the trigger: *Green Eyes!*

He mounted higher. She saw the rifle in his hand, and fury flamed within her. She knew at that moment the madness of the *heshkéé*, the need not just to kill, but to hurt, to wreak retribution in blood and fire.

Her finger tightened again. She didn't shoot. Tse'e had been firing too. She wanted to know, had to know, why her husband and the man he loved far more than his own brother had tried to kill each other.

Random stood above the body of Tse'e. Mariana had left him where he fell. For a long moment the tall blond man stood looking down at Tse'e, as the sky darkened to indigo in the east and the wind stirred his hair. Mariana sighted on the center of the chest, the spot where he had shot her husband.

Random flung his arms above his head, poised for a heartbeat like a great bird about to take flight, and dashed his rifle to the ground. *"Why?"* he screamed, and dropped to his knees. "Why?" He drummed hard scarred hands upon his thighs. His cry echoed long and lonely among the silent mountains. The sunset gilded the wet streaks that ran down his cheeks.

Slowly Mariana lowered her carbine. This man wept for her Tse'e like an Apache, wept as she would have wept but for the warrior's discipline that told her that her grief must wait. He had fired the shot that killed her husband. But somehow she could not tighten her grip that fraction that would send him tumbling down the face of the cliff.

The others crested the hill: a whiteman whose sweeping moustache failed to hide his youth, a smaller, older man with weasel eyes and sandy hair, and several black whitemen in tan soldier clothing. Silently they formed a semicircle, gazing at Random and the corpse over which he sat unmoving.

"Why?" he whispered. "Tse'e, why did this have to be?"

The weasel-man curled his lip but said nothing. The younger man shook his head in amazement. "I don't understand you," he said, his words plaintive and small. "Random, what are you? This man was trying to kill you!"

"He was my friend." Random spoke without turning his head.

"Are you crazy?" Brent Jordan looked at the others. "What's wrong with him?"

No one answered. Random got to his feet, painfully, as though he were an old man with stiff joints and a weary heart. He took a strange leaf-shaped tool from his belt and began to scrape at the hard sparse soil of the bluff.

One by one, the black whitemen unsnapped similar implements and took their place beside him. The two white-eyes looked on uncomprehendingly as they shoveled out a shallow hole and laid Tse'e inside, with the Sharps across his chest.

Mariana turned and fled. She could not bear to see the first spadeful of earth strike the face she loved so much.

She wandered aimlessly in the dark. Night was the time of ghosts, but only one ghost had meaning for her, and of that ghost she would never free herself. The night sounds, the soft-winging birds and the wind and coyotes yipping to the moon, reached ears as unhearing as Tse'e's. She fell again and again in the dark on the treacherous way down the slope, and did not feel the rocks bruise her. More by chance than intention she reached the place she had hobbled her pony and threw herself down, lost in a blackness deeper than night. At length she fell into a state too little restful to be called sleep.

A boot nudging her ungently in the ribs wakened her to a dawn the color of bloodstained cotton.

# CHAPTER FOURTEEN

*God helps those who help themselves*, Captain John Raker, late of the Texas Rangers and the Richmond stage, told himself with pleasure. *As the Bard says*.

It had been lean times there for a bit. His Rangers had taken Amos Cutcheon's death hard. Though they were mad as stirred-up yellow-jackets the first day or so after it happened, they soon began thinking more in terms of desertion than revenge. Not even Raker's suggestion that renegade niggers had teamed up with the Apache served to restore their martial ardor. The force of Raker's personality, backed up by his deftness with the worn-gripped Colt at his hip, had kept the Rangers together this far.

Then, too, there was a problem in the form of J. Ramsey Jordan. Jordan's patron back East was, it appeared, jumping the superintendent's ass about the lack of results in the form of a new Apache war. In turn, Jordan chewed on Raker's rear end, long-distance, and even in his present elevated frame of mind he found it in himself to abominate the invention of the military telegraph.

The day of Cutcheon's death Raker had gone into the San Carlos Agency for information. Jordan gave him an earful. He was, he would have Raker know, a man who required Results: to wit, an Indian war, and Random's head, platter optional.

Random's head posed problems of its own. The Apaches were getting wise. The last half-dozen camps they'd found had been deserted, and recently, by the signs. The San Carlos seemed to be consolidating their forces, drawing the clans together for support. He hoped that meant they were preparing to strike at the white-eyes, but he couldn't count on it. So the Rangers had swung south of the Gila Valley in search of bucks out gathering mescal. Instead they'd come within an ace of running into Random.

Sooner or later Random would have to be dealt with. But unlike Jordan, Raker didn't discount the mercenary's black soldiers. When well led, they would fight well, and Random was a good leader. Nor did Raker discount Random's ability with his damned Swiss long-gun.

If it came to open battle, Raker wouldn't bet a nickel on his Rangers' chances. He'd have to find a way to deal with Random the way he knew best: one on one.

Fortunately Raker topped a rise before his slow-moving party in time to see Random and his niggers splash through the Gila, heading south in a hurry. Traveling along the northern face of the Mescals, the Rangers managed to duck into the cover of the foothills without being spotted.

Not long afterward they heard gunfire to the east. Raker took Lew Anderson to reconnoiter. The firing died away, and they watched Random and his men ride to the foot of the bluff and climb it. As night arrived, the two returned to the wagon.

A vigorous debate awaited them. A faction headed by Lazy Ray Gunther wanted to slip away in the dark. Raker wanted to hold where they were, mindful of the second half of his assignment, though he couldn't admit his real reason. In an inspired moment he pointed out that the wagon couldn't possibly negotiate this rough, untracked terrain in the dark, so that flight meant relinquishing the whiskey. The vote to stay put was unanimous.

But his inspiration called to mind the worst problem of all: the whiskey was running out. When they lost their spirits, the Rangers would be no more. "The Moral is to the physical as three is to one," as the Bard said.

During the night Hodie Powell's big yellow-pinto gelding had pulled up his picket and drifted into the scrub. Searching for the animal in the murk preceding dawn, Powell had come instead upon a compact black pony tethered in an arroyo. And curled about herself in the weeds nearby (to quote Powell's own inimitable account) lay "jest the cutest little sharp-tittie squaw." Hodie did what any other God-fearing white denizen of Arizona would have done under the circumstances: stooped and reached out with big arms to scoop up his prize.

Mariana's knife went to the hickory hilt in the great muscle of his thigh. It missed the femoral artery, and Powell's branded-bullcalf bellowing brought the rest of the camp running to see what the matter was. Wounded though he was, the sandy-haired former foreman for the brothers Graham retained presence of mind to kick the woman's carbine into the brush before she could make a grab for it. But he let go of Mariana, who made a break for her pony.

So close were the Rangers that long-legged Lew Anderson scrambled into the wash in time to haul her back from the saddle.

Even unarmed, Mariana was quite a handful. Beneath her silky skin she was muscled like a bobcat. The lanky cowboy couldn't hold her, but he did slow her up enough for the rest to arrive and subdue her, none too gently.

Now they gathered around the well-trussed captive, commenting to each other huskily and wetting their lips frequently. John Raker contemplated her from his wagon-box throne with even greater pleasure than his men, and the certain knowledge that she represented the end of his troubles.

At his side old Jake LeDoux hawked lustily and spit. "Damnation, Johnny," he cackled. "The boys sure 'nough did right by you today." He favored the captive with a leer comprised of brown rotting stumps. "Now, was I ten or twenty year younger, you-all might just have to fight me for first crack at her, Johnny boy."

"How'd we do?" asked Sam McDowell, smirking with pendulous lips. "We brought you a nice li'l Injun piece. Done good, huh?" His comrades nudged one another and grinned. *They* knew they'd done good. This wasn't your normal run-of-the-mill squaw, red and wrinkled as an old boot or barrel-bodied with a face like a harvest moon. This was the Indian princess of every trail hand's dreams, well-proportioned and slim, high in the breast and small in the waist, and her skirt hiked up enough to reveal nicely tapered legs. Her face was oval with a chin just this side of pointiness, and despite the fact that it was puffed and bruised and split-lipped, and her right eye was purpling and almost swollen shut, it was a face of considerable beauty, as one of the Rangers observed aloud.

Raker nodded judiciously. "Her clan runs to fine features." Her gaze narrowed on him, as though she could focus her hate as a burning glass focuses the sun and crisp him as he sat. He laughed a dry laugh.

"You boys have done better than you know," he said. "Yonder dusky maiden is none other than Mariana, daughter of the White Mountain chief Thunder Knife. What's more, she's the wife of Juanito Aguilar, son of the same Chief Aguilar who broke out of Fort Sill last month." He stroked his long chin. "I shouldn't be surprised if she's become separated from the very pack of red wolves it's our sacred mission to run to ground."

The Rangers traded grins. Lazy Ray voiced the question poised behind every man's lips: "Who's first?"

"No one—yet." Raker let the words fall softly as leaves. "I've a more important use for her, my friends."

"You sayin' we cain't have a crack at her?" Black Jack Hutchinson demanded belligerently. Mutinous scowls replaced expectant smiles.

"No. It means what I said—not yet."

Chin in hand, Raker stared out across the chaparral. Somewhere out there Random was getting his party ready to hit the trail in pursuit of the war party. Raker had to stop him, and fast.

Random was as lethal a man as Raker knew of. But for all his case-hardening on half a thousand battlefields across the world, he suffered from one glaring weakness. He actually cared about his fellow beings, particularly those he called his friends—such as Juanito Aguilar and his wife Mariana.

While such sentiment was as alien to John Raker as the moon's bare backside, he could recognize it when he saw it. And just as you didn't have to have a game leg to know how to trip a cripple, he knew what to do to turn it to his advantage.

He saw it plainly as the gray day turning yellow and hot about him. But before he could act he'd have to let his loyal followers in on a bit more of the unvarnished truth than they'd been privy to before. Sighing, he reached behind him into an open crate. His strong fingers clamped on the necks of three of his remaining bottles and drew them out with a clink. "Here, boys," he said, tossing the bottles to the men like a juggler tossing bowling pins. "You-all drink up while I tell you a story about an Indian-lover named Random . . ."

Closing her ears to her captors' banter, Mariana sized up her situation with a sick, cold clarity. Tse'e's death had numbed her brain—and common sense. As an Apache, it was her right and duty to mourn her lost love with all the wild grief that raged within her. But she had let sorrow overcome her prematurely, and by so doing had betrayed her husband's memory, had forfeited her chance of doing that one last necessary service to Tse'e, and to herself: killing the man who had killed him.

She was trapped. The proper thing to do was die, if possible taking as many of her white-eyes tormentors with her as she could. But with a shaggy, scratchy hemp lariat cutting off the circulation in her hands and feet she was under no illusions as to how much she could accomplish toward that end.

Most of these men were fools, human scum washed up on this sandy shore of what the whitemen called civilization. But their leader—the tall long-headed man with wolf-gray temples and those strange dead eyes—he was no fool. He was soft of voice and manner, but Mariana was not deceived. Beneath the easy surface he was cold and hard as tempered steel. When he looked at her, those lifeless eyes held the hard ranging stare of a rattler getting ready to strike. And if he were a rattler, she knew with ice-cold certainty, then she was the leaping mouse, trapped against the canyon wall.

"Good morning, Captain Random." Random went dead still, his left boot raised and braced in the tapaderoed stirrup. The greeting had come from above, the cultured East Texas voice clear in the crisp cool air. He let his gaze travel up the face of the bluff.

On the heights overlooking the spot where the group had camped after burying Tse'e stood a man, tall and narrow as a gibbet. He wore a gray frock coat and Stetson. He waved a white flag tied to a dead scrub-oak branch above his head.

"*Merde*," Random said. Bits of fact began to slide into place in his mind like a lock's tumblers clicking open. "Raker."

Random's party had stopped in various attitudes of saddling and mounting their animals. He felt the pressure of their eyes. He had but to nod and the soldiers would send a volley crashing up at the cashiered Ranger. He refrained from giving the signal. He knew John Raker never played a hand unless he was sure he'd win.

Letting his boot slide back to the ground, Random crossed both arms on the saddle. "What are you doing here?"

Even from the foot of the cliff Random could read the theatrical surprise on the man's face. "Why, need I be doing anything? Might I not simply be out here breathing the desert air for the benefit of my delicate lungs? Or enjoying, perhaps, the beauty of the scenery?"

"In the San Carlos?"

Raker laughed. "Very well. I have a proposition for you, Mr. Random."

"I imagine you have some compelling reason I should listen to it," Random said. "If it's some nonsense about men with rifles trained on me from the rocks you're a dead man."

An eyebrow rose. "You wound me, sir." Raker half turned and gestured behind himself. "I do indeed have a reason to compel your attention, and it is nothing so crude as you impute. Or, to be precise, *she*."

Two men appeared at his side, holding a slim feminine form between them. The sight hit Random like a bullet in the gut. *Mariana!*

"You recognize this dusky desert rose, don't you? Mariana, lovely daughter of Thunder Knife." He shook his head. "' 'Tis beauty truly blent, whose red and white/Nature's own sweet and cunning hand laid on.' It would be a pity for such beauty to come to harm, would it not?"

"What do you want, Raker?" Random grated.

"Turn back. Ride out of the Territory and don't meddle with things that are none of your affair."

"Such as what?"

"Indian matters. Let them be, my friend."

"And if I don't?"

Raker's hands scrubbed one another. "I'm sure Thunder Knife would be most grieved should some . . . misfortune befall his daughter. To say nothing of her loving husband, and his father and brother." He smiled. "You're not the only one who's learned Apache tricks, Mr. Random."

"What the devil is he talking about?" Jordan demanded.

"He means if we don't give up he'll torture her to death."

Jordan paled. "No!" The soldiers looked stricken. Doroteo's face was clouded with anger. Cahill was looking off across the chaparral, seemingly oblivious to the scene on the bluff, which provoked a tugging at the fringes of Random's mind. But he could make nothing concrete of it.

"You'll let her go if we turn back?" he called.

"Naturally. You have my word upon it." He removed his hat. "I always strive to uphold the honor of a southern gentleman, after the manner of my late and respected colleague, Mr. John Wilkes Booth, of Maryland."

Unspeaking, Random rested his chin on his saddle. What was Mariana doing here? Had she and Tse'e willingly joined the war party? He still could not believe it.

Two things he knew: He could not give up his mission to stop the raiders. And he could not leave Mariana to her fate. Putting his personal feelings aside—which he was unwilling to do—such a move would doom his mission to failure. Even if Thunder Knife accepted Mariana's death as a warrior's sacrifice, his people and the other clans of the White Mountains would be outraged, would call for vengeance.

Two roads confronted Random, and both led to catastrophe. "We need time," he said. "Give us until daybreak tomorrow."

One of the men who held the silent, defiant woman protested. Raker cut him off with a peremptory headshake. "Gentlemen do not bicker, sir. Tomorrow morning it is." He waved his hand and Mariana was hustled back out of view.

"One thing more, Mr. Random," he said in his calm, carrying

voice. "Build your fire high tonight. My companions will be keeping an eye on you by its light, so you won't be tempted to do anything that might endanger the girl."

With that he turned and disappeared. Random dropped his forehead to his saddle. He felt time rushing past him like a river in flood.

Hot-eyed, Brent Jordan faced him across Malcriado's bony back. "You can't mean to give in to these ruffians!"

Random raised his head, and his eyes answered the boy.

"The white-eyes are camped at the foot of the cliff where we left Tse'e," Eskinyá said. The chubby Ndé'indaa who had accompanied him on the scout bobbed his head and said, *"Ha'aa, ha'aa.* Yes, yes," as he always did.

Bleakly, Aguilar averted his face. The firelight turned his cheek to a badland of deep shadowed furrows. "Do not speak my son's name," he said. "It will disturb his spirit."

"Don't talk that way, Father," Nducho said quickly. The raiders muttered and cast nervous glances into the darkness surrounding their mountaintop hideout, unhappy with this talk of ghosts. "He's merely hiding, waiting for a chance to rejoin us." He puffed out his chest. "You should be proud as I, Father. He's delayed the white-eyes a whole day!"

"And us as well," someone muttered darkly.

It was true. Their flight to Mexico had come slamming to a stop with Aguilar's sudden pronouncement of the day before. There were protocols to be observed on a raid, and the most ironbound was this: Under no circumstances was the word *death* to be mentioned. It was the worst of luck, bad as owls, worse than coyotes and lightning and snakes. War parties had splintered against that simple phrase, *daa'itsaa,* "there is death," like small ships driven against a rock. If those words were so much as uttered on the warpath, chances were good the warband, knowing its luck was hopelessly compromised, would simply break up.

It had taken all of Owl's persuasiveness to keep just that from happening here in the heart of the Mescals. The prophet had raised his skinny withered arms and promised ghost-sickness and the wrath of Yusn to any and all defectors—and so the danger passed.

But the words had been spoken, and now they lay before the war party like a dead, stinking thing. They must be buried. So two raiders were sent back into the north to learn the fate of Aguilar's elder son, while the rest of the party hid itself and settled in to wait.

Eskinyá's dark lupine face was sallow in the firelight, and he refused to meet Aguilar's gaze. "The white-eyes are thick on the ground as lice on a Navajo's sheep," he said. "But I left Ha'aa with the horses, and made my way to where . . . to where your son had been, Haastjj 'Ítsá." He hesitated, running his tongue rapidly over his lips. "I found a fresh-turned mound of earth, beside the rocks where he hid."

Aguilar nodded, unmoved by the tidings, as if they brought nothing new to him. Nducho's eyes snapped into slits of fury, and he shook his carbine under Eskinyá's nose, cursing him in Spanish as a liar and a fool.

Squatting like a gargoyle on a rock above the fire, Owl raised his head. "Have done," he said. "He speaks the truth."

An owl cried in the night. The raiders clutched their weapons and huddled closer around the fire. The Old Eagle's Power had been right. Ghosts flitted through the canyons and blotted stars overhead.

Like a cornered cat Nducho shook his head. "I grieve for my brother," he said, too loudly. "We must make the most of his sacrifice. We must press on, at first light if not this moment, go to Mexico and spread the word of Man our prophet."

Owl flung his arms high. His sleeves flapped like wings. *"No."*

Nducho recoiled from the shaman. "What do you mean?" he all but screamed.

"Your brother's death must be avenged," Owl said in a voice that rattled like bones. "Aguilar, will you let the white-eyes spill your firstborn's blood without claiming the price?" The old chief said nothing. "Aguilar's son fell in Yusn's service," Owl said to the others. "Do you think Yusn would have him go unavenged?"

"This is not the *time*," Nducho said desperately. "Let's gather our forces in Sonora. Then we can take revenge!"

Despite the bone-touching chill of the mountaintop Nducho's face was studded with gleaming drops of sweat. Owl talked as if he'd forgotten the nemesis that pursued them, the friends and clansmen of Temerario and his uncle, hot to collect their own blood-debt. And more than that, the shaman was forgetting Random, the witch, the evil sorcerer who had somehow reached out to strike down Tse'e for all his rifle Power. The very thought of Green Eyes leached the strength from Nducho's joints and turned his belly to water.

For Nducho was a coward.

He had hidden it well over the years. While the hit-and-run style of Chiricahua warfare paid dividends to a courageous, daring leader, it also made it possible for one less brave to acquire a warrior's name without unduly exposing himself to danger. Nducho dreaded death. The promise of the Happy Place was lost on him; he would be a ghost, condemned to an agonized eternity, as his brother had foretold that night in Española: *Murderer! You kill by night! You'll walk in darkness forever!*

The words tolled in his ears like Nakaiyé mission bells. If Nducho faced Random, Nducho would die. This he knew.

Yet there was one thing Nducho feared more than death. To be exposed for what he was, to lose his name and hope of greatness—not even the horror of his situation was worse than that. His limbs began to tremble as the horror of his situation swept him with blizzard fury.

"We'll attack a white-eyes town." Owl spoke in tones hot and dry as a desert wind. "They've grown complacent. We'll come on them as they sleep, run off many horses, fire many buildings and kill the occupants as they emerge. The bonfire we light will summon all true Apache to Yusn's cause. There will be no shadows for cowards and doubters to hide in."

His glittering black eyes reached straight down into Nducho's soul. The young warrior wanted to turn and flee into the darkness before the cowardice within him was dragged out, writhing and slimy, into the firelight. "What about the San Carlos?" he made himself ask, pushing the words out quickly lest they turn to squeaks and betray him. "If we have to fight them we'll lose our chances of recruiting these reservation Indians." *And Green Eyes, Green Eyes—if we fight him—*

"Doubt not the wisdom of Yusn!" Spittle sprayed over Nducho's face. "Listen to what He has revealed: those who pursue us, Green Eyes as well as the whiteman-lovers of San Carlos, expect us now to proceed to Mexico and the shelter of the Sierra Madre. We shall confound them all. We'll veer northeast, strike into New Mexico, while they stumble through these mountains and on into the south. In these mountains, and with Yusn's help, we'll lose even Nndé trackers."

A warm spot appeared in the pit of Nducho's belly, flowing rapidly outward. Owl offered him nothing less than a miracle. A chance to avoid the choice of death or disgrace—and a chance to become at one stroke a chief as great as Victorio or Cochise or Mangas. An army of devoted warriors would be his. Such had been the vision Owl conjured up for him months ago in the Sonora desert, and which had filled his heart and mind ever since. Now it could become reality.

*"Nzhǫǫ,"* he breathed. "It is good. It is very, very good."

Owl gave a piercing triumphal cry. "And the rest of you?"

Immediately Boca Negra and Eskinyá and García shouted assent. Ha'aa smiled and said, yes, yes, eager to please his comrades. But some of the raiders kept silent and turned troubled looks to Aguilar and the man called Wears-Red-in-the-Storm.

Chi''s cheekbones stood out like mesas in sunset, and his eyes were lost in pensive darkness above. "Does your Power tell you this is the wise course, Niishdzhaa?"

*"Yusn* speaks through me," the shaman returned pointedly.

Chi' glanced at the Eagle. Still the old man said nothing. "I'm with you," Chi' said.

Nducho touched Aguilar's arm. "And you, Father? What do you say? Do we make the white-eyes pay for my brother's death?"

For a long still moment Aguilar watched the flames in their dance. "If Yusn wills it," he whispered, and so it was decided.


"Can I go with you, sir?" Squatting Apache-fashion and staring moodily at the fire, Random glanced up to see Sergeant Brown standing over him.

"No, Sergeant," he said softly. "Thank you. But I can't risk you. You're the only man I can trust to keep these kids alive if I don't come back." Brown nodded once, briskly. As usual the mahogany eyes gave nothing away. Did he feel slighted? Random couldn't know.

He looked around him at the others. "Doroteo I won't ask to imperil his soul by coming along." Cahill showed jumbled teeth in a sneer at "Dorothy's" superstitions, but Jordan frowned at him and he quickly shut his mouth. "The replacement squad's got no experience in this sort of work. I do." He stood and stretched, wincing at the way his back cracked. "So I go alone."

He looked to the west, where the moon was almost down, and let his gaze slide toward the bluff. At the head of that bluff, he knew, lay Raker's spy, watching the campfire as promised. His presence, like that of the men who kept watch during the day, was no secret. Raker wanted Random to know his every move was observed.

Random had his own ideas about that, and accordingly had moved the party's camp two hundred yards north of where it had lain the night before. Now that the moon was going down it was time to put the rest of his ideas into effect. He harbored no illusions about his chances. Raker's men were no doubt barroom sweepings out of Globe, but there were too many of them for him to be comfortable about taking them all on single-handed. Nor did he underestimate Captain John Raker, Texas Rangers (retired). The man was mad, but no less lethal for that.

No, his chances weren't good. But they were all the chances he had.

Random walked around to the side of the fire opposite the bluff, where his bedroll already lay unrolled. "It's time, gentlemen. If you will, start piling the brushwood on the fire when I give the word."

Brent Jordan cleared his throat. "Just a moment, Mr. Random."

Hunkered down beside the blanket, Random cocked an eyebrow at him. "My promise holds. If I make it back, you can still take me into Globe for trial." He grinned savagely. "It seems probable you'll have a few more deaths to charge me with before the night's over."

The young man's eyes slid away, then returned to fix the older man's firmly. "That's not what I meant, Mr. Random. You see, I'm going with you."

"Oh, so," said Random, coolly. "You're actually willing to lift a hand against fellow Anglo-Saxons on behalf of a murdering red savage?"

"This is different." His cheeks were flushed in the firelight. "This is a—a woman they have. White men don't treat a woman that way, any woman. At least, not men I'm willing to acknowledge as my own kind."

"That may be the first thing you've said I could agree with, Mr. Jordan," Random said quietly. But he hesitated. *He's just a kid.*

"Green Eyes," Doroteo said. "You'll have to kill some white-men."

"No doubt."

The scout showed teeth in a worried grimace. "Yusn's a just God. He won't damn you to the darkness for this. It's a good thing you do." He raised a blocky, weathered hand to the crucifix that dangled beneath his Agency tag. "I'll pray to the Blessed Virgin and all the saints to intercede for you. And the great lost chiefs as well."

Random smiled. "*Ahtyi'ee,*" he said. "Thank you."

The Cibicu turned to face Brent Jordan. For several heartbeats he said nothing, unsure of whether to attempt what he had to say in his halting English. He decided on his own language, trusting that he would be understood because he spoke from the heart. "You're a brave man," he said, "to fight your own people for the sake of one of mine. I salute you."

Jordan smiled shyly. "I don't know what you said. But thanks."

Chin on chest, Random regarded the youth. Then he stuck out his hand. "Welcome aboard."

Jordan raised a hand, paused. Then he grasped the mercenary's hand in a strong grip and shook.

# CHAPTER FIFTEEN

Hodie Powell took a deep drag on his cigarette and watched the moon fall into the Pinals. When the last of the swollen disk was gone he sighed and tossed the glowing butt over the lip of the cliff.

Off to the north the campfire blazed suddenly higher. Powell grabbed for the field glasses lying in a hollow on a rock by his side, cursing as the movement sent pain lancing through his wounded leg. He raised the binoculars to his eyes and fiddled with the focus. A wavering blur of yellow light became a billowing fire, surrounded by the marionette figures of black soldiers piling on the brush. Tensely, Powell groped one-handed for his carbine. Was it a signal?

The flames ebbed. Lethargically the blacks seated themselves around it and wrapped blankets around themselves. It looked as if the kid and the man Raker called Random had already curled up in their own blankets to get some sleep. Powell sighed, farted, put the glasses down and pulled his own coat tighter. It was cold, that was all. Niggers never could take cold well.

He shivered. The cold bothered his stab wound. It reminded him forcibly of the slim lithe form of the captive held back in camp, the swell of her hips and the jut of her small breasts. It was damned unfair of Raker to make him come up here to watch over Random's camp. He was wounded. Besides, he was the one who found the squaw. He should have her first. It was only right.

*Well, shit,* he told himself. *Surely your pals'll leave enough for you.* But only because it was the sort of thing that was hard to use up, he reflected.

Hodie set the glasses down and picked up the bottle nestled by his hip. If he couldn't have the pretty Indian girl to keep him warm, he'd just have to make do. Raker would have shit green if he knew Powell had brought a bottle with him on sentry-go. *The hell with that sanctimonious son of a bitch,* he thought, and tipped the bottle back. Warmth cascaded down his throat.

He put the bottle down. It made a tiny clink. He fancied he heard another sound, equally small, as if in response to the kiss of glass on sandstone. *Imagination*, he thought. *Or an old coyote come to see if there's a chance of a free meal*. He thought uneasily of the mound not ten feet away. It was obviously a grave. Was the coyote drawn to that?

Shuddering from something other than chill he shifted so that the rock beneath wouldn't dig his ample rump so badly. With his arms clamped tightly about his chest for warmth he studied the camp far below. Looked like the niggers were going to bed now. Maybe he could catch a little shut-eye himself, and screw Johnny Raker.

His death came upon him soundless and swift. A hand came from behind and locked on his chin like a steel claw. His head was jerked up and back with such ferocity that his bull neck snapped, and he never felt the razor-edged touch of the knife at his throat.

The constellations seemed to have sped their procession, wheeling dizzily above Brent Jordan's head. Every breath he gulped down felt as if it was tearing something loose in his chest. The need for absolute silence hung above him like a weight, poised to crush him at the least misstep.

It had been a desperate scramble up the darkened cliff. A dozen times he'd known he was about to lose his grip and go pitching back into the rubble at the foot of the sheer face. But each time he paused Random was there, steadying him, helping him to better footholds and handholds and climbing on without a word, seemingly unencumbered by his heavy coat and the stage gun strapped across his back. Nor did the mercenary need to speak. His unflagging determination was challenge enough to the younger man.

Brent Jordan was a successful college athlete a decade and a half Random's junior. Yet Random went swarming up the treacherous face like a lizard while Brent was puffing like a locomotive on a long steep grade.

Still, huddled down uncomfortably behind a clump of algerita, Brent didn't think he was doing so poorly. He'd made it to the top of the bluff intact. And he'd sneaked so close to the heavy, pale-haired man keeping watch on the camp that he could almost touch one freckled arm. He could unquestionably smell the cheap whiskey that rode the man's breath like an off-key song floating downwind.

Having come this far, he wondered what he was going to do now. Random had assured him that he, Random, could deal with the sentry. Now, watching the big man keeping an eagle eye over a campful of black soldiers and two bedrolls stuffed with wadded-up ponchos, Brent was just as glad. While the sentry wasn't monumentally alert, at that moment Brent Jordan could conceive of no way on Earth of getting any closer to the man without his having a chance to raise the alarm. Whether by luck or not, the man was in the open, with no cover nearer than Brent's bush twenty feet to his left. Good thrustful Anglo-Saxon tactics didn't seem to cover this particular occasion.

A shadow loomed from the blackness at the lookout's back, like a gigantic bird of prey swooping out of the night. Brent barely choked back a cry of horror. He heard a thick crack, and then the splash of liquid gushing onto rock.

As the sentry slumped the dark figure stepped away. Starlight glinted briefly on thin steel and was gone. The figure melded into blackness, to reappear at Brent's side. He jumped.

"Did you have to do that?" he asked, more put out at being detected than by the killing itself.

"Yes," Random said. "Come on."

Brent kept pace as best he could, working back along the bony spine of the promontory. He soon fell behind. No matter how cautious he was, loose rocks always seemed to turn beneath his boots. Random, however, slid through the night as silently as thought.

The boy almost stumbled over the mercenary, who had stopped and hunkered down. Random pointed west. Below them, yellow light wavered and shifted at the foot of a hill a few hundred feet away.

The men made their way toward the restless gleam. At length Random halted and drew Brent down behind a dead dwarf oak. They could see the fire clearly now, with tall silhouettes stalking back and forth before it. Voices raised in merriment rang out stark and strange, profaning the stillness.

"I'll go left, along the hill," Random said in a low voice, not as carrying as a whisper. "You head straight in; it's easier going. Wait for me to call to them, and be ready to shoot. If we catch them in a crossfire, they'll cave in more quickly."

Brent frowned, puzzled. "I'd think you'd be ready to kill them all."

"Not so easy as you think, even with this." He patted the shotgun.

"What about revenge?"

Random cast a quick glance toward the campfire sixty yards away. "What about it? All I want is to free Mariana and send these jackals packing. I've a revenge to take, never fear—but not on the likes of these.

"Get as close as you can and still be covered. And remember, wait for my word before you shoot or show yourself." He gripped the young man's shoulder.

Nodding, Brent tried to think of a reply. When at last a suitably stirring utterance came to his lips, there was nothing but the skeletal tree to hear it.

Sneaking up on the Rangers' camp was even easier than getting near the single lookout on the bluff. That man had been dividing his attention between the campfire and the bottle. These men were engrossed in bottles and a fire of a different sort.

"Here, now, Johnny, be reasonable," Deuce Lewis said, shaking back black hair. "We done followed you all acrost this damn desert. I know it's fer the greater good of the citizens of Arizona—but, hell, cain't we have a little fun on the side?"

The others laughed agreement. But there was an edge to their laughter that Raker's wolf-keen ears did not miss. He leaned back in the wagon box and crossed his long legs. "Aren't you boys forgetting that *ranchería* last week?"

"That was *last* week," grunted Black Jack Hutchinson. " 'Sides, them gals weren't half so pretty as this one." He accepted the communal bottle from his friend Deuce Lewis and walked over to where the captive sat bound and gagged, taking a hearty pull. Mariana's eyes shone like obsidian flakes, hard and deadly, as she watched him approach. Grinning, he reached down to run his fingers through her hair. "Silky. I like it like that."

Crouching behind a bush thirty feet away, Brent Jordan bit his underlip till it turned numb. Seen up close the girl was lovely, breathtakingly so, her complexion, pronounced cheekbones, and sloe eyes lending her an exotic beauty that affected him like no white woman he'd ever seen. At some point her cotton blouse had been torn or slashed open, and a small brown breast protruded, vulnerable and soft-looking. The sight made his heart race and his belly clench in an emotion he told himself was outrage.

The balding squatty man caressed his captive's cheek with oddly slender, agile fingers. Brent's blood simmered in his ears. He was supposed to sit tight till Random made his move. But here was a lovely maiden held prisoner by brutes, palpably facing the fate worse than death—and Brent Jordan was being asked to cower behind a bush and watch. It simply wasn't *done*.

He asked himself the fateful question: *What would Theodore Roosevelt do?*

Unaware that righteous wrath was building pressure like a boiler with a stuck valve not ten yards away, Black Jack let one hand slip down to cradle the bare breast. "What about it, Johnny?" he asked, thick-tongued.

Raker's lips cut back into his cheeks. "Very well," he said. "I know a hawk from a handsaw. And all I agreed was to hand her over alive." He glanced round a circle of abruptly attentive faces. "Who goes first?"

*"Stand back, you rogues! Unhand that maiden!"*

The Rangers froze, as much at the bizarre grandiloquence of the words as their sheer unexpectedness. Tall and stern as Jehovah rousting Adam and Eve from the Garden, Brent strode grandly into the circle of firelight, holding before him a flaming sword as made by the Samuel Colt Company of New Haven, Connecticut, with walnut grips for the civilian market. Black Jack dropped Mariana's breast as if it had turned hot and leaped back.

Only Raker stayed unruffled. "Good evening, Mr. Jordan," he drawled.

"Huh?" Blinking, Brent spun to cover him. The penny dreadfuls he'd illicitly devoured as a child provided no ready-made dialogue for this turn of events. "Who are you?"

"A friend, my boy. And right now a friend is exactly what you need." He smiled paternally. "Now, why don't you put that away before someone gets hurt?"

Chaos churned behind Brent's startled eyes. This wasn't how it worked at all. He was a courageous young gentleman of fighting Anglo-Saxon stock. Such rabble as these should instantly recognize him as their natural master, and be cowed into cringing submission.

Besides, he had a gun.

"I've got a gun," he said. "Put your hands up."

"It works better," said Raker with infinite gentleness, "if you cock it."

Brentwood Jordan III just had time to feel a chill of surprise. Then the back of his skull exploded in white light, the scene went very dim, and hard sour-tasting earth hit him full in the face.

Behind him stood Russian Nick, a smile on his broad hairy face and a shotgun in his broad hairy hands. Using a skill he'd acquired in his youth poaching the czar's deer in Ukrainian pine forests, Nick had stolen up behind the boy and buttstroked him in mid-pontification. Now he knelt beside his victim and felt his neck.

*"Nix kharóshi,"* he muttered, rising. "Too bad. He live." The boy groaned. Nick looked expectantly at Raker. "Finish?"

"For Christ's sake no, you Russian ape!" Raker bounced upright in the box. "Saddle them horses, boys! It's time to cut stick and *go*."

"*Freeze*."

There was no prose or bluster to this voice, no adolescent uncertainty. It seemed to come from all around, belling out of the darkness itself.

"There! In those rocks!" Lew Anderson clawed for his gun.

A fireball half as big as a man blossomed from the rocks that walled the south side of the camp. Most of the charge of Number 1 buck caught the ranchhand in chest and belly and tossed him back into the fire. Across the span of flames Stu Hamill spun half around and fell as two big pellets smashed into his hip. Hunkering beside him Lazy Ray Gunther clapped hands to his face and screamed like a snared rabbit.

A shadow sprang from the rocks. Ex-lawman Jug Larrabee came out of his fog first. He drew fast and fired.

Springing aside, Random felt a bullet pluck his coattail like a devil's fingers. He dove onto his belly and shot Larrabee in the face with the second barrel of his stage gun. Stu Hamill forgot his own agony to cry out and then vomit in the dust as the headless corpse fell flopping at his side.

The Rangers scattered like quail. As Deuce Lewis vanished into the Mescals his partner, Hutchinson, lunged for Mariana, knife in hand. He grabbed her chin. She squirmed her head down and bit his fingers to the bone.

The gambler howled and slashed at her. She snapped her head back and the knifetip grazed her cheek, drawing a bright line of blood. Random was on Hutchinson in a panther rush. A strike with the butt of the shotgun sent the knife spinning. A swing of twin barrels caved in one side of Black Jack's face and dropped him whimpering to the ground.

An avalanche landed on Random's back. Reflexively he grabbed, ducked. Russian Nick lumbered over his head and went down with a crash. Unable to use his own shotgun for fear of hitting his own men, the bearlike Ukrainian had decided to destroy the intruder with his massive hands, a task for which they were eminently suited.

Though his fall knocked the air out of him he was back on his feet at once. Random got a foot under himself, and something struck the side of his head with a roar. Knowing he'd been shot glancingly, he flung himself to his left. A second shot fountained red dust by his heels.

John Raker had jumped into the wagonbed and was calmly shooting at the mercenary, holding his pistol in both hands. Rolling over and over Random fought to free his own Peacemaker left-handed. Raker fired again. A fiery line etched itself along Random's left side. Gasping in pain he brought his revolver up and fired once.

The slug plowed into Raker's right shoulder and knocked him on his back on the planking. His gun went wheeling into the scrub. Moaning, he rolled over the wall of the wagonbed, fell heavily, and began crawling into the covering dark.

A huge foot kicked the Colt from Random's hand. He yanked his head aside in time to keep the descending boot from crushing his skull, caught it one-handed, and jerked the Russian off balance with the energy of desperation. As Nick thudded to the ground, Random rolled away, came to his, feet and staggered toward where his stage gun lay.

Holding the weapon in both hands he turned to face Nick in a fighting crouch. The Russian laughed and spat. "Toy unloaded," he said. "You die now, I think."

He charged. The double muzzles of the shotgun speared into his solar plexus. The giant doubled, retching. His spasm bared the back of his thick neck to the classic killing stroke of the Legion.

The wrist of Random's shotgun splintered with the force of the blow.

Swaying, Random dropped the broken gun and walked to Mariana. She lay on her side, watching him with the same flat look she'd given her tormentors, while her blood dripped and made small balls in the dust. He knelt and slashed her bonds with his Moorish dagger. Then his legs gave way and he sat down heavily. His vision reeled. Objectively he doubted he was badly hurt. Subjectively he felt like hell.

Brent Jordan got to his feet, gasping at the pain. He recovered his Colt from a hairy mole of sideoats grama and went to Random's side, looking alertly if blearily into the surrounding darkness. "He knew me," he said again and again. "How did he know who I was?"

"I don't know." Painfully Random rose. He took hold of Brent's face and peeled back his eyelids with his thumbs. "Both pupils look all right." He felt the back of the boy's head. The bone felt firm. "No concussion, and I don't think your skull's broken. The sons of Eli have thick heads, it seems."

He let the boy go.

"Where's the girl?" Brent asked.

Startled, Random looked around. "Gone."

"Aren't you going after her?"

Random stooped near Stu Hamill to pick up a canteen, twisted off the top, sniffed, nodded, replaced the cap. He lowered himself gingerly to one knee. Hamill looked up at him with an animal's scared eyes. "I won't hurt you, boy," Random said. "But maybe you've learned something out of this."

Hamill nodded. His face was paper-white and drawn.

"Good. Perhaps you're worth saving. I'll tend to that leg in a minute." Straightening, he tossed the canteen gurgling to Jordan, who nearly fumbled it. "Don't worry, it's water," he said. "If Mariana wanted to talk to me she'd have stayed here. Not even Doroteo could track her through the dark. I'm not even going to try. Besides, she can take care of herself."

"How can you say that?" Jordan demanded. "She's only a girl!"

"She's a woman," Random corrected. "Quite a woman." He knew now whose horsetracks Doroteo had found, following an hour behind the war party. The realization filled him with admiration for Mariana's courage and determination, and most of all her loyalty. She had braved appalling hardships to follow her captive husband. Self-hatred surged in Random, and he wondered if she knew.

Shaking his head, he turned to face the mountains and cupped his hands over his mouth. "Raker," he called. The words boomed back and forth, retreating up the valleys and ravines until the hills murmured together like sleepy giants. "Raker, I know you didn't get far. Answer me, Raker. Don't make me come after you."

Hollow stillness greeted the echo's last grumble. "You left a blood trail a blind man could follow, Raker. If I have to come after you, you won't leave these hills alive. You haven't a chance with that broken arm."

In a moment the answer came back, laughing and carefree. "You're a shrewd young man, Captain Random. I fear I've underestimated you."

"Come down, Raker."

"What guarantee?"

Random paused. "My word as a gentleman."

Another pause. Then Random heard rock crackle under bootleather. Shortly the former Texas Ranger emerged into the firelight. Despite the mess that was his right shoulder, blood-soaked and caked with dirt and bits of vegetation from his crawl through the scrub, Raker scarcely looked rumpled.

"I actually believe you, Captain," he said in his low rich voice. "You're fool enough to mean that when you say it."

"Don't tempt fate, Raker."

Raker laughed. "As you wish. What may I do for you, Captain?"

"You didn't do this on your own, Raker. Who hired you?"

"Come now, sir. We are both professionals. Surely you don't expect me to violate a confidence?"

Random's eyes narrowed. "Your life's forfeit, Raker. You've murdered, raped, robbed, and burned. You've threatened the life of a friend of mine and shot at me." His voice dropped to a gravel bed. "Buy your life, Raker."

Raker raised an eyebrow. "You gave your word you wouldn't harm me."

"I won't. But I will tie you to your horse and deliver you to Burning Sky's *rancheria*, and I'll hand you over to the women whose daughters your men raped and whose menfolk you shot down. Then I'll swear to the agent I buried you by the Gila with a bullet in your head."

Raker went pale. "You wouldn't do that to a fellow white man!"

Random smiled. "You don't think so?"

The shark-eyed killer thought it over. His shoulder was causing him excruciating pain, Random knew, yet no sign showed on his lupine face. Random accorded him respect for toughness.

"It disappoints me that a man with your warrior's background should have so mercantile an outlook," Raker said. "Now, Mr. John Wilkes Booth, my esteemed friend and—"

"Raker."

He sighed. "Very well. What's your offer, sir?"

"The horses are picketed in an arroyo a little ways east," Random said sidelong to Jordan. "Go and bring the big whitestockinged black, if you please." The young man nodded and left at a run.

"Here's the bargain," Random told Raker. "Tell me who hired you and why. And ride out alive and free."

"You drive a hard bargain, sir. But circumstance compels me to accept." He told the story of being paid to prevent Random from heading off Owl and Nducho and their holy war.

"Why?"

"My employer was reticent as to precisely who it was, but he made it clear he had a sponsor, a very powerful one, in whose interest it would be for a new Indian war to break out."

"The Tucson Ring?"

"I doubt they'd be averse to renewed Army activity in the Territory. But the way my principal spoke, I believe his backer's interest was . . . political. In fact, I garnered the impression it concerned the upcoming Republican convention in St. Louis."

Brent had returned, leading the black by its silver-worked bridle. "Politics and power," Random said. "Just look at the good they achieve."

"I don't believe it," said Brent Jordan dauntlessly. "Who would hire you to do such a thing, Mr. Raker? A deed that would cause the deaths of dozens of innocent citizens."

For a moment Raker stared at him. Then he put back his narrow head and laughed. "You mean you don't know?" Incredulously the young man shook his head. "Why, it was your father, boy. Who else?"

Brent turned red, then white. *"You're lying."*

"Not so, son. How else would I know who you were?" He tipped his head at Random. "Ask him if I'm telling the truth. You obviously know Captain Random no better than you do your father; if he learned I'd lied to him, he would serve me the way he served those unfortunate bounty killers a few years past."

"He's telling the truth," Random said.

"No!" Brent shouted. "No, he can't be! It's a lie!"

Raker turned from him with a shrug. "And now that I've fulfilled my part of our compact, Captain?"

Random took the reins from Brent's nerveless hands and threw them at Raker. "Go."

Painfully Raker hauled himself into the saddle. He looked down at Brent Jordan's anguished face. "Boy," he said softly. "Get the hell out of the West. You don't belong here."

Fists tight, tears running freely down his cheeks, Brent stared at his feet. The lean gunfighter turned to Random. "You're a fool, Captain, as I said before. But I admire you, just the same. After all, wasn't it the immortal Shakespeare who wrote, 'To err is human, to forgive divine.'?"

"No," Random said. "It was Pope."

Raker's face stiffened. The dead eyes drilled Random. "I'll kill you someday," he said, and dug his spurs into the black stud's flanks.

With a wordless cry of rage Brent snatched his Colt from its holster and aimed at the retreating back. Random whipped the stage gun up under the revolver's barrel, and the shot took off for the Big Dipper.

"He's besmirched my father's name!" Brent screamed. "How can you let him go? He's a liar, a thief, a murderer!"

"He's all those things. And none of them is why you tried to backshoot him just now. You wanted to kill him because he told the truth."

He turned away. "But my father's honor—" Jordan shouted at his back.

"Honor." He gave a strange small laugh. "I'm glad we mercenaries have no such thing, Mr. Jordan." And he went to help the injured youth who lay beside the fire.

# CHAPTER SIXTEEN

"They'll head east," Random stated flatly.

The others looked at him in amazement. "But they were bound for Mexico," Brent protested.

"Yeah," said Cahill. "Done lost 'em, Random. They're deep in the Sierra Madre by now."

Firmly Random shook his head. "No. They'll have learned of the death of Aguilar's son by now. That will change their plans." He squatted by the low pale fire, bouncing slightly on his heels as though filled with restless energy.

The soldiers eyed one another over half-heated tins of beans. Above the Gila Mountains a gray line hinted at dawn. Now and then a nightbird ghosted overhead, returning to its nest after a night's hunting.

Neither Random nor Brent Jordan had slept that night. They'd returned barely an hour ago from the raid on the Rangers' camp. Random had found old Jake LeDoux hiding in an arroyo not far from the Rangers' horses, and sent him off driving the wagon to carry Stu Hamill back to Globe. Presumably the other survivors would catch them up sooner or later. The San Carlos would probably not molest them. Random had promised the Apaches retribution. The four corpses he'd left cooling for the coyotes redeemed his pledge; the blood-debt was paid.

In fact Random didn't deeply care whether the crippled remnants of Raker's Rangers made it home or not. He'd let them live. That was the extent of his magnanimity.

His companions passed a worried look around. He had been carrying a tremendous strain. And he'd been shot in the head, however grazingly. Was he starting to crack?

"You can't know," Brent persisted.

"That's true," Random acknowledged wearily. "But one knows nothing for certain in this life. Hear my reasoning, at least.

"Nducho and Aguilar will want revenge. They won't turn back to face us—that's poor tactics, to go against a larger, alert force, and they've no way to know we haven't got the entire male population of San Carlos riding with us. I think they'll want vengeance now, rather than deferring it long enough for a recruiting run into Sonora. Also, they'll assume their pursuers are making hard and fast for Mexico, and will plan to slip around our flank."

Jordan looked around. "He's crazy," Cahill said, but Brent had come to trust the little man less each day.

"So that makes sense," he admitted. "But what makes you think they'll head east? They might go west instead."

"They might. But they won't. Aguilar is very much an old-style Apache. You can't separate a Chíhéne from his land. He'll want to return to the place he was born. Nducho too, perhaps; I can't read him so well."

"Why didn't they go to Aguilar's birthplace at the start?"

"Owl—their prophet—told them the reservation Apache would rise and join them. Aguilar would rather go back to his homeland at the head of a liberating army than as a fugitive—as who wouldn't?" He shook his head. "He wouldn't go there first. But I'm dead certain he's going there now."

*"And how many will be dead if your certainty's wrong?"*

Brent tensed, expecting a blow or at least a stinging rebuff. Instead the mercenary merely nodded. In the dirty-wool light Brent saw that his eyes had sunk to hollows, and marked to his surprise that the beard stubble on Random's gaunt cheeks and jaws was streaked through and through with gray.

"You have a good point," said Random deliberately. "If I'm wrong, people will die. Yet I can only follow my judgment." He shrugged and stood up.

"I told you all before, I'll order no one. If you think I'm wrong, go your own way. Or even if you think I'm right—because if I am, we face a hard ride with a harder fight at the end."

Without waiting for an answer Random turned and briskly began saddling Malcriado. The others chewed their lips and thought. Even Doroteo was concerned, worry standing plainly on his broad round face.

"Well, you men heard him," said Sergeant Brown, rising. "He says to do as you will."

"What you gonna do, Sergeant?" asked Garrison with a touch of banter. He was hugging himself and doing a little dance to keep warm.

"Follow him, Private." He paused. "And you?"

The skinny recruit bent down and hefted his McClellan to his shoulder with a grunt. "Lead the way, Sergeant."

One by one the soldiers followed Garrison's lead. Shaking his head at Cahill's protests Brent began to load his own gear on his handsome stallion. "Where Random goes, I go," he said to his bodyguard. "I won't let him show himself the better man." So perforce Cahill had to go too, to keep watch over Jordan—and to try to salvage the other part of his assignment, which his hulking partner had failed to fulfill.

Sighing, Doroteo saddled his own mount. Tonton Macoute stopped beside the scout and nodded at Random as the mercenary climbed onto Malcriado. "He have Power on him," the Haitian said carefully, in the choppy English he'd learned from Doroteo.

Eyes widened slightly, Doroteo looked from Random to the *voudoun* practitioner. He broke into a smile. "You right," he said. Grateful that his friend had set his doubts to rest, he clapped the black man on the shoulder and mounted his pony to follow Random where his Power led.

For the first time since reaching Arizona Territory the war party set themselves the grueling, ground-devouring pace that had made the thousand-mile raids of Chihuahua, Nana, and Ulzanna possible in earlier years. They whipped their mounts through the forbidding Mescals with a grim urgency that could not be called eagerness, but would serve in its place.

Nducho talked incessantly of the triumph waiting at the end of their ride. Few believed him anymore. Yet they followed. For fear of him, for fear of Owl's magic, for fear of having nowhere else to go. Now they had three choices: surrender and the long death of captivity; return to the nameless hunted world of the fugitive; death. Even if the war party no longer offered an alternative to those bitter choices, it gave the illusion of one. At least it offered motion, the feeling of doing something.

Aguilar stayed silent through his son's ravings. He seemed to have shrunk since announcing Tse'e's death. His eyes had glazed and turned within. Likewise Chi' rode sunk in moody silence. From time to time he glanced at Owl, and his deepset eyes were troubled.

Before the sun was fully free of the eastern peaks they came upon a ranch huddled in a fold of the dwindling Mescals. Nducho leading, the raiders turned fear, exhaustion, and frustration into ferocity, and swept howling from the tree line. Two men, two women, and three children were in and around the doomed house. So swift and fierce

was the wildfire onslaught of the Apaches that all died without firing a
shot in their own defense. Nducho wept with anger that none survived
to face the torture, but he was mollified by the dozen excellent
remounts in the corral. On fresh horses, spirits buoyed by victory and
their appetite for white-eyes' blood whetted to a fine edge, the war
party hurtled on under skies growing dark with clouds.

In the rear rode two men, one late in middle age, one old and
growing older with every mile that passed beneath his horse's hooves.
Chi' and Haastjj 'Ítsá had not partaken of the slaughter, but only sat
their mounts and watched. And thought.

*"Bidáá dotl'izh,"* Doroteo shouted from the crest of a ridge.
"Green Eyes, look! There, to the south."

Random dropped from his saddle and scrambled up the grassy
slope. South of him rose the Gilas, and from the far side of them a
pillar of smoke rose to join leaden clouds. "You know what that
means, my friend?" Doroteo asked.

Random nodded.

"What is it? What's that smoke?" Brent Jordan had clambered up
after Random and stood beside him peering south.

"Lives and dreams and the labor of years," Random replied.
"That's the smoke of a burning homestead, Mr. Jordan. Once you see
it you don't ever forget it." He studied the young man's face. "That's
the glory of war, Mr. Jordan." He turned and trotted down the ridge's
flank.

By the time he slipped and slid to the bottom Jordan's pulse was
drumming a quickmarch in his ears. "Random was right!" he yelled.
"They're going east!"

"Look there," Random said, pointing. A solitary butte reared
against the sky and the blue line of mountains beyond. "There's a
Chiricahua watering hole there, where rain gathers at the top. A secret
place. They'll go to that. If we swing around and come down from the
north, we can get there ahead of them without much chance of being
spotted."

The column had dismounted when he went up the ridge. Now there
was a certain shuffling of feet and clearing of throats. He was
blueskying again, or so it seemed. "There are several tanks marked
on our maps between the Gilas and that butte, sir," Sergeant Brown
said. "Won't they stop at one of those?"

"No, damn it!" The sergeant took a step back. "Those tanks are
known to whites, used by them. The raiders will avoid it as they'd

avoid their mothers-in-law. A farm family got in their way this morning, and suffered. But they won't want to fight their way across the open."

"I dunno this damn tank," Doroteo said.

"I told you, it's Chiricahua." He was pacing to and fro as if consumed by the need to keep in motion. "The Chókánéń used to range this region. They discovered it, passed the word on to the Red Paints—though no doubt there are a few Chókánéń with the war party."

"How did you find out about it?" Brent asked skeptically.

"I was told." Random shrugged. "It was years ago. . . . Enough. Who follows?"

They all did, yet again. The rangy little *coyote* mustang set a killing pace across the open land. Here the country ran to volcanic drifts, red-brown earth overlying a razor-sharp skeleton of black lava. Five miles north and west of the butte Brent Jordan's big chestnut put his near forefoot down a frozen bubble and snapped his fetlock. Brent was thrown into a lava drift that gashed his legs and back like knives. His horse just lay there, flanks heaving in agony, staring at its master through yellowed bloodshot eyes. Crying unashamedly, Brent put a bullet between the pleading eyes. Then he loaded his saddle onto Harmony's mule, mounted Sutter's black, and followed, followed, followed.

The butte grew in the raiders' sight. As it rose, the sky lowered, and the sun sank, so it seemed that the war party, darkness, and the storm would all arrive at the same time.

They were half an hour from the old Chókánéń tank when the Old Eagle woke from his reverie and looked around at the red and black and ochre land, its colors muted under cloud, as if seeing it for the first time. He kicked his horse and brought it alongside Owl's crippled-seeming white.

The prophet gazed at him from the shadow of his painted hat. "Yes, Haastjj 'Ítsá?"

Aguilar pointed to the lonely jut of rock before them. "Do we go there?"

"You know quite well we do." Owl frowned beneath his hatbrim and eyed the old warrior sidelong.

"What does your Power tell you?"

"Yusn tells me: On."

He was worried now. The old fool had been perfectly malleable s long as he wrapped himself in the blanket of the past. Now there was something in his eyes, the way he held his head, that Owl did not like.

"Don't let your heart grow faint, old man," he hissed.

"Oh, no," said Aguilar. *My son, my son, you were right.* He lifted his eyes toward the red butte and knew what waited there.

"My heart has never been stronger, Niishdzhaa."

# CHAPTER SEVENTEEN

Eskinyá worried.

He had always believed the war party would succeed. Owl had
Power, though whether Yusn truly spoke to the hunchbacked shaman
Eskinyá neither knew nor cared. This raid would bring him glory and
riches, a chance to kill—a chance to hurt, to indulge that special taste
that made him *heshkéé*. He'd shared Nducho's frustrated fury that
there were no white-eyes left to cut and burn that morning. But the
wiry Ndé'indaa never doubted there would be many more opportuni-
ties for torture, and if that traitor Chi' interfered again, Eskinyá would
personally shoot him in the belly.

But something had happened today that spoiled everything. The
war party had no sooner debouched from the Gilas than a rabbit, a bi
torn-eared dusty jack, sat up behind a bush and spoke to Eskinyá.

"You die today," the jack said. "Rabbit will laugh." And laugh the
rabbit had, until Eskinyá's bullet knocked it kicking on its side
Nducho shrieked at him for wasting a bullet on a jackrabbit, and
risking the shot's drawing attention. In his misery Eskinyá wa
oblivious to the Mountain Lion's wrath. He left the rabbit where i
fell. None of the others had heard the animal speak, he knew; the sig
was meant for him alone.

For Rabbit had had it in for him a long time. Ever since he ha
caught a jenny-rabbit in a snare, out by himself in the Sonora desert
He had tortured the animal to death, and after it expired in squealin
torment he felt a strange wild release like nothing he had known in a
his twelve years. He was glad no Apache had seen him, for the Peopl
despised wanton cruelty.

But when he was done he'd seen a buck rabbit sitting tall behind
bush, like the one that taunted him this morning. The rabbit curse
him. Since that time, whenever bad things happened to Eskinyá, th
rabbits were always there, laughing.

Of course, he had Owl's Power to shield him from the harmfu
magic of the rabbits. But there was no point in tempting fate, so as th
party made its rapid way toward the butte and the hidden waterhole

he had drifted back until he was at the very tail of the line. If there was trouble, he would be the last in—and the first out.

But Rabbit was not so easily denied.

Fired from one hundred and fifty yards, the bullet from Random's Vetterli punched directly through Eskinyá's sternum. He felt the awful shock, the blazing pain as his heart exploded, and had just time to know that Rabbit had had his revenge after all.

At first the raiders thought the shot came from ahead. But Todéédi, riding just ahead of Eskinyá, happened to glance over his shoulder. His shout brought heads swiveling around in time to see the Mexican Chiricahua topple into the scrub.

Convinced the enemy was behind them, Owl screeched, "To the butte!" and the war party spurred madly forward.

They raced straight into the mouth of the semicircular firing line Random and the sergeant had laid among the rocks and brush at the foot of the mesa. Sergeant Brown's voice boomed off the sheer red cliffs: *"Fire!"* The growl of approaching thunder was lost in the crash of half a dozen rifles.

Men and horses went down in shouting, squealing confusion. Private Jones's shot knocked Todéédi's horse from under him, and the bandy-legged little warrior hit the ground running and vanished in the chaparral. Boca Negra's horse fell too. He leaped clear and began to run, only to stop, spin, and fall, as Random's second shot went through his head. Private Garrison shot García low in the stomach. The gangly soldier bounced to his feet shouting, "I got him! I got him!" and Delzhee shot him. Instantly Sergeant Brown was at his side, cursing Garrison's foolishness while he turned the boy over with a mother's tenderness to tend his wound.

Still believing themselves pursued from behind, the war party kept streaming toward the butte. Forty feet from Garrison and Brown, Doroteo lay on his belly levering shots at Nducho. "Hey, Dorothy," the scout heard Cahill call. He glanced at the little man crouched a few yards distant.

Cahill shot him through the body.

Doroteo let go of his gun. His fingers dug grooves in the dirt. "Serves you right, you red nigger," Cahill snarled, a tic twitching furiously below his right eye. "Now we'll see about that bastard Random." He rose to a crouch, ready to finish the task J. Ramsey Jordan had set for him and Sutter back at Apache: thwarting Random, and killing him into the bargain.

"Mr. Cahill," a soft voice said.

Cahill spun, bringing up his heavy Colt. Kneeling at Garrison's side, Sergeant Theophilus Brown fired his double-action .38. The red-haired gunman fell onto his back and kicked at the earth with his heels, strangling on blood from the hole in his throat.

Holstering his pistol, Brown returned to binding Garrison's shoulder.

Having missed his first several shots, to his immense chagrin, Brent Jordan cried out in delight when he fired his One-in-One-Hundred at a mounted figure that loomed out of the scrub at him. The rider screamed and fell at Brent's feet, clutching his belly. Brent stared at him. What he'd taken for muscular stockiness was baby-fat; the "man" he'd gutshot could not have been more than fifteen.

Ha'aa sobbed in agony and terror and incomprehension. Jordan stood over him, his mouth working soundlessly. He had no words for this. He'd been so eager to bring down his first man. It never occurred to him his trophy might be a boy younger than he, nor that his quarry would die so slowly and painfully, crying like the injured child he was.

He heard a sound and too late snapped to action. Brent saw a lean hate-twisted face, crossed by a white stripe already beginning to run from furious tears. He tried to bring up the 94, but Nducho's carbine spouted fire first, and a hammer struck Brent's right shoulder.

He reeled back, discharging the rifle into the dust at his feet. Nducho steered his horse toward him. The warrior dropped his empty carbine and drew a hatchet from his belt.

A brown-clad figure sprang from the bush into his path. Nducho shrieked as the black soldier aimed a Springfield at his chest from three feet and yanked the trigger.

The hammer fell with an empty click. Cornered, Nducho fought like the animal for which he was named. As Private Potassium Nitrate Monroe worked frantically to clear the improperly loaded round from the chamber of his trapdoor the Chiricahua launched himself in a tigerish leap and bore the boy to earth. Brent saw the hatchet go high and come down hard with a ghastly crunching sound. Monroe's limbs flailed once and were still.

Lithely Nducho sprang to his feet. His hatchet dripped blood and brains. Grinning madly he stalked Jordan. Numb with the shock of his wound the young easterner tried to bring his rifle to bear left-handed. Contemptuously Nducho swatted it away. Brent danced back to avoid the return swipe, tripped over a low bush and fell.

His face a triumphant death's-head, Nducho poised above him. The bloody hatchet rose. Brent Jordan stared up at his own death.

Thunder roared. A red flower blossomed high up on the front of Nducho's yellow shirt. He was thrown backward onto his rump.

Again the thunder crashed. Nducho's right shoulder exploded in blood and bright bone fragments and the hatchet fell from his hand. His eyes were huge, whites showing all around, and his lips formed one word again and again: *dah, dah, dah.* Brent understood no Apache, but he knew that word meant "no." He turned his head as a third shot roared by.

Ten feet away stood Mariana, holding a gigantic Peacemaker in both small hands. Working the hammer with one thumb, she fired the entire cylinder into the body of the Mountain Lion, slowly, while he wailed and wept and pleaded for her to stop. The way she stood with legs apart and shoulders braced told Brent that it was no accident Nducho lived until the sixth and final bullet burst his eye and the brain behind.

Brent stared at the riddled corpse. Nducho's hands were still raised, as though pleading even in death.

Mechanically Random fired the Vetterli. His first shot had served to drive the war party into the trap. Now he shot not to kill, but to convince the raiders that the time had come to forget this foolishness and go home. Except for Nducho. He scanned the brush for sight of the hated Mountain Lion as blue-white lightning stabbed down from the sky.

So intent was he that he didn't know one of the raiders had gotten behind him until the Apache leaped onto his back. Two more bounded from the scrub and grabbed him, trying to pin his arms.

But he still had the rifle in both hands. A stroke of the Vetterli's butt toppled a man from astride his chest, laying a mask of blood over the warrior's white and red paint. A muzzle-thrust dropped a second choking and semiconscious at his side. The final round in the ten-round tubular magazine exploded point-blank into the third man's groin.

Random heard a sound behind. Slowly he turned to stare into the barrel of a leveled gun.

"I greet you, Lightning-Strikes-Near," he said.

"I greet you, Green Eyes." The flat ugly face held no expression. "Will you shoot?"

Chi' frowned. "I don't know," he confessed. "I—"

A rustling brought his head round to see Owl, hatless and disarmed, scrabble out from under a bush. His shirt was torn, his hair in wild disarray. His eyes lit with joy as they beheld Random and the warrior in red.

"Kill him!" he crowed. "Kill him and we have won."

"I don't know if I can."

Owl gaped. "Of course you can. Kill him now, or—"

A white flash blinded Random, an earth-shattering blast deafened him.

His first thought was, *I'm shot*. But he'd had a gun go off in his face before, in Africa, and knew immediately that wasn't what had happened. Gradually sight and hearing returned.

Owl had fallen to the ground at the lightning stroke. Chi' was unmoved, sitting tall on the bony back of his buckskin, which like him seemed unaffected. "Kill him," Owl cried again. His words sounded distant and hollow in Random's ringing ears. "Kill him and Yusn will give you back your Power!"

Then Random heard a sound no man had heard for sixteen years, since Victorio fell at Tres Castillos: Lightning-Strikes-Near chuckled, deep in his throat. "Yusn *has* returned my Power to me, false one," he said. "And the lightning tells me you were running away, saving your filthy hide while you left the men you misled to die."

Owl turned to protest. Lightning-Strikes-Near shot him through his open mouth.

The red-clad warrior flung up his carbine in salute to Random. Then he turned and galloped off into the lightning-raked chaparral. In a short time the storm took him to its breast, and he was seen no more by red man or white.

The war party was dispersed. The survivors of the pursuit clustered round, caring for the wounded. Mariana looked up from helping Sergeant Brown bandage Brent Jordan's arm and smiled shyly. Random smiled tentatively back.

Then he saw the wounded scout and frowned. "Doroteo, what happened?"

"Cahill shot him," Brown said.

Brent winced. "Cahill was a traitor."

An ugly light appeared in Random's eyes. "What happened to Cahill?"

"Sergeant Brown shot him," said Garrison, who sat on a low

hummock nearby with his arm in a sling, smoking a cigarette. "Bang through the throat."

Random met Tonton Macoute's grave brown eyes across Doroteo's irregularly rising and falling chest. The Haitian swept his head slowly from side to side. Random gripped the scout's hand.

Doroteo smiled weakly. "You're truly of the People," he gasped, "not to try to soothe me with lying words. I'm going."

"You are," said Random in a rough voice.

"My wife and granddaughter? You'll see them cared for?" Random nodded. "And tell my Blossom Girl, her grandpa died a warrior? I am the last."

"You are the last."

"*Vaya con Dios, amigo*," Doroteo said. His hand clutched Random's hard and relaxed.

"And you, my friend," said Random, rising. "Go with God."

Brent touched him on the arm. "Aguilar," the young man said. "Where is he? Has he gotten away?"

"I know where he went," Random said. At the look on his face Brent fell back away from him. He walked forward, past the easterner, past Mariana and Sergeant Brown and the three surviving men. They watched him in silence.

The rain came down as he began to climb.

The rain washed Haastji 'Ítsá's face. He sang in a low voice. Farewell to the rain, farewell to the wind, farewell to the land of his birth, which he would never see again. After a time he turned to see Random standing behind him on the flat top of the butte.

"*Daa'ítsaa*," the old man said.

"It's done," Random agreed. "Come with me, Grandfather."

The old man got to his feet. "To what? The living death of Fort Sill?" He shook his head. "Don't you know me better than that, Green Eyes? Would *you* go back?"

"No."

The Old Eagle smiled. "Then you know my answer."

"Run, then. Go to Mexico. Live your last years in freedom. The Nakaiyé will never catch you."

"Life is a burden to me now," Aguilar said. "I have murdered my sons and many others. I almost brought destruction to the People. Because I have been blind."

He shook his head again. "No. I won't lie to myself anymore. I murdered my sons because I was selfish. I wanted the past to come back. I wanted to believe, and I did believe. My belief has cost me dear."

Tears ran down his face, mingling with the rain. "But Owl lied to you," said Random urgently.

"He did. Does that absolve me of my foolishness? I am Apache; I should think for myself. No, Green Eyes. I've failed, and must pay."

Random shook his head. "No."

But the old man was reaching to his belt. "Good-bye, Green Eyes. You're a good man. I wish—but no. I destroyed my sons."

He drew his knife. "See? Victorio gave this to me when I first married. I've kept it unblemished throughout my whole life." He held it up. "Now it's already spotted with rust. How soon it comes, how soon."

He turned the weapon in his hand and came at Random. "No, old man. Do not do this, Haastjį 'Ítsá." Random's own tears flowed.

The old man didn't hear. His eyes were fixed beyond the world. "My son," he cried, his voice an eagle's. "It's as I told you. I join you now!" He swung the knife, blinding fast.

A gunshot echoed long beneath the falling of the rain.

The Old Eagle's last flight was done.

# CHAPTER EIGHTEEN

Deadly combat was joined as Random stepped from the back door of the post adjutant's office into the afternoon heat. The 7th Cavalry was battling the 11th Infantry in a savage game of baseball, with regimental honor in the balance. For a moment Random watched them at play on the flat north of Fort Apache proper. The batter swung mightily and broke into a run. As he rounded first base and started along the adobe wall of the quartermaster's corral, Random heard the cheers and jeers of excited men. Smiling wryly, he shifted the weight of the saddlebags slung over his shoulder. They clinked as they moved.

"So you have your pay." Random turned to see Brent Jordan walking toward him along the boardwalk. His right shoulder was wrapped tightly in fresh linen bandages, his arm carried in a spotless sling. He was wearing his fawn-colored shirtwaist suit once more. It hung a bit loosely here and there.

"Have you spoken with your father yet?" Random asked. A look of pain crossed the younger man's face. He shook his head.

Jordan stepped close to Random. He started to raise his hand, then dropped it to his side. "No. I can't offer you my hand." He blushed behind his newly trimmed moustache and looked away. "I—I know we've been through a lot together. But you still stand against everything I believe in. I'm sorry."

"Don't take it too hard."

Bewildered young eyes searched Random's face. "Why do you do it? Why fight for money, when you could serve your country with honor? You're the bravest man I've ever known."

"So we're back to honor." Slowly Random shook his head. "The bravest man you ever met was a scared kid trying to save you from the Mountain Lion."

Jordan clutched Random's sleeve with his free hand. "Why don't you join us? Our time's coming, Mr. Random. The time when men of ability will grasp the reins of power and turn this country around." Spots of color glowed on his freshly scrubbed cheeks. "Join us.

We're the wave of the future, Mr. Random. You can't stand in the way of progress."

"Maybe that's all the more reason I should stand up for the things *I* believe in, Mr. Jordan."

He walked past the young man. "What will you do now?" Brent asked.

"I've some unfinished business to attend to. You?"

Brent shrugged, winced, grinned sheepishly. "Go back to New Haven, I expect. Go to law school. Impress the girls with my war wound, even though I can't tell them how I came by it."

"You can tell them. You just won't be believed. The killings in the Territory these last few weeks were the work of *federale* deserters out of Sonora. Didn't you know? The State Department has filed an official protest with Mexico."

Jordan bit his lip. "I guess I'd better go see my father, shouldn't I?"

"What will you say?"

"I don't know. I—" He shook himself. "No. This is all a terrible misunderstanding. And my father has friends who'll stand by him— influential friends. Did you know he was personally acquainted with Mr. Roosevelt?"

For a moment Random stood very still. "No," he said at length. "I didn't know."

He slung the saddlebags over Malcriado's cruppers and fastened them in place. "Good luck in law school, Mr. Jordan."

"Thanks." The young man hesitated. "Good luck to you too," he said as Random mounted. "Whatever you are."

"Thank you." Random nudged the little mustang to a trot toward the ridge where the scouts' families built their wickiups, and there he tied him to a cotton wood.

"Do you have a moment, Sergeant?" Brisk in his gleaming bleached-linen fatigues, Sergeant Brown came to a halt as he rounded a corner of the nearly deserted barracks and found himself facing Random.

"Certainly, sir."

"You don't have to 'sir' me, Sergeant. How's Garrison?"

"Has most of his sass back. I can't say I'm sorry, sir."

"Nor I." He pulled a rolled blanket from his shoulder. "Here. There's something I have to give you."

Brown almost dropped the roll. "My God, what's in this thing? It weighs like lead." He set it on the ground, unrolled it, and settled slowly onto his heels, his eyes wide.

"Two thousand dollars in gold," Random said. "Your share, and your men's. I've already given a share to Doroteo's family."

Brown's face was gray beneath the flat brim of his hat. "You can't."

"It's yours."

The sergeant stood up. "I'm sorry, sir. I can't speak for my men, but I cannot accept money for simply doing my duty."

"You weren't doing your duty. Technically you were absent without leave."

"I don't want charity," Brown snapped.

"It's not charity, damn it! You earned that money. I didn't order anybody to follow me. You weren't along officially—or legally—as soldiers of the United States Army, so you were acting as private citizens, and you're entitled to the money."

The sergeant's jaw stayed set. "I'm being selfish," Random said. "I can't accept all this money. I feel some of it's blood money. I'll take pay for stopping a war. But not for killing a friend. So I ask you, Sergeant Brown, if you and your men will do me the favor of accepting the money you have earned?"

Brown lowered his head. "If you insist, sir."

"I do. Take it or I throw it in the White River."

For the first time since Random had known him, Sergeant Brown grinned. "We can't expose the men of Fort Apache to that temptation, can we, sir?"

Random laughed. "Naturally not."

"Thank you, sir. For the men, and for me."

"I'll leave it to you to get Monroe's and Harmony's shares to their families." He walked toward Malcriado, who was stripping leaves from the lower branches of the cottonwood to which he was tied. Halfway there he stopped and turned back.

"Some advice for you, Sergeant—with your permission." Brown nodded. "Get out of the Army. The whites won't thank you for fighting their wars. They resent you. If they can, they'll destroy you. But they'll never, ever, acknowledge you."

"Thank you, sir." Brown's face showed no emotion. "But the Army's all I know. I'm staying, whatever happens."

"And the others?"

"They've been offered early release. I think young Garrison will accept, and MacHoot wants to go back to his island, I understand. Jones is an old warhorse like me, sir. He doesn't know anything else."

"Good luck. To all of you." He reached to untie the reins.

"Captain Random."

Turning, he saw Sergeant Brown standing rigidly to attention. The sergeant saluted sharply. "A pleasure to serve with you, *sir.*"

Random's body snapped taut and his heels clicked resoundingly. He flashed the crispest palm-out Continental salute Brown had ever seen. Just for an instant, he was Captain Random of la Légion Etrangère, on the white parade ground of Sidi-bel-Abbès. And despite disillusionment, despite his hatred of regimentation and colonial wars, just for an instant, it felt good.

"And you, Sergeant!" His hand came smartly down.

Then he was mounted on Malcriado, loping lazily around the dusty quadrangle of the fort, bound for the Northwest and a final rendezvous, a final settling of accounts. He wondered if he would be alive to see the sun come up again.

To his surprise, he found that he cared.

With an odd delicacy, fussiness almost, the heavyset man smoothed the thin yellow sheet on the green blotter before him. Squinting through his elliptical glasses, he carefully read the message through again. The words did not change. They obstinately continued to inform him that the Apache chief Aguilar, who had escaped from Fort Sill in late March, had been killed in southern Arizona, his raiding party scattered and driven back to Mexico. His Army informant was pleased to relay that the danger of a new Indian war was past.

Theodore Roosevelt sat back in his chair and blinked at a piece of plaster flaking off the opposite wall. *It's the end of the dream,* he thought. The end of his hopes for St. Louis.

Quick as a snake he snatched up the paper and crumpled it in one huge hand, as though crushing the life from some offensive insect. He hurled it into the wastebasket at the end of his desk. "Miss Kelly!"

A worried staccato of footsteps answered his bellow. His secretary opened the door and peered tentatively in, her lower lip quivering.

"Miss Kelly," he said again, soothingly this time. The tremor stopped. "Miss Kelly, has Intelligence sent up those reports I asked Captain Bakke to compile?"

"I'm not sure, sir. I'll check." Instead she hovered in the door.

"Yes, Miss Kelly?"

"Is—is something wrong, sir?"

His face clouded. He sat back in his swivel chair, and his knuckles beat a slow march on the walnut desktop. "There's something wrong with America, Miss Kelly. I've just received further confirmation of the rot that's eating out the nation's heart from within. But I don't intend to stand by and do nothing!" He swung his body forward, and his fists came down with a bang.

"Those reports I asked about, Miss Kelly. They contain irrefutable documentation of corruption on the part of an official of the United States government. This man has used his position as superintendent of Indian Affairs for Arizona to defraud the American people and enrich himself at the expense of his charges. But he isn't going to get away with it, Miss Kelly. No, he isn't going to get away with it at all."

He leaned back again and gazed out the window. "When you return, I'll ask you to take a letter for the Commissioner of Indian Affairs. We'll soon put a stop to *this*." He chopped the air with his hand. "Vamoose, Miss Kelly."

"Yes, sir." But she paused a moment, looking at him with adoration radiating from her blue eyes. *He's such a great man*, she thought. *The country needs him.*

She turned and left him sitting with his shoulders braced under the burden of greatness.

# EPILOGUE

The Fort Apache Indian Reservation
Arizona Territory
April 30, 1896

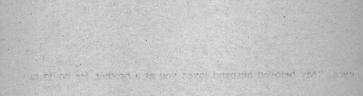

A voice called softly to him from the darkness. He halted Malcriado and waited. In a moment her pony stepped from between the trees to stop facing his in the small clearing on the side of the mountain named Gaan bích'it'izhé, Crown Dancer.

"I've come to pay the debt I owe you, Mariana," Random said.

"What's that?" she asked.

He drew his Colt, reversed it and held it out to her. "My life. I killed your husband. Now my life's yours to take."

Solemnly she looked from the proffered weapon to his face. His features were calm in the light of the arc of moon that showed above the ridge to the east, calm and somehow boyish. So serious, so sad. Yet composed.

"I have a pistol of my own, Green Eyes," Mariana said. "As I had a carbine, that day you shot my husband. I was there on the bluff and saw it happen. I was ready to kill you then."

He stared at her. *She saw!* He felt sick, not at the close approach of his own death that day, but that Mariana was forced to see her husband die. "Why didn't you shoot?" he asked.

"You cried for him. Cried like an Apache, cried as I longed to cry. He shot at you, and you had to defend yourself and those who rode with you. But you didn't kill my husband."

"Mariana—"

She would not be put off. "You did not! Nducho murdered my husband. And yes, I name him; let his spirit try to haunt me! I killed him. His death paid the blood-debt for my beloved in full. You owe me nothing."

Wetness gleamed in her eyes. Random urged Malcriado forward and took her in his arms. Leaning from her saddle she clung to him as the crying wracked her body. Tears soaked his shirt and were cool and wet against his skin.

"I'm glad you didn't shoot," he said quietly.

She drew away. "So am I," she said, wiping moisture from her eyes. "My beloved husband loved you as a brother. He could have taken your life, but didn't. He wouldn't want me to." She looked abruptly down at the ground. "But why did he throw his life away?" she asked in a rough voice.

Random said nothing, knowing that was not a question asked to be answered.

"What will you do?" he asked.

"Return to my father for now, I suppose." She was looking at him intently, her eyes oddly bright in the light of the moon. "Perhaps some young man will want me for a wife. I'm not so old, and there is still prestige to be had from marrying the daughter of Thunder Knife, though the government has tried to take his influence from him."

"I'd think any man would be honored to marry you," Random said, surprised at the bitterness in her voice. "For your own sake, not your father's name."

"Perhaps." She looked away. "But if I'm asked to marry for whatever reason, I think I will refuse. I'd rather live alone than sully my husband's memory by marrying a lesser man."

Random nodded. It would take a remarkable man indeed to be worthy of this woman. Looking at her in that cool, quiet clearing, it occurred to him that he'd never known a man who was braver or more resourceful than Mariana. Nor had he known a lovelier woman.

He grimaced. Such thoughts were less than honorable. His friend was scarcely buried with Random's own bullet through his heart.

"Come," he said. "I'll accompany you to your father's camp." She nodded. He turned Malcriado's head toward the rising moon.

And stopped.

At the crest of the ridge to the east stood a young buck. Antlers covered in winter velvet raked forward from his high-held head. He was looking straight at Random and Mariana.

Slowly the antlered head dipped, once, twice, three times. Then the animal sprang across the face of the moon and was gone. Without turning his head Random reached out his hand. Mariana gripped it tightly.

So they rode away together, the warrior named Green Eyes and the warrior woman who would live long in the legends of her People as She-Walks-Alone, to seek the camp of Thunder Knife.